Copyright and Dedication

---

1. http://www.erinthorntonauthor.com

2. https://d.docs.live.net/d431b832a6171c86/Documents/Erin%20Thornton%20Publishing/Dangerous%20After%20Dark/www.facebook.com/authorErinThornton

Other books by Erin Thornton
Dangerous Series (Romantic Suspense)
Dangerous After Dark
Dangerous Calculations

• • • •

Standalones
Disaster In Love (Romantic Comedy)

This book is dedicated to my children. Without whom I might not have lost the necessary amount of sanity to begin writing, to begin with.

Chapter 1: Trish

Another late night at work, Trish wondered if she would ever catch a break. She was the only female in the office, and as the newest she was left with all the grunt work. What the others didn't want she got. That meant long days and late nights. She was supposed to meet up with Grace tonight to catch up but was forced to cancel. It had been weeks since she had been able to spare enough time for a girl's night.

Thunder struck outside her office window. She didn't have an individual office; she had a cubicle that sat close to a tiny window near the bathroom. Nothing fancy or extraordinary for the lowly "wo"man on the totem pole.

Great. Now I will be soaked while walking home. There is no way I'm going to find a cab this late in this weather. It was the stormy season. She should have planned better. She lived close enough to work that walking wasn't usually an issue. This time of year though, she was more likely to get caught in a storm.

About eleven o'clock she finally wrapped up her long list from her extended day and was more than ready to be home. Unfortunately, the rain hadn't gotten tired yet. She was going to have to trudge back cold and wet.

Halfway home Trish was freezing, and the walk seemed longer than usual. She would need a hot shower before she could go to bed or she would never fall asleep. As Trish turned the corner, a car pulled up and stopped. In this storm, she just kept her head down and walked faster to avoid any unnecessary attention. It wasn't unheard of for her to hear a few catcalls and wolf whistles on her way home.

"You should have called. I would have been more than happy to come and get you. Unless drowned rat is the look you were going for, then I'd say you hit the nail square on the head," a familiar deep timbre rang from behind her.

She turned, and as she expected Brian Thomas was leaning against his Dodge Challenger Hellcat. Trish always thought that car was so sexy, but she wouldn't ever tell Brian that. He didn't need any extra help with his large head. There was a time when his interest had gotten to her, but that quickly changed after their one and only date.

Trish agreed to go out with him a few months ago after they first met. That was the biggest disaster and worst decision ever. They went to a new cocktail bar in town, and she thought it was going to be a good night. He had other ideas. The place was so classy, and she felt instantly comfortable there. Unfortunately, the bartender was more intriguing than Trish because Brian couldn't keep his eyes off of her or be bothered to stay in the conversation. He proved that night that he was more a player than she ever thought. It wasn't that Trish was ready to settle down yet, but she wanted her date to care more about her than whoever he was going to sleep with next.

From that night on she swore off Brian and the thought of how attractive he was in everything he wore. This instance was no exception; Brian was wearing a dark t-shirt that fit him snugly, but still comfortable enough he could move with ease. He covered it with a black leather jacket to keep dry. His jeans curved around his legs and left her wondering what his butt looked like, not that she couldn't picture the image from memory.

"Not that you deserve an answer, but I didn't call anyone because it was late and I wouldn't call anyone at this hour."

"Really? You know I'm always up this late doing something. This hour is the worst time for you to be out walking home not to mention in this storm."

"Doing someone is more accurate. I'm not stupid. The last thing I want is to witness your extracurricular activities first hand."

"That is what you say, but we both know you are dying to know firsthand what you're missing."

Rolling her eyes, she let out a huff, and without another word, she turned back to her walk home. She didn't have to put up with his version of crazy. She chose to opt out of that months ago.

Moments later she heard his door slam and the car start. Trish assumed she had made her point and he was driving away, so she continued her trek home. At the next intersection, she was startled by the Hellcat. It was sitting across the crosswalk and parked. The passenger window was rolled down, and Brian was grinning at her.

"Get in the car before you get any wetter and I can't drive you because you will ruin my leather. Just try and keep your dripping hair towards your lap. I'd hate to have any unnecessary puddles to clean up."

Tired and fed up with his antics Trish gave up. Intuition told her that no matter what she said he would follow her home anyway under the guise of protection, railing on her all the way. Crude comments about the rain leaving little to the imagination were not what she wanted right now. The only thing Trish wanted was her bed and pleasant dreams before she had to repeat this process the next day. Perhaps she would remember her umbrella just in case.

Trish opened the car door and plopped inside. Only she didn't do anything special to avoid leaving puddles in his seat. She had left her hair down that day, and so it was long and stringy, dripping everywhere. She didn't care in the least. If nothing else, the ride was under duress, and she didn't have the energy to fight with him. That didn't mean she had to concede to all his demands. She smirked to herself.

"Why are you walking home so late anyway?" Brian had already started the drive to her house. It would be a short drive now that she was already halfway there.

"Some of us have jobs that make us work and don't always have a set nine to five plan. Besides, I'm the newest, so I'm left to do all the grunt work." As much as she didn't want to talk to him, her mother raised her not to be rude even when she wanted to.

"What could you possibly need to do that was so time sensitive that couldn't wait until tomorrow? Don't you just crunch numbers and analyze spending habits?"

Sometimes she felt people underestimated her and her work. She was more than just a glorified number nerd. She helped businesses figure out why they weren't showing a profit or new ventures understand where they were making the most money to help in future inventory purchases or adjust their business goals based on profit. She helped families with their household budgets to become debt free. Most people didn't consider all the aspects of her job.

"Well not that it's any concern of yours, but I'm working toward a promotion so I can get off the bottom and start having a bit more freedom. We just took on a new case from an old family business that is trying to see what they actually have to their name. They want to know what they can legally split between the children for inheritance."

"Seriously, you work too hard. I liked you more before when you knew how to relax and have fun."

"Fun? I know how to have fun I just don't have time these days. I'll have more time when this project is done and can get back to going out and meeting people."

"Meeting people? Are you looking again?" He sounded a bit hopeful. "Well with that outfit, you are sure to garner some attention." Once again, he let her down by saying something crude.

Trish looked down at her soaked appearance. She realized that she was wetter than she thought her blouse looked completely soaked. Covering her puckered nipples, she huffed and turned toward the window away from him.

A few moments later, Brian pulled up in front of her apartment building. She lived on the second floor, but the building was a nice one and had a doorman on staff one of her mother's stipulations for living on her own. If Trish ever decided to move, she would have to find a roommate or her mother would gladly take the job. Thankfully, she liked her apartment building, so that wouldn't be a problem.

Brian came around and opened Trish's door. They may fight like cats and dogs, but he was always a gentleman. His mother had raised him right. "Well, thanks for the ride, I guess," she reluctantly said as she leaned out of the car trying to avoid flashing him further with her transparent top.

She made her way inside, but Brian followed her to the door. "You're welcome, but I'll still see you to your door safely."

"You don't have to come inside; the doorman has my safety covered. That is why I chose this place, among other reasons."

Picking up the pace she made her way to the door that was being held open by Sam, the doorman. They had a good rapport, but nothing more than a little friendly banter and some inquiries into each other's health. He was a large, intimidating man and would gladly step in if necessary.

"Of course, I'm not going to walk you all the way up there this time. My mother didn't raise me to leave a girl at the car. Even if you are a short-tempered one."

She visibly relaxed. Sam saw the change and eased up as well. She didn't realize how tense she was until she realized he wouldn't actually follow her to her apartment door. The last thing she wanted was to feel obligated to invite him in. No excuse was out there for her to refuse him entry. She was also brought up with proper manners.

Her mother was an old debutante. Therefore, so was Trish. She didn't advertise that fact at all. It wasn't a time in her life she wanted to be known for or remember frequently. Trish still suffered from life-altering aspects of that point in her history. All things she didn't discuss with anyone. Not even Grace, her best friend. Grace had enough on her plate since they'd been friends. Grace didn't need to take on Trish's problems as well. Now that Grace had found her happily ever after with Patrick, she was in a good place. Trish wanted nothing but happiness for Grace's future. To ensure that, she kept her problems locked away.

"Good night then, Brian. I'll see you another time. Just not too soon, okay?"

"Oh, you'll see me. I promise. Stay out of the rain." With that, Brian turned on his heel and headed back to his car.

Making her way inside she covered herself as best she could in her current situation. Without making eye contact, she acknowledged the ever-present doorman, "Evening, Sam."

"Looks like you've had a rough night. You need to quit working such late nights. It's not safe for a girl like you out there after dark."

"A girl like me? What exactly does that mean?" Trish said as her tired brain escalated quickly to anger, skipping all other rational emotions. After dealing with Brian, this was the last thing she wanted to deal with or hear.

"No, I just mean beautiful girls tend to draw unwanted attention. I'd hate for something to happen to you. I'd imagine you were so caught up in hurrying home in the rain you wouldn't have heard someone come up on you. You're my favorite tenant. I'd hate for something to happen to you." Sam was a genuine person, and it was evident that he was being his usual straightforward self.

"Okay, Sam. Thanks for your concern. I obviously have friends in low places and got home in one piece. I'll see you tomorrow. My shower and bed are calling my name." Chuckling softly Sam said his goodbyes and got back to his desk.

Unlocking her door, she walked inside slowly. Even though she wanted to be in bed more than anything, the activities of the evening had depleted her energy. To avoid dripping water all over her carpets, she stripped out of her blouse and pants making her way straight to the bathroom. All she could think about was hot water sluicing over her entire body.

Brian got back into his car soaked to the bone. That wasn't the plan for this evening. He was on his way home from the bar and was pleasantly surprised to find Trish walking home alone. He knew she wanted everyone to see her as an independent badass. However, Brian was sure there was a side of her that she didn't show anyone. He wanted to be the one she showed that side. Unfortunately, he had screwed that up already, but he was determined to win her over no matter what it took.

As Brian drove home, his phone rang. "Detective Thomas," he said in a business tone. That was his standard response when his cell rang no matter what. One was never officially off duty as a detective. He was always ready to be called in for a case.

"Brian, it's Patrick. We caught a case. DOA. Meet me at the old paper warehouse on Benedict Street." Patrick didn't give him a chance to respond. He just hung up and knew Brian would be there posthaste.

Brian made a quick U-turn in the middle of the street and sped off.

Ten minutes later, he skidded to a stop outside the paper warehouse. He hadn't been here in years. It was on the outskirts of town. This area was mostly treated as living quarters for the homeless or digs for punks to run their drug rings.

He quickly made his way inside and found Patrick. "Hey, I got here as fast as I could. What's the story?"

"You got here faster than I expected. I can't imagine you were in the neighborhood."

"No. When I finished up with my date tonight, I found Trish walking home in the rain. I had to convince her to let me drive her home."

"Convince? I can't imagine what it took for her to make that decision. I know how she feels about you. Anytime she has any interaction with you, she calls Grace and vents for a minimum of an hour. How long were you with her this time? I'm asking so I can try and be gone for that phone call."

"Oh, please. It's no big deal. I wasn't going to let her walk home in this weather if she could just climb in my car and stay safe and dry."

"Whatever you say, man. We should get back to work. I'll just wait until your evening plays out into my life later." Patrick made his way back into the crime scene and motioned for Brian to follow him. "A couple of kids found the body in here. They said they were dared to come in here by their friends, but I'm betting they are here a lot for recreational activities."

"So, you're saying they are drug dealers."

"Pretty much. The body seems to have been dumped here. That will limit our evidence a bit, but this one appears to have more of a story to tell. It's as if they were trying to get information out of him or maybe there was money owed. It looks like they were trying to scare him by inflicting injury. His kneecaps are shot out, and there is a knife wound in his right leg. It looks it might be a loan shark or a mob-related connection somehow."

"It looks like they really worked him over. What could he have done that would cause them to inflict so much damage and then go ahead and kill him?"

"That is going to be part of the puzzle, isn't it?" Patrick said with a smirk. He always did love the challenge of the case. Patrick was the one who decided in their downtime to pick cold cases to solve. He wanted the ones that no one else could work through and prove that it could be done. He was a fixer to the truest sense of the word. That is how he met his wife, Grace. She was in trouble and started out as a case. He took care of her problem in the only way possible at the time, and they fell in love. Now they lived happily ever after.

"Has the M.E. given an educated guess on what cause of death is?"

"Well, he won't commit until he gets him on his table, but my educated guess is a gunshot wound to the back of the head."

"Hmm, that would do it. I guess he pissed them off. Guess he should have paid up whatever he owed them. The things we've seen that stemmed from money are unfathomable. I'd put my money on a debt of some kind was owed." Brian started to walk around the scene taking everything in. Patrick seemed to be right; someone had definitely relocated the body here. If it was a blow to the head, which Brian couldn't make out from the position of the body, there wasn't enough blood for it to have happened here. The dirt was stirred from where foot traffic had moved it around, but there was no guarantee that they were going to find anything directly linking to the case. Not to mention, the rain that night would make finding forensics that much more challenging. It was clear the murderer knew what they were doing dropping the body that night. Hopefully, the forensics team would pull a white rabbit out of their hat.

This was going to be a difficult one, but they lived for that. He and Patrick had been partners from the beginning. They were like-minded, so they clicked from the start. They were both single when they joined the force and had their sights set on the grand career. They both worked hard and through the process had made it to detective. They were both very driven and had a one-track mind. Now that Patrick had settled down, it had Brian wavering on his bachelor status. He couldn't decide if he was ready to give up his freedom and be a one-woman man, but the thought had crossed his mind.

· · · ·

LATER THAT NIGHT, BRIAN was sitting at home enjoying a beer. It had been a long night. It was already late when he got called to the crime scene. By the time he got home, he was so keyed up he needed a drink to wind down. More than anything tonight he couldn't get his mind off of Trish. She was a witch who cast a spell on him. He was hypnotized and couldn't focus for days when he had spent any time with her. There wasn't a day that went by that he hadn't wished he wasn't such a player by nature. If he hadn't screwed up by trying to figure out if he knew the waitress on their first date he would probably be in Patrick's shoes by now.

To this day, he was still pretty sure that he dated the waitress at some point. She was overly friendly to him that night, but she was different when he went out with her. She was a brunette then and had a weird tick. Something about the need to swish her beer every time she took a drink. It was distracting, and frankly the thought of it was disgusting. By the time he satisfied his itching brain and figured out the mystery waitress, Trish was a woman scorned. There's a saying about those women too.

Now he had to figure out what he was going to do to win Trish over. She was the most beautiful creature he had ever seen. They say eyes are the window to your soul. Trish's eyes were proof of the storm that was brewing in her night and day. The only question was if it was a beautiful summer storm that you wanted to run through because it was warm and balmy or a spring storm that would cause destruction bringing with it dangerous additions like tornadoes and hurricanes. The curves that made up her lithe body made him want to reach out just to touch her. She had a way about her that made people want to be around her. If her body spoke to him in that way, then he was sure that most every man who saw her got the same message. The thought of another man touching her made him very protective, jealous even. He had no rights to her, but he was working to change that.

Lately, his dates have been leaving something to be desired. It would probably help if he stopped comparing them to Trish. He just needed to work on a plan to get her to give him a second chance. That was the most important thing right now.

Early the next morning, Brian made his way to the office. On a whim, he decided to take a quick turn by Trish's office. He wanted to be sure she made it to work. A gut feeling told him she would be there bright and early even though she had been there so late last night.

Parking his car, he got out and made his way quickly inside. He had never actually been to her office, but today he was making an exception. There was no reason for him to be there, but he decided to go with the truth, even if it made her mad.

Walking into the lobby he had no idea where her desk was, but it was early enough in the deserted office no one would be in for awhile. He just followed the sound of a clicking keyboard and hoped for the best. As he rounded the corner toward the back across from the window, he caught sight of the vision that was Trish. She dressed in a pencil skirt that hugged her hips so perfectly; he could see it even though she was sitting ramrod straight in her office chair. A pale pink blouse draped over her shoulders and flowed like water over her skin. While it was made to accentuate her body, on her, the effect was alluring and made him want to touch her. It seemed her aura was screaming for him to touch her. Everything about Trish was calling out to him.

As if she felt him watching her, she slowly glanced over her shoulder to look at him. Immediately her face changed from calm to shocked and angry. "What are you doing here?"

"Just checking to see that you made it back to work all right after the late and eventful night you had last night."

"Eventful? Are you serious? The only event that I had happen was a self-assured asshat decided he needed to intervene on my life and rescue me like some kind of knight in not-so-shiny armor. Besides, what made you think I would be here now? It is well before opening hours. Obviously, I'm the only one here. No one starts work this early."

"I know you, Trish. I knew you would be here and that makes it easier to stalk you," he said with a smirk and a wink. "Whenever you need a knight in shining armor, I'll be there any chance I can get. Not to mention, after that rain last night my car is shiny enough for the job. You could just thank me for not making you walk all the way home last night. I figured you'd at least appreciate being able to get to your bed a little earlier."

"What I appreciate is when you don't insert your plans into my life. I was perfectly fine walking home even if it was raining. I walk that path every day by choice. I could drive, but I don't see the point. I also don't see the point in you following me around."

"I love it when you lie to me. Getting to see me is a highlight of your day, maybe your week. That is whenever I decide to grace you with my presence."

"Ugh, you are so full of yourself it's a wonder you even fit through the doorway to get in here, and it's a double door. Care to tell me what you are really doing here?" Trish turned back to her work and gave him her back to continue talking to. She didn't kick him out though, so he rolled with it.

"I thought maybe I could swing in and see what time you were going to head home tonight and I would save you from getting wet. Pretty sure the weatherman is accurate today saying it's going to storm again. I'd hate for you to ruin those shoes," he added glancing down at her three and a half inch black heels that gave him many other ideas, that were not proper in their present location.

She joined him in looking at her shoes as though she'd forgotten which ones she put on this morning.

"I can't imagine walking that distance in those shoes was very comfortable anyway. Do you change your shoes out when you get to work?"

She rolled her eyes at him, "I've been wearing heels like this most of my life. I was brought up to understand that the right shoe for the occasion is to be worn the entire event no matter what it is. You are to dress the part from the beginning to the end. To remove a pair of shoes because they may or may not be uncomfortable is heresy. After a period of time, it is like walking in tennis shoes, and one doesn't even notice anymore.

Brian could tell there were some seriously indoctrinated beliefs buried deep in that answer, but that was a side of Trish he'd never met before. They were friends because of Grace and Patrick and by no means were they close friends after his epic lack of judgment. "I'll take your word on that, but I obviously will never know from experience. Seriously though, let me take you home. I want to know you get home safe. At least let me see you into the care of your grizzly bear of a doorman again. I'll take that if you will give it."

"Why are you so concerned all of a sudden of where I am and how I get there?"

"It's not all of a sudden, but last night opened my eyes to a few things and not just when I was with you rescuing you from torrential rain."

"What is that supposed to mean? Are you saying you had an epiphany? That's rich. You believe that something that happened last night would change the way I see you?"

Brian didn't want to have this particular conversation yet. He was still trying to figure out what exactly he felt and how he was going to win her over. "Let's just say I had a call last night that opened my eyes. You have my number call me when you get off, or I'll just camp outside after five o'clock and see you whenever you decide to go home."

Trish scoffed at Brian's statement, "You are going to wait outside my door for hours for a chance to take me home? You are going to give up your evening and sit in your car for however long it takes for me to finish my day? I don't understand you."

"The choice is yours. I can wait, or you can save me the trouble. And don't even think about telling me the wrong time so I will miss you. Remember, I know exactly where you live."

"Threatening me now? That is not very becoming of an officer of the law." Trish loved taunting him with his job, but he secretly enjoyed giving her reasons to do it. It was a game for him, but she hadn't figured it out. She just thought she was getting in one dig after another.

"I'm always gonna threaten you with your safety. You are on my radar now. That is good and bad for you."

"You are unbelievable. This is probably why you can't hold a girlfriend. You have serious stalker tendencies. Perhaps you should seek professional help to look into overcoming that nature."

"Well, I'm gonna head into the office now. Patrick and I got a new case, and I'm anxious to see if we have any new developments. I'll be awaiting your call." With that, he made his way back out the door without another word.

Brian arrived at the office twenty minutes later, with the same smile he'd had on his face since he left Trish's office. She had a way of making him happy just from being around her. Even if all they did was fight, he was satisfied with the morning's encounter because he had goaded her into continuing their conversation. She was absolutely gorgeous when she was fuming. One day, he would kiss her scowl right off her face and shock the hell out of her.

Rushing to the bathroom, Trish didn't know if she would make it. She was more than used to this process, but this time it was different. Today took longer to get there, because there were so many people in the house more than normal. No one knew what she was doing, but it's the only way to get rid of it.

Fitting into the right dresses for the right events was always the most important, at least to everyone else. She had been brought up with this mindset but had to work harder than anyone to achieve the goal. Her mother didn't see the struggle; she didn't want to. That was a choice she made. Trish was left in the darkness, alone to figure out the answer to the inevitable puzzle. If she were to stop she would just pack on the pounds and be an outcast to her mother and her mother's friends stopping was not an option. That is not how the women in their family operated. They're expected to live up to the standards set before them and not complain. They were practically Stepford Wives from birth. The past few months had been the same. Eat regularly, so everyone saw from the outside the perfect specimen that they expected, but then purge moments later in the bathroom to make the perfection an actuality.

Trish's debutant ball was that weekend, and she was supposed to be the belle of the ball at whatever cost. For her, that cost was her appetite. Since she couldn't just stop eating - since that would raise suspicion - she had to adapt. So for the past few months, after realizing that she had a propensity for gaining weight, Trish started throwing up the excess that her body didn't need. It started out small, just her largest meal of the day, but after a week she saw amazing results. Unfortunately, after about a month it began to level back out. Trish realized it wasn't working as well anymore, so she escalated to two meals a day. In another months time, she moved to; all food consumption was immediately followed by a trip to the bathroom. It had worked quite well, and she was easily going to fit into her dress as planned. Her mother would be *the proud peacock displaying her wares. She could show Trish off to all of her friends as Trish was introduced into fine society. It's an old tradition, but their family had upheld it because it was a rite of passage. All the women are released into the privilege of courting just like all of their ancestors had been for centuries.*

As the weekend came, her family was in a whirlwind of preparations. Everyone except her father. He was merely supposed to show up and walk her into the room. His job was the easiest. Her mother, on the other hand, was more like a drill sergeant, calling out orders and commands left and right to any and everyone who crossed her path. Trish chose to stay out of her way as much as possible so as not to take on any extra duties or be scrutinized any further than she did herself.

It was the party of the year for their community of friends. By order of her mother, everyone who was anyone got an invitation. They would all show up just to watch her every move and to be seen by the best of the best in town. Her only personal goal was not to disappoint her mother and look like a fool in front of all these important people.

As the evening approached, Trish took to her room. She expected the makeup and hairstylist would be arriving soon to fine tune her mother's vision. That night should have been an exciting moment for Trish, but it was actually all about her mother. Since the focus was skewed, she was dreading the rest of the night. Perhaps her father would help her escape unnoticed early. She had a date arranged, but it was set up by her mother as well, and she wasn't concerned about what Trish wanted. Trish didn't even get to choose her date for the biggest event that had ever happened in her life so far.

By the time she had finished being fawned over from top to bottom, she was the epitome of the pristine princess. She was wearing a fitted white gown that could double as a wedding dress. If she knew her mother at all, it probably cost something comparable as well. Her naturally blonde hair was fashioned in an elegant chignon and clipped with a diamond comb fanning out the side. Her makeup was applied lightly to accentuate her best feature, her eyes. They used a dark eyeliner to draw attention to them, and a thick coat of mascara left her feeling almost seductive. For someone so young she wasn't sure that was the right word, but she imagined this was how it would feel.

Making her way into the ballroom after being chauffeured to the hotel was a quick process. She wasn't supposed to make her appearance until after the guests appeared so she made her way to the designated room on the upper level to wait. Her mother planned her grand appearance to the minute. She wore the tallest heels she'd ever worn in her life, but her mother assured her it was necessary. Everything she had worn up to this point was training for this main event. She still feared that she would trip and fall down the stairs humiliating herself and her family, most of all her mother.

After what felt like an eternity her father knocked on the door. "Are you ready dear?" he asked as he walked inside.

"As ready as I can be, given the situation," she replied diplomatically. Her father knew this wasn't how she wanted this to happen, but they both knew her mother would get her way no matter what. "Is there any chance of sneaking out the back, daddy?"

"Don't I wish. Your mother wouldn't speak to either of us for a year or more if we did that."

"Would that really be so bad?"

Her father laughed and offered her his hand to guide her to the staircase. He would make his way down first to make the announcement and then guide her to the front of the crowd for greetings. She was so nervous that she had to grab a tissue to wipe the dampness from their surface before taking his hand.

With a peck on the cheek, her father made his way down the stairs to announce her to the crowd. She gripped the rail so tightly her knuckles were white. Fear was over-taking her. She would survive tonight on sheer willpower.

"Attention ladies and gentlemen, I'd like to introduce to you all my beautiful daughter, Trisha LeAnn Montgomery." As her father finished, the room broke out in a resounding applause. That was Trish's cue to begin her descent. One foot in front of the other. She had to force herself to keep her shoulders squared and face looking out. A broad smile on her lips was putting on the front that said she knew what she was doing and she feared nothing. A few steps in her heel faltered, but she quickly stabilized her footing. With a renewed vigor, she made her way down the stairs without another misstep.

Getting to the bottom, her father took her hand in his and guided her to his side. He looped her hand over his arm and pressed another kiss to her cheek. He understood what she was fighting for to get down the steps and please not only the crowd but ultimately her mother as well. Having survived her entrance, now she needed to spend the next few hours greeting and speaking to her guests. The only problem at this point was she didn't feel like they were her guests but her mother's.

Hours had passed, and she spent the entire night on her feet. They hurt beyond measure, and all she wanted to do was take them off. Her date had moved on to a group of girls that Trish wasn't familiar with, but was side-eyeing her the entire night. She excused herself to go to the bathroom. While Trish was in there, she heard the door open and close. A couple of girls walked in, and she remained silent to not draw unnecessary attention to herself.

"I can't believe she is wearing that dress. White might be a traditional color for debs to wear, but she looks ridiculous. Her hips are huge in that fitted cut, and it doesn't flatter her at all," the first girl spoke up without remorse. Trish instantly knew they were talking about her. Tears pricked at her eyes, but she held them back for fear of being found.

"Exactly. I know what you mean. She should have opted for a cut that hid all that extra around the middle. No wonder Lucas decided to abandon her and come hang out with us. He was being forced to slum with her anyway. Too bad their mothers are such good friends. I bet they

were hoping for a wedding after all this." The girls laughed at their inside joke. Trish didn't want anything to do with Lucas or any of them. She just wanted this night to be over so she could crawl into bed and forget any of it ever happened.

The girls finished primping in the mirror and Trish was left alone. Instead of leaving the stall and heading back out, there wasn't anything that could keep her from throwing up right then.

• • • •

AFTER BRIAN LEFT, TRISH didn't get much work done. Her mind kept wandering to the past. All things fit together to make her the way she was. Her mother's rearing, her father's love and doting, but ultimately agreeing with whatever her mother wanted, her weight issues that have continued to this day, and now her inability to keep a man in her life. She dated but felt like no one was good enough for the way she was brought up. If they liked her, then they most certainly would turn away running upon meeting any of her family. Her mother was a tough one to crack, and her father was so sweet to her that no man was good enough for his little girl. There wasn't much middle ground with either of them. Now that her father passed a few years ago from an unexpected heart attack, they would only have to worry about her mother. That just gave her mother more ground to cover, and she was more than up to the challenge.

Why did she think about her family meeting the men in her life? She wasn't dating anyone right now. She didn't have time for that fiasco. She was working on case right now that was more important than her social life. She'd get back to that once she wasn't the one doing all the grunt work, putting in long hours on project after project to get her to a point where the partners noticed her. They worked with some very prestigious clientele. The case she was working on was just the tip of the iceberg. None of the rest of the team was working on this with her. It was her first solo case, and she was planning on making herself a name with it.

The Castenellos Family was an old family in the city. Everyone knew who they were, but they specifically requested a new set of eyes on this one hoping to garner some extra attention. They were worried they wouldn't have enough money to leave down the line to the grandkids if they didn't get their books in check. It seemed they were making money, but they were having a hard time seeing the actual profits physically. The books always said the numbers were high, but the actual account numbers were just floating. There was an underlying concern that there was someone skimming money off the top hoping no one would notice the differences.

Trish was determined to figure out the discrepancies, but she was worried she was missing information. Instead of spending countless hours working on it she decided to go and have a conversation with her boss. Making her way to Mr. Phillips office, Trish considered what she was going to say. She wanted to sound like she knew her case very well, but not like she was whining about needing help. She was just missing some vital information. She made a mental list of what she believed was missing. Arriving at his door faster than Trish had hoped, she still felt ill- prepared. She should have stayed at her desk and made a list, but she could still smell hints of Brian's cologne every once in a while when the office vents kicked in.

Taking a deep breath, Trish knocked on the door, mentally hoping he was out of the office for a meeting or an early lunch. Dashing her pleas, she was called in. "Come in," Mr. Phillips called through the door.

She pressed her way in, slowly opening the door, "Ah, Trish, to what do I owe the pleasure?"

"Good morning, Mr. Phillips. I was hoping I could pick your brain for a moment and see if you agree before I bother a significant client with this."

"Trish, you know you can call me Wyatt. It is an informal office even though we have grown so much recently. I'd love to help. I assume you are working on the Castenellos Family project. What seems to be the trouble?"

He was always so easy-going unless you upset him. If you didn't want to pay a high price, then you needed to duck and cover. He had the worst temper you could imagine. You didn't want to be on the wrong side of it. "I was just thinking I must be missing some information. I would like to see the actual time sheet and payroll information from the inception of the business. I think there is a discrepancy there, but I can't find it with the limited information given to me. I also believe there is something off with their logs. While I'm glad they aren't handwritten because those are so much harder to go through and more common with old business, something isn't adding up with all the ones I have. Is there by chance something else I should ask for?"

"I'm glad you came to me. I agree you should ask for the payroll information. It honestly should have come over with the original files. My only concern is they aren't tracking everything on the ledger, or someone is getting paid cash for work to hide something. As for your other concern, if I recall correctly, one of the kids takes the log books and transfers them by hand to the computer files. The grandmother likes to do all the books longhand just because 'that's the way she's always done it' rather than give up her job or force her out, they just relay all the information to the electronic side for easy record keeping. They are happy, grandma is happy, and she gets to stay busy. I'd ask them for a copy of grandma's books. I bet there is something that has been left out or accidentally overlooked."

"That makes sense. I'm glad we are on the same page, Wyatt. I was worried I was missing something obvious in the existing files. I'll go and call them right now."

Trish excused herself from Wyatt's office and felt a lot better about the situation. She made her way back to her desk and quickly dialed the Castenellos' number. On the second ring, an older woman answers the phone, "Hello?"

"Good morning, this is Trish Montgomery at Phillips, Baker, and Associates. I'd like to speak to someone from the Castenellos family."

"This is Mama Castenellos."

"Oh perfect! I'm the advisor working on your case, and I've run into a couple of hiccups. I need a bit more information, and I heard you keep copiously detailed logs by hand."

"Yes, I don't trust those newfangled computers the kids are determined to get me to use. I like my good old-fashioned pencil and paper. There is less chance of error if I know I was the one who wrote it down."

"Even better. Then is there a chance I could get a copy of those books? If you sent over the books I could have copies run and the books back by the end of the day if that is easier for you."

"I think I can make that work. That will still allow me time to do the end of day numbers tonight."

"One other thing, do you keep records of your payroll hours or some sort of timesheet? That would make crunching some of these numbers easier too. I could come by and grab it all within the hour."

"Sure, I can pull all that together for you. I may not have all the payroll, but what I don't have for you when you get here I can send over with Little Timmy when he gets in later to run his deliveries."

"That should work for me. I'll get my things together and be over there soon." Trish hung up the phone and was very pleased with herself. She seemed to have been worried for nothing. Now she could grab a quick snack and head to the restaurant. Today was going to be a productive day after all.

Right at an hour later, Trish pulled up outside Abuela's Pequeño Restaurante. It was evident that Grandma was the highlight of this family. She must have been the founder of the family business. Trish quickly went inside and was promptly face to face with Mama herself. It was obvious that she was the woman that Trish had spoken with on the phone. Mama carried herself with an air of superiority. She was a tiny woman, but her presence commanded respect. It was as if she never thought anyone would do anything, but treat her with the utmost honor. It wasn't just her age that was the reason. She was the boss here, and everyone knew it.

"Mama? I'm Trish from Philips, Baker, and Associates. We spoke on the phone. I hope I gave you enough time to pull together the paperwork."

"Oh dear, of course, I did. I'm a very organized person, so it wasn't an issue of where, but merely the time it took to box it up for you. Little Timmy will bring over the older stuff. I took the liberty of only boxing the most current files in this one for you now. If I sent them all with you now, you would be overwhelmed. Don't worry about running copies of everything. I only need this current ledger back for tonight. So just get what you need from it and send it back with Little Timmy." Mama handed her a standard banker box filled to the top, but the lid still closed with ease.

"This is perfect. It will get me started, and I'll wait for Timmy to make it over. No hurry, though. From what I see in this box, it will take me a while to line these up with what I have."

"*Little* Timmy," Mama said, simply correcting Trish's slip.

"Oh, I'm sorry. I didn't realize it was important."

"Not important, but it makes it a lot easier to be sure who you're talking about because Big Timmy is already frustrated to be sharing a name with his brother." A small smirk played at Mama's lips.

"Oh, did the boys all get named after their dad, Tim Sr.?"

"Nope, their mother just loved that darn name, and no one could persuade her to name them differently."

Trish laughed because it couldn't be helped. She knew what it was like to have a strong-willed parent. Her mother could rival many others out there with ease. With that, she thanked her for her help and made her way back to the office.

The rest of the afternoon was spent doing a lot of checks and balances. Trish made notes that showed her which figures were missing from the electronic file. After she couldn't stare at the ledger anymore, she moved on to the payroll pages hoping that the change would give her a much-needed boost in energy.

Progressing through the payroll sheets, Trish started to realize some of the line items on the electronic side listed as payroll weren't coinciding with the time sheets given to her. Could some of the employees have been paid under the table, but later recorded in the electronic log to show all expenses? She started to notice a pattern the longer she looked at these numbers. The employee who supposedly got twenty-five hundred dollars a month was the highest paid employee by far. That wasn't the only one that was like that. There were six to seven different payroll listings over a thousand dollars each that didn't show in the paper logs. Something was definitely wrong.

How could that many outgoing payments just be omitted from the internal log? This seemed to be a regularly occurring thing too, so Trish couldn't just chalk it up to absentminded Grandma. Trish decided to take copious notes. If something was awry, then she was going to have all her ducks in a row before presenting any findings to her bosses. Mr. Phillip may have a sweet side, but Mr. Baker was old school in his thinking. The customer wasn't just always right, but they were made of gold too. He wasn't going to lose an old client because of something a minion found. He would take the clients word over hers any day of the week. Trish could easily get fired over something like this.

"I thought this was my ticket to moving up off the floor in this company. Little did I know it was going to be the case that solidified my job or took it away. Why did I volunteer for this? I don't need the money. My trust fund would cover me for as long as I need," she muttered to herself. That was where she stopped, because she always got like this when things didn't go her way. The moment Trish was thinking about living off her trust fund was when she pulled the emergency brake on her wild thoughts. She vowed years ago never to touch that money. She was brought up in wealth, and the only reason she'd gone to school was for the prestigious ability to say she had her degree. Her mother never intended for her to use it. She was old-fashioned like that. A woman was to run the household and not run around outside of it. Trish was supposed to be settled down years ago with a man who was beyond wealthy and living in their inner circle. Her mother hated when Trish came home from school with her degree and announced that she had an internship straight out of school. That was over five years ago now. When Trish got offered this job two years ago an entry-level position at Phillip, Baker, and Associates, she jumped on it like a ravenous dog. Without a job, she would be forced to live off her family wealth. Something she swore she wouldn't do. Trish wanted to know what it was like to live life to her standards, her own rules. Not the kind of rebellious teenage behavior she showed before college, but the kind of young adult independence that one needs to feel complete.

Lost in her thoughts, she didn't hear someone approaching her desk. When she turned around, she was startled to see a giant of a man standing behind her. "Excuse me. I didn't hear you come in. Can I help you?" Trish feigned professionalism now that she was a bit scared of this huge man before her.

His hulking figure wasn't the only thing that was terrifying. When he spoke, his deep voice nearly vibrated everything around him. "I'm Little Timmy, and Mama sent me over to bring these boxes." It was only then that she drew her attention to the stack of boxes on the floor beside him. Did he carry all of them in here by himself? There were at least four boxes similar in size to the one she brought in with her earlier. What kind of a man could carry that many boxes at once?

"Of course. I'm so glad you were able to bring them. There was no way I could have gotten all of those in here on my own. Can I have the office write you a check for your trouble?" She didn't know the relationship to the Castenellos family and didn't want to assume he was related until she knew for sure.

"No, Mama would kill me if I let you double pay me for this. I'm on the clock, and I am already being paid to run deliveries. This was just an added stop after I delivered the last order." He wasn't the chatty type but more direct and to the point. He also seemed to be more than ready to leave so Trish decided she would put him out of his misery.

"Okay. Well, thank you so much for adding me to your list of stops. It helped me out a lot even if it does mean extra work on my part," she added with a smile which he didn't return. He just turned and walked toward the door without so much as a goodbye.

"Well, isn't he a real joy. If that was 'Little' Timmy, I'd hate to meet 'Big' Timmy," she mumbled turning back to her desk. After what she found in the files she brought back herself, she was dreading even opening the boxes he'd delivered to her.

It was approaching five o'clock, and she was just at the tip of the iceberg on the Castenellos file when she remembered she didn't call Brian. Truthfully, she didn't want him anywhere near here when she got off work. She just wanted to go home and relax after her exhausting day. Some people may think she had it easy, sitting all day with no weather to stop her from work or inhibit her day. They were beyond wrong. Staring at a computer all day crunching numbers and comparing line items with other files got monotonous and was very tedious work. Most don't take that into account; they just wondered why she wouldn't go out with them after her extra-long hours. Tonight would be no exception. The problem was, did she want to call Brian's bluff or just suck it up and let him drive her home. The more she thought about it, she wanted Brian to just go away as usual. She had seen enough of him the past two days and definitely more than she wanted. Making the decision, she was going to call his bluff and ignore him. If all went according to plan, he would be busy at work with his new case and forget all about her.

Chapter 4: Brian

Evidence was currently lacking in their case. The man had been identified as Peter Shoal, thirty-eight. A local man who worked as a freelance accountant, but hadn't had an official client in a while from what they could tell. That was odd because he seemed to be living quite high on the hog. They still hadn't been able to track where the money came from at all. He seemed to have a few different accounts, and all the money was transferred in from off-shore accounts.

"Why do we always get the weird cases that don't make any sense?" he asked Patrick as they were going over their notes from the night before.

"They know who they're dealing with, don't they? Only the best for the best." Patrick was always the cocky one. He was aware that they would solve whatever case crossed their desk. They had an incredible track record, and the department had given them countless accolades for their reputation.

"You think we might not get enough evidence on this one? They really did plan that dead drop perfectly. The storm last night washed away a lot of evidence. Not to mention anything that might have been on the body while transporting would have been washed away on the way inside."

"Evidence has never been a problem before. Something always turns up. Criminals are stupid, they are notorious for leaving something behind. Even in Grace's case that guy was so smart, he was bound to screw up at some point. We just have to look where we aren't looking now for evidence."

"Where do you suggest we start?"

"I think we should focus on the victim. If we can figure out who was paying him to keep him in that lifestyle, we will probably turn up something. I'll put money on it that whoever he was working for is involved in this somehow."

"Now we just have to deduce who that is. Peter was a very secretive man. He didn't let anyone in his life much, and he lived alone with no known family."

"What if Peter Shoal is an alias? He could have been hiding family to protect them from the people he was working for. That is something we could consider."

"Always another angle. You always seem to find them, too." With that, they went their separate ways. Brian hadn't heard from Trish today, but that just meant she was playing hard to get. He would wait until five o'clock, and then go camp out in front of her office so he wouldn't miss her. Knowing her, she would try and sneak out the door in hopes of avoiding him. He wouldn't let that happen.

When he got to her office, he had a new plan. He would just sneak up on her again. As he made his way to her office, it was now after five, and everyone seemed to bail out of her office on the nose. She was obviously an overachiever. Following the sound of her keystrokes again, he made his way to her desk. As before, she was engrossed in her work, so he snuck up on her. Boxes surrounded her that weren't here this morning. What could she possibly have going on that required all these boxes? He glanced at the name on one of the files, and it read Castenellos.

"Are you doing a project for the Castenellos family?" His voice startled her out of her working fog. Sneaking up on her was becoming a fun pastime for him. Lost in her work, she didn't hear him come in. He hoped she didn't do that with everyone, but it would be some great entertainment the longer he could keep it up.

"Can't you wear a bell or something?"

"Nope, that doesn't really fit my style."

"You have a style? I would never have guessed that about you. I just thought you just wore whatever you found on the floor as long as it didn't smell too badly." It seemed like she was deflecting his original question. He wouldn't let her get away with it, but he would indulge her a little longer.

"I only do that on the weekends, during the week I wear all my clothes freshly pressed from the dry cleaners. There is a dress code for the office, even if it is a more laid back one." He glanced over her desk and took in a few notepads covered in notes. Whatever she was working on, she was working quite hard. He feared she was going to be in over her head if she wasn't careful. The Castenellos family was a well-known crime family. How did she not know that? They'd been trying to find something to stick to that family for years. Somehow no matter what they were connected to they were able to keep their hands clean.

"What are you doing here, Brian?"

"I told you if you didn't call I would come at closing time. My phone never rang, so here I am."

"I didn't call, because I didn't want you here. Not to mention, I'm still hard at work. You aren't needed here."

"Then I'll wait around and keep you company. It will be better than sitting outside waiting for you. Now tell me about this case."

"I'm not going to tell you about a private client's case. That is a breach of contract. I don't know how long I will be here. Having you here will impede my ability to work."

"Oh, so you're saying I'm a distraction to you now? I knew you'd succumb to my charms eventually. I'm like a magnet you can't resist."

"You are so full of yourself. How do you ever have room for anyone else in your life?"

"I always have room for someone else. I just have to fill the space in the meantime," he replied cockily. He knew he was digging in deeper and she would get fired up.

"I can't even begin to have an adult conversation with you. If you insist on staying, go ahead and wait in your car, then I won't have to look at you and won't have to listen to your insane dialog or your breathing down my neck."

"I will wait in here, because if I wait in my car. You will try and sneak out. This is easier for me. If you are working on a project for the Castenellos, I plan on sticking really close to you from now on." Trish rolled her eyes at him. This was becoming a common reaction for her when he was around.

"You aren't going to be a shadow because of an ordinary case. There is nothing about this project that would warrant you hovering around like a bad ghost. You can just be on your merry way right now. I'm a big girl. I can get myself home like always. It's not even raining, see." She gestured toward the window across from her. The rain had pushed out, and it had been a beautiful day. Contrary to her beliefs, that wasn't the only reason Brian was here. He was going to be around a lot more until she realized there was more to him that his constant reaction to the fairer sex.

"How about I just take up residence in this chair and wait until you are ready?" Brian pulled out a rolling desk chair and reclined drastically back as far as the chair would allow. He placed his hands behind his head in a very relaxed pose making himself more than comfortable. "I have nothing else to do tonight. This seems like as good of plans as any.

"Only you," Trish turned her back on him and tried to ignore him. If she thought that would make him go away, she was infinitely wrong.

Another hour passed. Brian was thankful for his ability to stay awake in incredibly boring situations. He had to do that here and there on stakeouts with Patrick, but even those were getting worse than normal since Patrick married Grace. Instead of talking women and horror dates, all Patrick had was cute stories about Grace and what she made for dinner the night before. Not that Grace wasn't a good cook - he always accepted her invitations for dinner - but a man could only take so many happily ever after stories.

Trish turned in her chair barely sparing a glance at Brian. She had been doing a good job of ignoring him, but he had had enough of it. She leaned over the stack of boxes and started to down stack them to reach a lower box. Brian jumped up quickly, "Here let me get that for you. It's the least I can do." He grabbed the box out of her hands and began to lower it to the wall beside the stack. He motioned toward the next one to see if she needed it moved as well. She nodded, and he lifted it with ease. They weren't too heavy, but it was more than she needed to be lifting especially if he were here to do it for her. He repeated the previous gesture until he'd restacked them all, save one. She rummaged through it to find a file, then returned to her desk in silence. She couldn't even muster a thank you for him.

"I thought your mom brought up better than that?" Brian was trying to poke the bear. If he got lucky, she would speak to him. No luck she continued to scribble notes and click away at the keyboard.

"My mother would wallop me if I grumbled in that situation, let alone showed no gratitude." Again, she didn't take the bait. He would need to up his game.

"What would your mother say? Something tells me you are sucking on vinegar right now trying to hold back your ingrained manners." She turned abruptly in her chair. BINGO! He had her right where he wanted her.

"What do you know about my upbringing? You don't know anything, that's what." He could practically see the anger radiating off of her. He had her right where he wanted her - talking.

"I'm a cop. It's my job to know everything about all the people I'm around. It wouldn't be smart to make friends with a criminal and not know it, would it?"

"You thought I was a criminal?"

"No, but it makes for a good excuse when I run a background check on people."

"That can't be legal. That is a horrible invasion of privacy. I can't believe you did that." She was on fire now. All the heat had turned into licking flames, and there would be no quenching them quickly.

"Invasion of privacy? Yes. Illegal? Not as much. Frowned upon? Probably, yes." He kept his answer vague, but still answered just to keep her talking.

"You are so infuriating. Do you know that?"

"I'm completely aware. You aren't the first person to tell me that. It doesn't change the fact that I know plenty about you. You come from a rather wealthy family. Your education was paid for from kindergarten all the way to your degree. You wanted for nothing and always got the best of everything. You haven't lived off your parents for many years, but that is probably just a show of your independence and are likely welcome to that wealth at a moment's notice. So your workload is unnecessary at best, but you do it for some sense of self-worth." The longer he continued he could see the stunned expression change on her face. The anger didn't subside, but it morphed into a surprised infuriation. He knew he was getting to her. "Am I somewhere close?"

"First of all, my life on paper may look a certain way, but don't even attempt to act like you know my reasons for doing the things I do. My life was not all roses and sunshine at all. I may have lived a life of ease from the outside looking in, but it was far from it. That is all you're going to get out of me. You and I aren't friends, and we aren't sharing secrets, not now and not ever."

He knew he was getting somewhere, but he hadn't broken her yet. She would require more time for that. This was just the tip of the iceberg. Apparently, she was hiding something, but he wasn't going to push her now. She would tell him...eventually. He knew it.

He broke out his phone and dialed, not bothering to respond to her rant. He let the phone ring as she looked at him puzzled. "Yes, I'd like to order a large pizza," he said into the phone. "Do you have a preference or any major dislikes?" he said glancing over at her while pulling the phone back away from his mouth. Her mouth opened slack-jawed. Then, as she tried to regain her composure, she resembled a codfish opening and closing her mouth.

"What are you doing? I'm not eating with you. I'm working."

"Oh, okay." He returned the phone to his mouth, "I'd like a large pizza with everything on it. Extra sausage and pepperoni, I like my proteins with a sprinkle of veggies." He wrapped up the order and hung up the phone. Without another word, he placed his phone back in his pocket and returned to his relaxed position in the chair.

Trish, on the other hand, wasn't returning to her work, "What do you think you are doing?" she repeated.

"Since you are going to work late, I figured food would be necessary. If you aren't going to eat, I'm going to enjoy as much of it as I can put away myself. No sense in starving because you have an insane work ethic for reasons I don't understand or you won't make clear to me, by your own admission."

"No, you are welcome to leave at any time. I've made it clear that you aren't needed, and I can work as late as I please without you."

"I'm aware. I'm just a terrible listener. My mother hated that trait when I was a kid, but I never outgrew it."

Silence came over the room; they sat that way for a long time. Brian just decided to let it linger in the air and see where it went. Unfortunately, she seemed to be as stubborn as he was. They didn't say a word until there was a knock at the door. It startled Trish out of her work.

"That must be my pizza."

"Oh, then by all means, please go handle that. Feel free to take it to-go." Quickly, she returned to her work.

Brian got up and made his way to the front door. He paid for the pizza and locked the door to keep out any unwanted visitors. Not waiting until he made it back to his designated chair, he opened the pizza box and grabbed a slice knowing that the smell alone would make her hungry. Watching him consume a hot cheesy bite would send her over the top.

"Mmmh, this is the best pizza in town. I don't order it anymore because I'm never over here. They don't deliver to my place." He could see her shoulders tense. He knew she was having trouble ignoring this delicious aroma. She hadn't even seen him take a bite yet.

"I wish you would have taken that to your car. I can't eat any of that and smelling it just makes it worse."

"What do you mean you can't eat it? Are you allergic to something on here? I did ask you what you wanted on it."

"No, I just can't eat it."

"Please, don't tell me you are on a diet. You are the last person I know who needs to lose any weight."

"I refuse to discuss my weight with you good or bad. Your opinion is of no consequence to me." She turned in her chair attempting to ignore him once again. He left her be. For now.

Smelling the pizza was torture, but she refused to give in and eat a meal of any sort with Brian. Going over to Grace and Patrick's for dinner was bad enough, and there were other people there, so she didn't have to speak directly to him most of the time. This felt too much like a date, and she didn't like that. She felt trapped as though he was forcing the issue when he knew very well that she wouldn't be caught dead on another date with him.

"Mmmh! This pizza really is good. You sure you don't want a slice? I could probably eat the entire thing, but then Patrick will make me go the gym. I hate the gym."

Brian was physically fit from what she could tell, but the fact that he didn't like to work out blew her mind. She couldn't figure out how he stayed so fit without putting forth the effort. "You hate the gym? How is that possible? You are on the police force and, granted, you are a detective, so I'm sure you don't walk around like a beat cop, but you look like you're mostly in shape."

"Round is a shape, Trish, so being in shape is a relative term."

"You know what I mean. You are physically trim and from what I can tell you have enough muscle mass to hold your own." She blushed slightly. How did he get her to admit that?

Smirking with his very cocky attitude, "Are you saying you have been checking me out?" Wagging his eyebrows in his signature way, he leaned forward to look at her better. His eyes bored into hers making her instantly feel uncomfortable and perhaps even a bit tingly in her lady bits. If she could rub her legs together to ease the sensations without being noticed, she would.

"No, I'm just saying to the naked eye someone would think you worked out, is all."

"Naked eye? Have you been picturing me naked?" He was doing this on purpose, but there wasn't much she could do. She might have thought down that road a time or two. If she denied it, he would assume she was lying, and there was no way she was going to admit it. That'd be suicide for her. He would latch on like an alligator and never let go. She was in a catch twenty-two, nowhere to go and no way out. Hesitating just a split second longer, she decided to take her chances, because she had to give him an answer.

"No one would picture you naked; they would probably get a disease just from imaginary contact."

"So, you're saying what exactly?" Brian was playing dumb wanting her to draw this conversation out further. That was the last thing she wanted. So instead she stood from her chair and marched over to him. He was taken back by her abrupt change of location. She launched her hand toward him making him flinch slightly not knowing her intentions. At the last second, she jerked toward the box and retrieved a slice of pizza. Quickly, she stuffed the slice in her mouth and took a bite. With her mouth full, she wouldn't have to respond.

"See. I knew you were hungry," Brian teased as Trish chewed slowly, savoring every delicious inch of the bite. She and food had a hot and heavy relationship. Without particular rules and watching, she would easily overdo it. The first time Trish lost control and went on a binge, it was scary. She just couldn't consume enough food. When it was over, she felt so remorseful that the only thing she could do was purge it all. She threw up that time for so long, and then she realized how much better she felt afterward. That was when she realized how thin the ledge was that she stood on every day. The edge between just eating what was necessary and letting her body take over her mind. Today wasn't going to be that day. She would retain control just like every other day, because that was how she trained herself.

"I'm not hungry. I'm just refusing to speak to you any longer," she said around her mouthful. Still wanting to take in every flavor, she was still chewing her first bite.

"What did I do to deserve the silent treatment?"

"The easier question is what did you not do. You are a self-centered jerk who thinks the world would stop spinning if you weren't in it. I'm a realist. That means I know not everyone feels one's presence is necessary all the time for people to be happy. Yours is one of those. People can be perfectly content with you somewhere else, anywhere else." With that, she turned back around to enjoy her pizza in peace.

Without warning, Brian was up and standing directly behind her. He placed his hand on the back of her chair and leaned in close to see her computer screen.

"What are you doing? I already told you this is none of your business."

"This is a big crime family in the city, and you are doing work for them. I'm interested in what you are doing."

"Do your ears work or are they full of cotton? I said, stay out of it." Trish was beyond frustrated with Brian. Without another word, she saved her document and shut down her computer. Then she filed her notes into her desk drawer and locked it. "Since you are a Nosey Nelly, I guess I'm going to call it a night. I'll just plan on working extra hard tomorrow in hopes I can get this finished. After dealing with you tonight, I think I'll need happy hour Friday drinks. Which means you won't need to meet me after work tomorrow, because I'll have the girls meet me straight at the bar."

She only hoped that appeased him. With that, she made her way to the door without a backward glance at Brian. Assuming he was following her, she held the door so she could check to be sure it was locked. From there he led the way to where he parked his car. She wasn't going to fight with him about the ride, because if she relented he would be out of her hair sooner rather than later.

The drive home was quiet, just how Trish wanted it. The last thing she wanted to do was continue a conversation with the thorn in her side. He had already caused enough trouble in her evening.

As Brian pulled up to her apartment building she spoke, "You don't need to get out. I have Sam to see to me getting inside. You have done your good deed for the day and got me home safely."

"My mother raised me to be a gentleman. What would she say if something got to you between here and the front door?" Brian moved to get out of the car before she could respond.

As he opened her door she glared at him, "She'd say that you have overstayed your welcome, and the gentlemanly thing to do is not to press your luck." Trish climbed out of the car ignoring his outstretched hand waiting to help her. Pushing past him she made her way to the door. She figured ignoring him was the best plan, and it had been working so far.

Making it to the door, Sam held it open with a grim look. Anyone else with that face would worry her, but that was just his look. He was always in security mode when he was here. She never really saw him smile as though his goal was to intimidate everyone. Luckily, she was fully versed in all things Sam. He no longer scared her, and she usually brushed off his behavior. Trish brushed past Sam and made her way into the building. She wasn't even going to thank Brian for the ride then her upbringing started to twist in her gut. Barely glancing over her shoulder Trish said, "Thanks for the lift," as though he were merely a cab driver.

Trish went to bed without another thought about Brian. Well, maybe that was a stretch. He might have made his nightly appearance in her dream, but does it really count if it's only his face? Her dreams usually consisted of people she knew or had seen that day, but Brian was always in them. He was sometimes a Scottish blacksmith, wearing only a kilt of his family colors. Other times he was a cowboy, hot from a hard day's work and usually shirtless. She had a vivid imagination, and she was an avid reader. There was never a limit to what she could conjure up in her dream world. Nevertheless, it wasn't worth complaining about because she was always well rested after those dreams. If he kept her up tossing and turning, she might have to take it out verbally on the real thing.

Waking up the next morning, Trish shot off a message to each of the girls, Grace and Abigail. Since Grace's stalking and abduction, Abigail has stayed close to the group. Not to mention as Grace's sister-in-law now, they were pretty much stuck with her. Not that that was a chore. Abigail was an absolute joy to be around, and she could practically light up a room just by hopping into it.

Hey, let's do happy hour tonight. I'm feeling overworked and under relaxed.

Grace was the first to respond, as always. She was happily married and worked in an office by herself, but she wasn't at work yet. Trish had set her alarm early so she could make up some work she had lost last night when she was interrupted.

That sounds perfect. It feels like ages since we've hung out.

Abigail was always a late riser. Since her husband, Ted, owned his own construction business, she didn't have any reason to be up this early. She would respond later when she woke up. She would probably be up for anything as long as she got home in time to make Ted dinner.

Trish busied herself with getting ready for work. Knowing she would be going out tonight straight from work, she wanted to dress accordingly. She weeded through her closet for a something a little nicer than her everyday work clothes. Toward the back, she found a pale pink flowy dress. It was a lot fancier than she would usually wear to work, but she remembered it to be very comfortable and it swishes when she walks like a flowing current on the water. As Trish put it on, she gave it a couple of swishes for good measure.

• • • •

TRISH HAD A BUSY DAY; she made a lot of progress on the Castenellos file. By lunchtime, she was starving. Since she planned on drinking her dinner, a lunch break was in order. While she was at the local deli Trish's text alert sounded. Glancing at the screen, she smiled. Abigail was always a colorful creature.

Do you ever have to ask? Just tell me when and where, I'm always up for a girl's night. If I have to spend another night in with Ted, I'm going to lose my mind. He is such an old fuddy-duddy. I'm much younger than he is. I need a social outlet.

Trish laughed out loud, drawing a bit of attention her way. Embarrassed, she ducked her head slightly. She never did like to have all the attention on her, but if it were a steamy guy she'd take it. She wasn't a nun. She quickly relayed all the details and made her way back to the office.

At five o'clock sharp she was making her way out of the office. A few people looked at her surprised, because lately she was usually nose deep into her computer and barely glancing up to see her coworkers leave.

Since she dressed for this, Trish made her way straight to The Fainting Goat. It was a bit of a kitschy bar, and it was laidback enough the girls could go for drinks and not be attacked by potential suitors not aware of the fact that over half of them were already taken. Girl's Night was exactly that, a night for just them. They were never on the prowl, and they most certainly didn't bail on each other for new men or the existing men in their lives, unless there was an actual emergency. They weren't completely heartless, but there was a time and a place. They wanted to have time uninterrupted to catch up and talk. They deserved a time to themselves to share with each other the good and bad things in their lives. Give advice and share laughs. After a few drinks, they were sure to be laughing and perhaps engaging in side-splitting fun.

She picked a table closer to the back of the bar. She wanted fewer distractions and a little more seclusion. The waitress came over directly; it must not be too busy yet.

"Hey stranger, where have you been?" the waitress asked Trish as she bumped the table with her hip.

"Oh, Danielle, I didn't know you were working tonight. Don't you ever take a day off?"

"I could ask you the same thing," Danielle put her hand on her hip looking like a mom scolding a daughter. She wasn't old enough to be Trish's mom, but she was in her forties and seemed to be happy as a waitress. It suited her personality. She didn't have any kids of her own, so the hours were perfect for her. Outside of work, she didn't have anyone to worry about. That meant she could take on whatever shifts she wanted.

"I know I've been working a lot of hours, but I'm trying to get a promotion which won't happen if I don't put in the time to accomplish it. This case has been day and night. Even though it started out seeming small, it might turn into the biggest one I've ever worked on."

"Well, it sounds like you've been busy, but I'm glad you took a night off. Who are you expecting? An unknown beau or the girls?"

"The girls, should be Grace and Abigail. Just the three of us." As if on cue, in walked the girls. But as they approached the table, Trish saw another familiar face that she hadn't seen since Grace's wedding, Sal. Her full name was Sally, but she had been introduced as Sal because that is what everyone called her since she was a kid. She worked as a barista at the Brewing Bean. Grace met her when she was hiding out from her attacker. Patrick was trying to track him while he stalked Grace. Sal is becoming one of the group by default.

"Hey, surprise! We ran into Sal on the way over here and invited her to tag along. We knew you wouldn't mind," Grace said as she took her seat.

"Of course, I don't mind. I feel like I haven't seen you in forever. This will give us a great chance to get to know each other better. I could always use another single friend since Grace abandoned me for a handsome detective."

"Uh, I remember you were pushing me to explore my options with him not too long ago," Grace chimed in with a touch of feigned offense.

"Yes, but I didn't expect you to leave your single status so quickly and leaving me with no wing-girl," Trish joked lightly.

"What did you expect her to do? Leave my brother on the market for someone else to scoop up? Now she has her territory marked without having to pee on him," Abigail was the one who had the least filter. She had been married the longest and was Patrick's sister. She joined the group when Grace and Patrick started dating. Even though Grace has worked for her husband for what seems like forever now. That office would be a disaster if not for Grace and her mad skills.

"No one had scooped him up yet, who's to say he wouldn't have taken anyone up on their offer? Grace had him right where she wanted him." Sal added to the conversation, and everyone looked at her. She looked a bit startled that she let that slip. Obviously, she still wasn't completely comfortable with all of them at once.

"You're so right, Sal. On second thought, I think I'd rather have you as a wing-girl in most situations. My brain seems to have forgotten that she wasn't the best in the major social settings. She was a bit of a homebody back then and didn't want to go out when I was ready to be on the prowl. You and I could get into so much trouble if we wanted to, but it would be too much fun." Trish wasn't a big partier, but she had her day back when she was younger.

Abigail started laughing out of the blue, and all the girls turned to look at the nutcase in the room. "I'm sorry, I couldn't help it. You girls sound crazy fighting over who is better in this situation or that.

If my memory serves me correctly, none of you have been "out" for a while. Grace is taken, Trish you've been a workaholic and Sal I'm not sure about you, but if you are friends with these two, you have climbed aboard the wrong ship."

They all crumbled into laughter, and Danielle took their drink orders and left to tend to other customers.

"I don't know about you girls, but I am ready to drink tonight. I know I've been locked away, but if I don't finish this project soon, I feel like I'll be old and grey before I see another promotion opportunity. I just want to get off the bottom even if it is just a step up. This grunt work would kill the strongest person." Danielle came back quickly with their drinks and Trish took a long drink of hers.

"What is so great about that project that will result in a promotion?" Abigail asked genuinely interested. She was a bit of a meddler, so she wanted a little bit of a hand in everything.

"It's supposed to help a family pass on their legacy to their children, but the further I get into it the stranger it gets. Like money is appearing from nowhere. I can't tell if something is wrong or they are just trying to live outside of their means."

They were about to continue when Danielle returned, "Now that you've got some liquid in you, do you ladies want to try some of our appetizers?"

They all exchanged glances and nodded. Soon they had placed an order for every appetizer option on the menu. Danielle left their table pleased to have upsold their table, but there was never a question because these girls loved their food.

Quickly picking up the conversation where they left off, Grace added her two cents, "What do you mean outside of their means? You have their books. You should be able to see how much money is coming in and what their bank account says. I'm not much of a money guru like you, but even I can tell that sounds hinky."

"That's what I thought, so I asked for their paper copies of the ledgers. Apparently, the grandmother of the family has kept the books for years. So now I have to differentiate whether it's the paper copies or the electronic versions that are skewed. There just aren't enough hours in a day. I'm going crazy. I have stacks and stacks of notes, and they are almost more confusing than the books themselves." Trish dropped her head into her hands in frustration. "Okay, no more work talk. I came here to relax and catch up. That is exactly what I intend to do. Grace, I need to know what the latest is with you, Abigail you need to tell me about the upcoming charity auction, and Sal tell me about the most recent man in your life even if he isn't current." Saying it all in one breath, Trish took a deep breath, and her eyes settled on her drink. Quickly, she slugged down the remaining liquid and held it up for Danielle to see which worked flawlessly. The waitress nodded at Trish to acknowledge the brazen drink request.

The girls all looked between them deciding without words which would go first. Abigail took the honor, "Well, you know I try and do four to six charity events a year, but this is the big one. The Snowflake Ball is the grandest affair, and we treat it as such. There is an elegant dinner to set off the black-tie requirement. I figure if I'm making people go above and beyond their standard dress-up attire then I should spring for fancy food."

"How long do we have to prepare for this? You know there will need to be a shopping trip, and the guys are going to need help. Not to mention, Sal and I might need time to plan for dates." Trish winked at Sal, but she didn't want her to think she overstepped, "Unless, you already have someone in mind, girl." Sal blushed as if on cue.

"No, I don't have anyone in mind. I haven't had a decent date in a while. The last one I had was too perfect, and I paid for it later." That was a very vague statement, and Trish would need to dig deeper to get to the bottom of that. But first, she wanted to finish with Abigail. Then she would sic the wolves on Sal.

"Good. Then you and I have to find perfect dates. If nothing else, we need to make other potential suitors jealous. So, Abby, when is this elite soiree?"

"I like to get started on the big one early, so that means you have two months. I've already booked the venue and planned the food, but I have to start selling plates. Each plate goes for one thousand dollars. All the money this year is going to RAINN."

"What is that?" all the girls asked in unison.

"Rape, Abuse, and Incest National Network," Abigail answered without hesitation. She said it as though it were nothing, but then she glanced toward Grace. "Patrick and I thought it would be perfect in honor of Grace and her journey." A tear slipped down Grace's cheek. Obviously, this was news to her. Abigail leaned over and hugged her.

"I don't want any attention, but I think it is perfect. I know the struggle I have gone through, and Patrick has been there for me. There are a lot of women out there who don't have that same support group. You are a great sister-in-law. Do you know that?" Grace wiped her tears and hugged Abigail back.

"I was born for this role. It just took Patrick too long to find you." Abigail was always good at bringing the subject back to happier topics.

"So, Grace, what is new with you?" Trish steered the conversation to keep it from falling back to her. Danielle snuck in and brought Trish's new drink and placed their buffet of appetizers around the table with plates for everyone. They all started filling plates to eat, and Grace dropped a bomb.

"Well, Patrick and I have been talking babies." Conversation erupted, and they started talking over each other.

"How exciting!"

"I'm going to be an aunt!"

"I'm so happy for you two!'

They were all caught up fawning over Grace's news. Grace continued, "Unfortunately, Patrick has been caught up with a new case, so it hasn't gone much past talking." The disappointment in her voice was palpable.

"I'm sure he'll be finished soon," Abigail reassured. "You know my brother. He is a regular Sherlock Holmes. Cases in his hands don't remain a mystery for very long at all."

"Well, maybe if Brian didn't seem to have a new love interest they could put their usual hours into things. He seems to cut out early every night, but I guess according to Patrick he's coming in early too. So, he is putting in hours, but not their usual ones." Trish was startled by her words and immediately looked down at the table and the food. She started shoving food into her mouth like it was going to disappear before she could consume it.

"Oh, this spinach dip is amazing. Have we had this one before? I'd think if we had, I would remember it. This is the best. Ever."

The girls looked at Trish confused for a moment. Then Sal piped up and broke the ice covering the conversation. "Is there something you want to tell us, Trish?"

"What? Me? No!" Trish hedged non-convincingly.

The girls smirked and then pounced on her like ravenous cats. They were determined to dig out every bit of information possible.

"Obviously, you have some knowledge of this mystery girl. Care to share?" Grace questioned in hopes of getting it out of her.

"He doesn't have a new girl, but he might have a pet project." She was opting for vague in hopes they would take the bait and let it go.

"What project could possibly be more important than solving the case they have acquired? Patrick said there was a murder, and it looked like it might be related to some of the known crime family cases that we have heard about over the years. Granted they never pin anything on the crime family; they're involved somehow." Abigail was very knowledgeable about the case. Then again, she always was very aware of the cases in this town since her brother was on the force. That didn't mean he told her; she had her sources and she was always well informed because she was worried about her brother.

"I heard about that one," Sal was starting to become more comfortable with the group and decided to join the conversation on a chatting level. "I heard they smashed his kneecaps and stabbed him before finally killing him."

"I hope it isn't anything too serious or a serial. I do okay thinking about Patrick at work, especially when he has a cold case, but most of the time I try not to think about all the dangers he encounters in the line of duty," a shiver ran over Grace's skin causing goosebumps to pucker all over her arms.

"If Brian is out gallivanting every day than I'm sure it's nothing so terrible." Trish regretted her words as soon as she said them. The girls were back on the hunt for information. After a few more questions, Trish decided to cut the head off the dragon and spill her guts. Besides she had had enough liquor to feel like it was her girl's night duty to share.

"FINE! Brian has been stalking me." That was the best thing she could think of for what Brian was doing. It wasn't as though she had asked him to do so.

"Stalking you? That doesn't sound like Brian. He usually has a different girl every night and doesn't have to chase them. They typically throw themselves at him. Why would he be stalking you?" Grace was as confused as Trish. This was out of her wheelhouse, and she didn't know what any of it meant.

"How should I know? He followed me home after work the other night when it was storming. I was fine walking. It's my time to decompress in the silence of the evening and no one to bother me. I admit it was later than I usually came home, but it didn't explain why he was there. He refused to leave until I got in his beautiful car so after I put up a significant fight, I caved and purposely soaked his seats with my dripping hair." She laughed maniacally showing that the alcohol had reached all the way to her brain cells. They could ask her anything at this point, and she would probably answer.

"I bet he appreciated it. He treats that car like a person and babies it as though if anything happens to it, he'll be crushed for life. I'm sure it has a name, too." Abigail laughed, because honestly, it was a hilarious mental picture.

"I might have enjoyed it a little too much. Well, if that wasn't bad enough he showed up at my office the next day, under the guise of checking to make sure I made it in alright. It wasn't even regular working hours. I was there early more like six o'clock. I needed to get back to work, and there just aren't enough hours in a day. So, after I finally convinced him to leave he swore he would be back to take me home regardless of whether I wanted him to or not. I was to call him, or he would be there waiting at five o'clock."

"Are you serious? What has gotten into him?" Grace had leaned in to listen to Trish's tale in detail.

"I don't know Brian that well, but I do know he looks like a lady's man. This sounds out of character for someone like that." Sal was spot on. Everyone nodded their agreement, because she was right on track.

"I'm not sure. Needless to say, because it's me, I pushed my luck and didn't call to tell him when I would be finished. Mostly because that answer is relative these days, and usually I take off whenever I feel I am at a stopping point or have gotten enough done. He showed up as promised but didn't wait outside. He snuck up on me again at my desk. Then he actually ordered a pizza while he was waiting, because I still refused to leave."

The girls couldn't contain their laughter. Trish couldn't blame them in the least. Retelling this story she could certainly see the humor, so she joined in with them.

"He is up to something; we should watch and see if anything changes." Abigail was all for her secret missions. Anything to liven up her life as a housewife. That is why she always puts on charity functions within her circle. She is an old pro, and everyone wants to be a part of all of her projects no matter how heartfelt or mischievous they might be.

"Well, I'll be glad when he gives up. I don't know how much more I can take. My lady bits can only tell him no so long." Trish's eyes got large as though it took a moment for it to sink in that she had said that out loud.

"Girl, no one can blame you. I thought that Grace was a goddess when she came into the coffee shop with both him and Patrick two separate days. He is one fine piece of man meat. If you are a red-blooded woman who swings for that team, no one can blame you." Sal was quickly becoming Trish's favorite person.

Grace and Abigail agreed wholeheartedly even though they both had their husbands to go home to tonight. Girl code distinctly states that we are allowed to notice the hot level of a man until the day we die. The only problem is if we cross the un-crossable line and act on those observations. Nothing will ever stop this group of girls from telling each other who is worthy of lingering looks or the occasional taste.

"Trish, have you ever taken that leap with Brian?"

"Oh no. Don't get her started on this one. They have a standing rivalry, and now they love to hate each other." Grace simply stated, and Trish would usually shy away from this story, but for some reason - probably the alcohol - she found herself jumping into the story.

"So, you're saying that he just ignored you the entire time? Who would do that? You are drop-dead gorgeous. Any man would kill for a chance to talk to you, let alone the opportunity to go out with you." Sal was a keeper. She knew how to boost a girl's self-esteem.

"I lurve you!" Trish's words were starting to slur, but everyone knew what she meant.

The evening went over really well, but Trish needed to call an Uber to get home. Grace called Patrick because he was still very protective, and she didn't trust service transportation after her attack. Before Trish's ride got there, the boys strolled in, and Trish took a double take. Patrick and Brian made their way to the girl's table.

"What are you doin' here?" Trish asked feeling her lady bits start to tingle at the sight of him. Without him here, Trish was enjoying her relaxed alcohol-induced state. Now she was more dreading what she might be open enough to do that she wouldn't typically allow herself.

"Patrick and I were together at the house, reviewing the case. He said he was on his way here to get Grace from girl's night. I assumed you would be here too, but I'm also pleasantly surprised you took a night off. Anyway, I decided I'd come and be your ride for the night."

All the girls exchanged knowing looks, "I have a ride on the way."

"Cancel it. No biggie. They don't charge you for cancellations if you can do it before they arrive. How far out are they?"

Trish opened the app, and it said fifteen minutes. Rolling her eyes, she flipped the screen so the others could see. In her inebriated state, she couldn't think of any other excuses. She was so far off her game it was ridiculous.

"See you can still cancel and save yourself money. You are the financial advisor here. It should be a no-brainer to save money and accept a free ride from someone you know."

"I wish I didn't know you," that was the best she could come up with at that moment. It was a pathetic comeback.

"That is just the alcohol talking. You know you love me, and you also know this is the smart thing to do."

"Ted just texted and said he is here, but he stayed outside waiting for me. Sal, want us to give you a ride?" Abigail started gathering her things and threw her money on the table to cover her drinks and part of the food. They had done this enough she knew the drill without question.

"She can ride home with me," Trish was grasping at straws trying not to be alone with Brian right now.

"Nonsense, we brought her, and her place is right on our way home." Abigail winked at her. She was obviously plotting, and there was nothing Trish could do to stop her. At least not in this state. She just wanted to be home, at this point. It's not worth a fight if she gets home sooner. She will just leave him in the car like she usually does or at least tries to do.

The drive home Trish tried to be quiet. Much to her dismay Brian had an unrealistic need to keep the conversation going. "It looks like you've had a drink or two tonight."

"Wow. You really are a detective, aren't you?" Trish said sarcastically. "If I hadn't, you wouldn't be driving me home." She maturely followed that with an eyeroll that he most likely couldn't see. Drunk was really not a good look on her.

"I'm glad you let me drive you home. I would have been worried about you if I didn't get to see you back."

Trish was confused, "Sometimes you make no sense at all. Aren't you supposed to hate me? We have been battling for months."

"You have been battling, as you put it. I've just been letting you, because I think you look hella sexy when you're angry." He turned back to the road with a sexy smug grin on his face.

Trish's intoxicated mind was trying with a lot of effort to calculate what he just said. It sounded a lot like he thought she was sexy. That couldn't be because he paid her no attention on their date. He spent the entire time checking out their waitress. Trish had spent months reliving that night and comparing herself to the other woman.

"You make no sense to me. I don't know what to say to you."

"Say yes." Brian was laying it on thick.

"I don't recall hearing a question, but it is possible I blacked out for a second and missed it."

"Give me another chance."

"Again, I could be mistaken, but that wasn't a question either." Rather than answering his request directly, she opted to deflect him. It was easier than admitting that she wanted to give him a second chance more than anything.

"Come on Trish. I want to make everything up to you. No other girl compares to you, and they don't do anything for me now. I've decided I have to have you or no one."

"Wow. You know how to tell a girl what she wants to hear just to get your way. You have a funny way of showing it. I let you have a chance, and you spent the entire night focused on another girl. That is the last thing a girl wants to see is her date lost in another chick."

"You have still not given me a chance to explain what happened that night."

Trish interrupted him, "I'm not sure I can handle the explanation in my current state of mind."

"This will be one of the only times I know I'll have your undivided attention because your brain isn't fully firing. So, buck up and listen. I admit I spent the entire night distracted, but it wasn't for the reason you think. I wasn't checking her out. I thought I recognized her, and I couldn't place her. It turns out that she dyed her hair, and it was a crazy psycho I dated a few years back. I will never forget her now. She wasn't only a psycho in the light of day. She was worse behind closed doors."

"You do realize that story doesn't help your case. It just means you are such a player you can't tell which girls you have slept with and which ones you haven't. People should be able to recognize the faces at least and put them together with a situation, even if you don't remember their names. I'm sure all their names are relative to you and mean nothing. One girl is the same as the next if they serve their ultimate purpose beneath the sheets. I don't even want to think about the fluids that may or may not be on the seat beneath me."

"I draw the line there. No matter how hard up I am I refuse to contaminate my car. This sacred piece of machinery won't be damaged in that way."

Trish couldn't help it; she burst out laughing. Brian just looked at her with a blank look on his face. That last statement broke her. She remembered what the girls said about his car, and she lost it. He was so attached to that car he treated it like a spouse or a child.

"You should pull over."

"Are you gonna hurl?" Brian quickly made it to the side of the road. He rushed around the car and got her door.

She turned to exit the car, "Nope. Just thought you needed a moment alone with your baby."

He let out a groan of frustration. "Maybe you were right; this wasn't the best time to have this conversation. You can't take anything seriously."

"I can take things seriously, but you are over the top funny tonight. I can't combat that with anything in my arsenal."

Brian made his way back to the car and climbed back into his seat, but he didn't take off right away. He turned to Trish and just looked at her. She was growing very uncomfortable. There was no way she was going to be able to stand against his smolder for very long. She hoped he wouldn't press the go steamy button before he decided to resume their drive to her apartment.

Looking away from his stare, "What? Why do you keep looking at me like that?"

"How can I not? You are truly the most beautiful creature I've ever seen, and no one compares to you or even comes close," his voice was barely above a whisper, and Trish instantly got goosebumps. What was she supposed to say to that? When she didn't respond, Brian started the car and drove on in silence. He didn't try to talk to her anymore the rest of the trip. Trish felt confused. What did he mean he thought she was the most beautiful creature? He dated a variety of women, and their date had been a nightmare. He must be delusional to think she could believe him. Unfortunately for her, she wanted to believe him more than anything. Her life had been a mess her entire life. She was always trying to make herself better to please others. Why couldn't she be allowed to be happy for once?

Brian dropped her off at the door and didn't even try to walk her to it. He was obviously out of it and barely grunted a goodbye. So lost, Trish was ready to go home and pass out. Sam tried to talk to her, and she just brushed past him and went home. After the ride and discussion with Brian, she didn't want to talk to anyone.

Safely locked away in her room, Trish made her way to bed. She could shower in the morning there was nothing she wanted more than to sleep. The night with the girls was fantastic, but the drive home was stressful. Now the safest place for her was locked away inside her dream world.

It was late afternoon, and Trish was getting ready to head out with friends. They had a long day at school after finals, but she was ready for the weekend. They all decided to go the mall and kill some time. They were planning to go to a movie later that evening. They shopped and bought a few small things they could carry easily with them, but really the mall trip was about being seen. She was popular in high school and had to make a certain showing of herself. Public appearances were mandatory to keep her status. If she locked herself away in her bedroom, her status would fall from social princess to agoraphobic troll. She knew the latter wouldn't fly with her mother and her social circles, so she made every effort possible to be the best daughter she could be and tried to keep up appearances.

This trip was no different. The longer she spent out, the more difficult it was to hide things from her friends. She felt like they could see the sweat beading up on her forehead because any food she ate was stressing her out. She thought they could see her clammy hands, because all she wanted to do was go throw up. The girls stopped for dinner in the food court whenever they were out, but that was the last thing Trish wanted. There was no way she could keep up her façade with them so close and breathing down her neck. No matter how much she protested, someone - if not all of her friends - followed her to the bathroom. It was as though they were unable to go alone.

Trish, as usual, tried to eat the least amount of food possible, but the less she ate, the more questions they asked. Trish, are you on some kind of diet? Trish, did you not like your food? She knew they weren't going to relent, so to avoid further questions, she took a huge bite out of her sandwich. Her stomach rejected the idea of food immediately, but her tongue came alive under the flavor. She had deprived herself of foods and such to keep the temptation to binge was under control. She never wanted to experience that lack of control ever again. Nothing had changed. Her mouth watered with the taste. As she forced herself to swallow, her stomach - which had been trained to reject all food - was immediately trying to go to work. She had to do something to keep her secret hidden. Without much thought, Trish grabbed her drink and started to force fluid down her throat to reverse the action her stomach wanted to take. If the liquid made its way down, then it would stop anything from coming back up, at least for now.

Crisis averted, for now. The girls finished up quickly to make it to the movies. There her problems would begin anew. The girls all went to the snack counter to order drinks and popcorn. They all ordered larges under the guise that in the dark no one would know they ate so much. When Trish's turn rolled around, the girls were bothered because she ordered a bottle of water and the smallest popcorn. She covered it up as best she could through their whining of unfair and such. She said that she had an event coming up. She needed to fit into a dress for her mother's circle. That seemed to calm them down a bit. That didn't get her off the hook for finishing the popcorn. With every bite, Trish fought her revolting stomach. It was a battle of wills, and she had to be stronger. There was no explanation great enough if she failed to stay in control.

She survived the movie, barely. By the time it was finished, she felt feverish and nauseous. Walking outside was a chore in and of itself. She said her goodbyes to her friend and quickly as she could she got into her car to leave. She made it around the block before she had to pull over. She barely got her car door open before she lost everything she had eaten that evening. It felt like a relief to release all of it and not have to fight anymore. On the other side, she was torn because she felt like a monster. Who does this? Who can't go out with their friends without struggling to keep their body under control? What have I done to myself? These were all running on a loop through her mind as she purged all the toxins from her body. As she finished, she felt her body return to its version of normal. Was she going to be like this forever?

Trish awoke the next morning feeling awful. She had drunk enough last night to ease her tension, but unfortunately, she also drank enough to be a bit hungover. She had gone straight to bed last night and neglected to drink any water or take any aspirin. Now she was paying the price, her mother had always been a day drinker, but Trish never developed that kind of taste for alcohol. She was a good time gal and limited her drinking to social gatherings. Although, she had been known to adhere to the saying 'where two or more are gathered'. She and Grace might have had a drunken night or two in the past, just the two of them, but only under dire circumstances. A little 'hair of the dog' was out of the question.

Trish made her way to the bathroom to medicate her throbbing head. Blindly, she opened the medicine cabinet and pulled out some pain relievers, quickly shaking out two and throwing them down the chute. Turning on the faucet, she stuck her face into the sink and got a drink of water to wash down the pills.

Before closing the cabinet, she hesitated. The part of her morning she hated was looking in the mirror. With all the alcohol and food she consumed last night, she could feel how bloated she was. After coming home and to bed straight away, she didn't have time to rid her body of any of the toxins she consumed. With a flash of bravery, she closed the mirror and slowly raised her eyes to take in her appearance. Still clothed in just her underwear from last night since she only bothered to rid herself of the clingy dress, she saw everything without barriers. Her face was thicker in her cheeks than she wanted, though to any other person they would seem gaunt. As her line of sight trailed down her body, she observed her curvaceous figure. In her eyes she filled out in places she wished she could stunt the growth forever. Her hands traveled over her ribs. Even though she couldn't see how thin she was, others would say she was almost too bony. Her clothes covered her well enough, but slim was a word used by others often. As she got to her stomach, she leaned over slightly and pinched off close to an inch of what she assumed was fat. She had been told by health professionals in the past that even the most toned person with a six-pack could lean over and pinch skin. She didn't care. This was disgusting in her eyes and everything she had seen made her sick to her stomach.

She rushed to the toilet and purged everything that she could. She attempted to rid her body of anything left over from the night before. To her dismay, all she threw up was the small amount of water she had and her pain pills. Then the only thing left was the acid in her stomach that burned as it came back up. Her throat screamed for her to stop, but the dry heaves were all that she had left. Her body racked with tremors as her body convulsed attempting to rid herself of any small morsel remaining.

Before she stood up, she turned on the shower. Now she needed to wash off the layer of sweat that was clinging all over her body to every inch of skin. What little clothing she had on was suffocating her just from the closeness. Ripping her bra and panties from her body as quickly as she could, she stood in her bathroom naked as the day she was born. Glancing in the mirror one last time she thought, *when is enough going to be enough?* She was beyond abhorred by her appearance. Trish knew she was going to be causing her body more harm than good eventually, but every time she looked at her body she couldn't bear it.

Each time was worse than the last. She tried to limit her eating so she wouldn't feel the need to vomit so much. After a while, though the neglect takes over, and she loses control. Those are the times this disease scares her. She gorges on everything in sight, and she can't stop. By the time she has reached her limit, she throws up so much that she either passes out or just stays in the bathroom for hours on end. That has only happened a few times in her life, because she does everything she can to avoid it. The control is her sanity. Without her sanity what does she have left? This illness had already taken most of her dignity, but she had done well to hide it from all of her close friends. Her mother was aware, but that is the difference between her mother and her friends. Since she has found a way to please her mother by staying the daughter her mother needs, her mother ultimately doesn't care how she accomplishes it. This was working so it must not be altogether wrong. No one ever said her mother was the most intelligent person.

Instead of lingering on it any longer, Trish stepped into the warmth of the shower. The water sluiced over her body as she attempted to absorb the heat. Showers were one of her favorite things in life, and there was never such a thing as a cold shower. She preferred them skin melting hot, and nothing less would satisfy her craving.

Today was no different. As she ran her hands over the skin on her arms, she realized it was time to shave again. Most women don't shave their arms, but she knew an Asian girl in college who did. Apparently it was a cultural trait. Not long after meeting her, Trish took up the habit and never looked back. The doctors told her that the extra hair grown on her arms was her body trying to find new ways to warm itself. Since she wasn't allowing her body to build up any fat at all, it had nothing to protect her from changing temperatures. Her body had compensated, but Trish didn't like how she felt when it seemed people were staring at her apeish arms. She took it upon herself to remove all visible signs that she was different or something might be wrong. She never wanted to be one who stood out for any other reason than her face or who her mother was. She never thought she was exceptionally beautiful. Half the time she left the house in sweats with almost no makeup on her days off from work. Grace always told her women probably envied or hated her, but Trish didn't see it. Then again, who sees their own beauty flawlessly?

After Trish wrapped up her shower, she decided she would get ready and run to the office for a little while. Since it was Saturday, she would try and get in a few hours at work, but not before she enjoyed a nice cup of joe. She pulled up the Uber app on her phone and placed a request for a ride to the Brewing Bean. The girls had spent a lot of time there since Grace made it her office on the go a few months back. Even better than that, it was where Sal worked. Trish didn't know if she would be working today or not, especially since she was out with the girls last night.

Walking into the shop, Trish scanned the room for familiar faces. She didn't get all dolled up since no one would be in the office with her. She wore yoga pants and an old t-shirt, threw her hair up in a messy wet bun, and didn't even bother with makeup beyond mascara and lip gloss. Having come from a family of society, people assume she is going to look glamorous all the time. As soon as she got out of her mother's house, she loved nothing more than to prove them all wrong.

"Hey there stranger. Long time no see," a familiar voice drew her out of her thoughts. She looked up and saw Wes Bowman, owner of Five Alarm Security. She hadn't seen him since he performed Grace and Patrick's wedding a few months ago.

"Well, hi there. Fancy seeing you here. What have you been up to?"

"You'd know if you weren't such a worker bee. I hear you are practically chained to that desk at work. You haven't been out with any of us in a while." This statement was odd for Trish to comprehend. Even though he had performed the ceremony, she didn't think anyone was close friends with Wes. Initially, Wes tried to make a play for Grace and was shot down by her initial interest in Patrick. Honestly, who truly knows? If he had met her first, maybe things would have changed. Wes was a good-looking guy. He just wasn't a Patrick.

Wes was wearing what looked like work clothes, himself. "I could say the same about you. It's Saturday, and you appear to be getting ready to go to work."

"I'm in the security business; my job life comes on with a phone call. If I can avoid it, I try, but every so often my Saturday morning gets invaded by work."

"So, what have you all been doing lately without me? I didn't realize you had all been so busy in my absence."

"Nothing too exciting, but I hear from Brian that you used to be quite the party girl. He'd see you from time to time frequenting a new bar or club." There was that cursed name again. She couldn't go anywhere without hearing about him or seeing him. At this rate, she'd have to relocate to a new town to get away from him.

"Oh, well. Your information came from an unreliable source. He doesn't know much. Next time try a different rat, and see if you can get some better cheese."

"Am I sensing some bad blood?" Wes winked at her and came a little closer. Did he think he stood a chance with her?

"Understatement of the year. As you said, I'm a workaholic. I'm going to the office for a bit to catch up on some work I missed out on this week because of your new best friend." With that, she made her way to the counter to place her order and was happily greeted by Sal.

Sal wore a pleasant smile, but Trish could see a little deeper and saw underlying tiredness in her eyes. She had also paid this morning for last night's excursion.

"Hey lady, what brings you in today?" Sal asked while grabbing a pad to take down her order.

"Need a bit of the old brew to kick my butt into gear. I have a killer hangover, but I still need to get a bit of work done today."

"Hangover? I can't imagine why. The way you were pounding back drinks last night I expected you to be passed out all day. How are you even moving this morning?"

"Probiotics and vitamins," Trish stated flatly trying to hold a straight face.

"Seriously? That can't be right. You look healthy, but I don't think any of that will ward off a hangover from hell."

Trish started to giggle, "No, you're right. I'm a mess and nowhere near that healthy. Grace gets mad at me over my diet choices all the time." It was true Trish made poor dietary choices, but since she wasn't actually going to digest her food, she decided she would enjoy it as much as she could on the front end.

"Well, at least you can hold your figure. If I choose not to eat healthy for too long, I swell up like a sponge. Now enough about that, what kind of fattening coffee can I get you today?"

"That is where I will surprise you. I might like my food heavy on the fat, but my coffee I prefer a bit more natural. Can I get a Crimson Stamp black, please?"

"Of course, and you are right. I would have pegged you for a foofoo drinker. Honestly, I love this blend. It comes from Costa Rica and Columbia, but that isn't what makes it unique because so much coffee comes from Columbia. Am I right?" Trish nodded enjoying listening to Sal's trade knowledge. It was fun for her to hear someone who was proud of their work. Sal continued, "No, what makes this blend so unusual and unique is how it actually has a naturally creamy body with chocolate, nut, and fruit undertones. It is perfect for a morning after and allows you to have all the sweetness of life without having to doctor it up to alter the pure flavor. I knew I liked you just like I did Grace the first time I met her. You girls know how coffee is supposed to taste. Those people who want me to color it up for them with milk, creams, flavor shots, and sugar don't appreciate the true nature of the beast. It's wonderful to know, that you can handle the animal contained inside coffee, the way it should be."

"Wow! Girl, you are a poet of coffee. Do you know that? I could listen to you talk about the bean all day and never get bored."

Sal blushed slightly at the compliment, "I guess I'm just passionate about it since I work with it all day and sometimes night."

"You love your job, and it shows. It's a relief to know someone with your knowledge and background is the one who makes my favorite cup of joe."

Sal went about brewing her cup glancing up over her shoulder she watched someone leave the shop. "Did I see you talking to Wes when you walked in?"

"Oh, yeah. He caught me as I was scoping out the joint for familiar faces. One, in particular, I was thankful not to find. Why? Are you guys friendly?" She was poking around a little because Sal left her hanging a bit last night in the relationship talk department."

"I wouldn't say friendly. At least, not anymore. We went out once."

"Oh, I have one of those, and those are usually the worst stories." Since the line wasn't too bad and there were two more baristas on duty, Trish pressed a bit harder. "Care to share? I told you mine last night or at least enough to get the gist."

Sal hedged a bit and stayed silent. Trish assumed the answer was no until she started, "We went out once. I told Grace this before, but she must not have shared. Not that it would have mattered, but I'm kind of glad my dirty laundry wasn't aired all over the group."

"You don't have to tell me if you don't want to."

"No, you should know. We are friends, and friends tell each other things like this. That and I'd hate for you to try and fix us up again or, even worse, fall for his crap the way I did."

Trish wondered where this was going as Sal placed her coffee in her hand. She leaned against the counter and listened like a good friend, but really, she was eager to know the details of this sordid tale.

"Wes asked me out a couple of years ago when I first started working here. I thought he was dreamy. and I was young and naive. I couldn't believe he wanted to go out with me. I was nobody, and he was a handsome business owner. What more could a girl ask for? Right? So, we went out, and I had a great time. The conversation was never lacking, and we seemed to hit it off really well. I broke my cardinal rule and let him come up for a nightcap. One thing led to another, and we ended up in my bed. That was probably the best night of my life. I came to work the next day on cloud nine. Thought my life had finally peaked until he came in for his morning cup. He waited in line allowing people to go ahead of him until I was busy, and another girl helped him with his order. He never even looked at me let alone spoke to me. Now when he comes in, he might get his order from me, but still to this day keeps conversation to a minimum. We never went on another date."

Trish couldn't help her slack jaw. She couldn't believe that Wes would have ever treated her that way. At least not the Wes she had met a few months ago and had spoken to just moments before. She quickly regained her composure.

"Well, I say good riddance. He didn't deserve you. There is someone else out there who will be much better and probably more attractive. I'll just have to keep my eye out for you." One thing Trish loved to do was to fix people up. It had been a long time since she'd had a friend with whom to play matchmaker. Grace was her last one, but that was no fun. When she fixed her up, it seemed more like a chore than something exciting for her. Grace went through the motions, but nothing ever came of it. When Patrick came along, Trish wasn't sure if she was going to take the bait. Thankfully, it all worked out in the end, but Trish did do her fair share of nudging.

Waving goodbye to Sal, Trish made her way to the office. She sipped her coffee and enjoyed the delicious flavors as they permeated her mouth. She was a sucker for a good cup of coffee, but this one was exceptional. She'd never been a store brand coffee kind of girl. She liked hers exotic and full flavored.

That got Trish thinking about other things that would be good in full and exotic flavors. She walked along daydreaming of muscular, tan, foreign men when she absentmindedly ran into a tall, strong body halting her in her tracks. Slowly she looked up and into pools of deep, dark chocolate.

Brian was going to go into the office today to work on the case that he was obviously neglecting, but before he headed that way he wanted to check on Trish. After seeing the file she was working on, something felt off. He couldn't quite put his finger on it, but he didn't want to leave anything to chance.

On his way over to Trish's apartment, he decided he'd stop by and see Sal and grab a cup of coffee to go. Before he could go inside, he saw a familiar face. Walking up the street away from the Brewing Bean, was Bobby Castenellos. He had become the face of the family over the past few years. If anyone said anything about that family, that was the person you thought of and who you didn't want to upset. He never got his hands dirty, but he always had a hand in everything good or bad. The family restaurant was a cover. Granted they couldn't prove all the illegal activity that was going on, they could still smell a rat.

What is Bobby doing on this side of town? Brian wondered right before he saw another face he didn't expect this early on a Saturday morning. Walking up the street seemingly in a dream world, was Trish holding a steaming cup of coffee from The Brewing Bean. He started to walk towards her, but before he could get there, she ran right into the back of Bobby. Brian's heart clenched. She didn't need a run in with that beast. Increasing his speed, he made it over to them and picked up a portion of their conversation.

"Oh, I'm so sorry. I was distracted, and I should learn to pay better attention when it's this busy out." Trish placed her hand on his forearm to steady herself.

"If you are the worst thing that disturbs me all day, then I'm having a good day." Bobby placed his hand over hers, but not out of necessity. This made Brian's blood boil. The last thing he wanted was this guy, or any guy other than him, touching her. Bursting toward them from the corner where he had paused, he appeared before them as though by magic and startled them both.

"Hey stranger," he said feigning a casual tone. By no means, did he want her to know he had been watching her.

"What are you doing here?" Trish started, sounding her usual upset self whenever Brian was near. He was sure most of it was a front, but he never called her on it outright. He just enjoyed watching her sizzle underneath the collar whenever he was near. He knew it was just her fighting her own emotions and the conflict causing her frustration.

"I was in the neighborhood and saw you. Who is your friend?" Pretending not to know full well she was talking to Bobby was a ploy to see if they already knew each other.

Trish hesitated glancing at Bobby; she was clearly at a loss for words. Bobby came to her rescue putting his hand out to Brian first since he was the one who asked.

"Bobby Castenellos. It's a pleasure to meet you."

"Brian Thomas. The pleasure is mine." He then turned to Trish to see how they would act. Bobby didn't turn to her right away to introduce himself, but Trish was processing this information slowly. Brian knew the instant it clicked, because her face morphed into one of shock and quickly masked itself into her signature smile.

"Castenellos? That can't be a common name around here. You must be related to Mama." The statement was left hanging in the air and Trish gave him a moment to acquiesce.

"Guilty as charged. Mama is the matriarch of our family, and I'm apprenticing under her to take over the family business." Brian was slightly relieved that she didn't know him before now, but it didn't put him at ease that she had since made his acquaintance.

"That makes me your new financial advisor, Trish Montgomery." She thrust her hand in his direction eagerly as her eyes lit with excitement. Brian didn't know if it was because she was meeting a client for the first time or if there was something more there he couldn't see.

"Well then, I'm thrilled you are the one who ran into me today. I couldn't think of a better person, not to mention a beauty like you, to attempt to run me down on a day like today." He motioned toward the sun that was shining uninhibited by a single cloud in the sky. Brian rolled his eyes at the theatrics. Bobby Castenellos struck fear into the hearts of the strongest man. There was another reason he tolerated Trish running into him, and it wasn't her beautiful face.

"Trish, after last night," Brian let the innuendo hang thick in the air like fog, "I figured you'd still be limp in your bed. What has you up so early after such a busy night?" He purposely made it sound like there was more to it than just over drinking. He also made it sound like he had been there, even though he most certainly hadn't.

Trish glared at him for the inaccurate tone and directed her attention to Bobby, "I had a few too many last night with the girls, hence the rather large coffee." She held up her coffee cup as if it needed to be addressed. "I'm actually on my way into the office to work a bit more on your file. I didn't get as far as I wanted to last night. It is in a bit of disarray. Whoever took over for Mama and tried to go digital has mixed a few things up. I'm having trouble getting through it all, and it feels like double work half the time. No worries though, I'm amazing at what I do. It will be all sorted before you know it." There was her award-winning smile again. She was definitely putting on a show for Bobby. Something was up with her and Brian needed to get to the bottom of it. Now.

"It's Saturday. Whatever is in that file can wait." Before Brian could continue, he was rudely interrupted by Bobby.

"Byron is right. You should have a day off from work. Why don't you let me take you out for some breakfast?" Now it was Brian's turn to be steaming from beneath the collar, and this time it wasn't confusion causing it.

"Brian! My name is Brian!" he spat out with anger. Bobby knew who he was Patrick and he had investigated enough cases over the years that stank of Castenellos dirty laundry.

"My mistake," Bobby replied with an air of nonchalance.

Trish jumped in to end the banter between them, but she didn't say what Brian expected.

"I'd love to have breakfast with you, Bobby. Perhaps you will be able to shed some light on some of the more challenging portions of your file." She glanced back at Brian, and her eyes shown with rebellion. If she had been eight, she would have stuck her tongue out at him.

Without another word, she placed her arm on Bobby's proffered one, and they were off. Brian didn't have a chance to counter or voice his displeasure. She had gotten what she wanted - to upset him - but what she didn't bargain for was he was green with envy. That was what he had planned to do, but how ridiculous would he have looked if he shouted, 'no go to breakfast with me'? She wasn't a toy to be fought over. She was a lady. He would have her, but in his own time and by his own standards. She would choose him when it came down to brass tacks.

Without a good reason, he couldn't stop them from running off to breakfast, but seeing as it was broad daylight, he wouldn't press the issue. For now. Bobby did get her to quit work, at least for the day.

Brian made his way to the coffee shop to see Sal. He loved popping in to see her now and again. She was a sweet girl, and ever since he met her while guarding Grace, he was intrigued by her. He wasn't interested in her to date her, but she made a good friend now that she was a part of their inner circle. He never understood how she was still single. With her sense of humor and pretty face, she was a catch if he'd ever seen one.

As he walked in, Sal looked up and smiled at him followed immediately by an eye roll. Brian laughed out loud, "I see you're slacking as usual."

"No more than you would be, lover boy," Sal responded with a knowing grin and a wink. What did she think she knew? The girls must have been talking about him, and this piqued his interest.

"I know you're not referring to my amazing skills in the bedroom, so I have to assume you are referring to something else that was said last night during your drink fest." He tapped his finger to his nose in a knowing gesture.

"What happens during girl's night, stays at girl's night. I'll never break confidence on account of someone like you."

"Actually, that's only if you're lucky. If you're not, it ends up all over the internet," Brian winked at his humor. "You know you love me. You'd even marry me under the right circumstances. I'm precisely the kind of guy you should break confidence for."

"In your dreams. You aren't suitable husband material in your condition for anyone."

Brian loved to banter with her, even if it was at his own expense. "What condition is that now?"

"I'm not sure what diseases are present in your bloodstream, but I want to find out. Nor would I allow any of my friends to find out either."

Shaking his head, Brian leaned against the counter, "You wish you knew first hand that is all. You know as well as I do that I have a clean bill of health. Someone in my line of work has seen the horrors that can befall someone."

"We'll just have to agree to disagree. What can I get you this beautiful morning? I'm sure you didn't come in for my glowing conversational skills."

"You know that half the reason I come to this particular establishment is your glowing everything. The other half is I don't have to give you my coffee order. You already know it. Most likely have gone ahead and fixed it while we were shooting the breeze." Brian threw his money and tip on the counter to prove his point.

"Aren't you the confident one of the bunch. One of these days I'm going to surprise you with a different coffee, just to bring you down a notch or two."

"You wouldn't do such a thing. What if I reported you to the boss?"

"I'd tell him you were lying."

"I'm a member of law enforcement. Why would I lie?"

"Why wouldn't you? He's known me a lot longer, and I have no track record for him not to believe me."

"And I do?" Brian knew she was playing with him, and he was equally involved, but this was entirely too much fun to let go.

"No, but until he has a reason to disbelieve me, I still rank higher than you. I'm like the daughter he never had, even though he has three daughters at home," she smirked at him and scrunched her nose in a way a little sister would her older brother when she thought she'd won an argument. Instead of pushing it further he did the only thing he could at that moment. He took his coffee from her and with his other hand ruffled the top of her head and messed her hair.

"See ya later, Sal. Pleasure as always." With that, he turned and made his way through the front door and back to his car. Now off to the office to find a murderer.

* * * *

ALONE AT HIS DESK, Brian was sorting through all the gathered evidence hoping that miraculously something would stand out that they had missed previously. The body wasn't identified yet, but the fingerprints were in the file. Forensics wouldn't be back for a couple of days, but there were things he could do to speed up the process.

Fingerprinting was just a process of waiting and since he wasn't doing anything else and wasn't in a time crunch, what did he have to lose?

Flipping the card over, he quickly scanned them into the computer. No matter how long it took, he would wait for it to come back. Flipping through the case file, he thought about reasons why someone would have been beaten and abused in such a way. He'd already considered owing them money or digging for information, but could there be anything else that would result in such violence?

He looked a little deeper and realized the M.E.'s report was back. As they had thought, the cause of death listed was a gunshot wound to the back of the head. Since he already knew that, he went a little further to see what they didn't know. "Hmmm, that is interesting," Brian said aloud to the empty room. The report stated that it was a low-velocity gunshot. However, it wasn't a direct shot to the knee, but to the knee pit and didn't shatter the kneecap as expected. That means he must have been standing at the time of impact. *Who interrogates someone standing up?* That means his heart would beat faster due to stress and cause excessive blood loss than if he were sitting down.

This case was getting more and more weird by the second. Scanning down the page, Brian saw a note about shoulder damage similar to a rotator cuff injury but very recent and showed no signs of healing.

"That could be why they shot him in the back of the leg instead of directly into the kneecap. Either that or the shooter was completely inept." While he was looking through the remaining report, everything else was consistent with what they saw at the scene.

A moment later his computer dinged, alerting him that the fingerprint system found a match. Flipping screens, he was face to face with their victim. He was none other than Seymore Hamilton. That name meant nothing to Brian which discouraged him slightly. He had hoped that the person who was beaten and shot would be someone of obvious consequence. His fingers flew across the keyboard, and he pulled up another search to find out who this man was and why he needed to be removed from life so tragically. What he found left him feeling less than thrilled and a little sick to his stomach. Seymore was none other than a local accountant that, according to social media, was working for the local, not-so-friendly crime family, the Castenellos. He might just have the evidence he needed to pursue the investigation on the Castenellos family after all.

Now Brian knew why the family had reached out for a new financial advisor, and he wanted nothing more but to get her fired.

Chapter 7: Bobby Castenellos

I'll take this girl over Seymour any day of the week, Bobby thought while looking Trish over from top to bottom. He lingered on her ample bust line and perfectly trimmed bottom. Walking with her to the restaurant was almost like taking one of his harem on a date. He didn't date much, but would happily take this woman out anytime he needed to keep her in line.

"So, Trish, not that I want to talk business, but do you think you might be able to handle this job long term?"

Trish stood there staring at him slightly stunned.

Bobby continued, "We have found ourselves in need of a permanent financial advisor, and after meeting you I can honestly say I wouldn't mind having you around more often."

"Bobby, I'm flattered that you think I would be a good fit for your needs. I'm not sure yet how well I think I fit with your situation. I'm still slightly overwhelmed by everything. Perhaps if I get through it and realize I can maintain it better on a regular basis, then I don't see why not. It's too soon to say just yet." Trish looked so timid like she didn't know how to handle him. That was ok because he planned on handling her and Bobby never left anything to chance. He played every card in his deck before they had an opportunity to do any damage to his hand.

"In the meantime, let's forego any shop talk. I want to know more about you. Do you have a boyfriend I should be watching out for?" He knew the answer would be no, but he asked anyway to sound polite.

Trish giggled and covered it with her hand. *Women are so easy to play,* Bobby mused while she gathered herself.

"No, I don't have a boyfriend. I've not had a lot of time to socialize since I'm trying to make a good impression with your project."

Trish ducked her head obviously embarrassed that she divulged that last tidbit of information.

"Well, I'm all for making a good first impression, but I can't have you running yourself ragged on my account. I'll just have to personally make sure you are taking your personal time as well as working hard. You are much too valuable to be burnt out after such a short time on our team. I've got big plans for you if I can persuade you to stick it out with us." Big plans indeed. Bobby intended to use and abuse her just like he did all his employees, but he could tell this one would be special. Unlike Seymour, Trish was a diamond in the rough. He had done some research on her as they did all their up and comings.

She was a gold mine in and of herself. She came from an old society family and had money stashed in a trust fund that, as far as he could tell, she had never touched. It was ripe for the picking and Bobby would be the one picking if he had any say in things.

• • • •

BREAKFAST HAD GONE smoothly. Trish had opened up a bit and relaxed around Bobby, so he counted that as a win. Unfortunately, he had to wrap things up quickly when his phone rang. It was Bobby's right-hand man, Mickey Menasco. If he was calling, something was definitely wrong.

"Talk to me, Mickey," Bobby said into the phone right after he placed Trish into a cab on her way home. He had slipped the cabbie one hundred dollars to get her there without incident.

"Hey, Boss. I just wanted to call and let you know it sounds like they found the drop from Seymour. A couple of low-level junkies were walking through and called the cops."

"Do we know who the junkies were?" Bobby was fuming, although he never let his lackeys know he was ever anything but cool as a cucumber. He saved his anger for the nobodies who tried to cross him but only in exceptional circumstances. He preferred to scare them with an eerie sense of calm.

"Yeah. they were a couple of Morley's guys. We got a handle on them, and they didn't know anything. We shut them up anyway." When Mickey said he shut them up, that usually meant he made them unable to speak for a while with a broken jaw or a stopped heart. Either way was okay with Bobby, because he never had a hand in it. Nothing could be traced back to him, and he paid his guys off the books. No paper trail or physical one meant no leads for the coppers to follow. They always assumed, but could never prove anything allowing Bobby to stay relaxed about everything.

"Good. How is five-O handling Seymour's body?" Never one to leave it to chance, he wasn't going to be unprepared for his inevitable conversation with whatever detectives they had on the case.

"They are chasing their tails as usual. We moved the body after he stopped bleeding and wrapped him up. Them knowing who he is wasn't an issue for this one. When we got to the drop site, we kept the plastic so there wouldn't be any trace evidence on the body. Bing, bang, boom. Easy as that. You know how we do things, Boss." Mickey was a professional in all things, but this was his favorite. He loved finding new and creative ways to dump a body. Bobby couldn't even fathom where those ideas came from or what the next one would be. Honestly, it was better if he didn't. There are some things you are better off not knowing.

"Okay, keep tabs on them, and let me know if I should prepare for anything. You know I hate surprises." With that Bobby ended the call. He never had time for the pleasantries of hello or goodbye. All he wanted was information and to be left to his own schedule.

Chapter 8: Trish

Climbing out of the cab at home, she felt like she had wasted her day. The plan to go into the office was destroyed when she crashed into Bobby Castenellos. Not that she was complaining about that in the least. He was incredibly sexy and made her a little tongue-tied. She still didn't know much about him since she could hardly answer his questions without embarrassment let alone ask her own.

Habitually, she made her way to the bathroom to rid herself of the poison in her stomach. She couldn't not eat around Bobby, but each bite tasted sour on her tongue as she thought about how he must see her. She tried to order the lightest thing on the menu, but breakfast food was by far one of the heaviest meals as far as she was concerned. Eggs were high in fat unless you just order whites, but if you do that, people always ask if you are on a diet. If you answer with yes, they follow with you don't need to lose weight. Trish didn't ever want to start an argument, so she avoided those. Pancakes, her arch nemesis of foods, were always delicious, but they were nothing but useless carbs. Bacon or sausage were options, but they were both very greasy and therefore going to cause significant weight gain. Though in this case, it would work for what she was attempting to convey. She ordered a side of bacon, cooked with added crisp, and an order of oatmeal. At least she would balance her choice of flavor with a healthy option.

Now that she was home, she needed to get rid of both from her body. Nothing sat well on her stomach after all these years, not even the healthy options.

Trish couldn't take her mind of Bobby. Who would have thought she would find her client so attractive? That was something she always considered unethical, but he interjected himself into her day so smoothly that she didn't know what else to say or do. She just followed him away from Brian. That was a bonus since it seemed like

Brian was stalking her at this point. It was more than a little annoying. Everywhere she went, he was bound to show up. Trish was even surprised that he didn't try to crash breakfast for some concocted reason.

Either way, she had a pleasant breakfast and Bobby was excellent company. He kept the conversation going flawlessly and never let it slip. *Even if I was distracted by his insanely handsome face and imagining what was beneath that tight shirt he wore.* Bobby was one of those guys that were ripped all over, and his shirts couldn't contain him. Trish assumed that even if he wore a larger shirt size, he would still be spilling out muscle somewhere. With his defined jawline and slightly pouted lips, Trish found herself missing half of what he was saying lost in the features of his face.

After Trish had had plenty of time to clean up and relax, she got incredibly bored. She wasn't used to having so much free time on a weekend.

What am I supposed to do? Grace and Patrick are probably busy with each other on a Saturday. She had already stolen Grace last night from Patrick. *Sal, is the only other person I could call that wouldn't necessarily have someone at home expecting them, but she is working today.* That gave Trish an idea, "I know Bobby said he didn't want me working on his file today, but what could a little while hurt?" she muttered out loud to the empty room.

With that Trish grabbed her purse and headed into the office to work for a few hours.

• • • •

AS TRISH SAT AT HER desk, everything felt normal again. *I am becoming a workaholic. I hope I can push through and finish this project quickly so I can snap out of it.*

She continued working through the file diligently until once again she started to notice discrepancies. Not just payroll numbers were differing, but now inventory items and even a company party or two hadn't been noted on the original logs.

"They must be a great company to work for; they have an employee party every month. I wish Phillips and Baker thought so highly of the little people they were stepping on to get to where they are today. They live high on the hog while us minions do all the work." Luckily Trish was the only one in on a Saturday afternoon since she was berating the bosses while sitting at the desk they had provided her.

She dug a little deeper and realized that a cleaning company was paid as well, but in a higher amount that she had ever seen before. Perhaps she would mention that they were being ripped off and suggest another company in order to save money. With that, she jumped on Google and searched, *A Bloody Mess.*

"Must be a European company. What a cute name." Trish blindly searched for their website, so she could get an idea of what they offered. She was hoping to find a company who offered similar features for a more reasonable fee.

"Oh. My. God." Trish said each word slowly. She couldn't believe this is what she was seeing. *A Bloody Mess* didn't offer traditional cleaning at all, but a broader spectrum of the term, if the website she had found buried deep in the search engine was to be believed. Splashed across a black background, the website featured blood running from the edges of the screen with the occasional rolled up carpet or garbage bag that hinted at what unthinkable thing it might hold.

"What have I gotten myself into?" she whispered, not because she thought anyone would hear her. Trish feared if she said it any louder it would become real. The things she saw scrolling through their webpage were unthinkable. The script was worse because it explained all the things their services encompassed. Things as basic as cleaning up a manhandled room that needed to be righted to moving and cleaning up a body. The limits of goriness were endless with different pricing listed for each.

When the shock had lessened a bit, Trish had enough where-with-all to put her skills to the test. She looked at the most recent payment to the 'cleaning company' as she was going to continue to refer it. Comparing the charges, she sat frozen with fear. She realized that it was the exact amount as would have been billed for a body removal and an apartment cleaning for mass amounts of pooled blood including splatter. In addition to the gorier aspects, it included a room cleaning to right it to its normal appearance.

"Who are these people?" Trish whispered still in shock from what she had seen. Then she remembered a backhanded conversation with Brian, something about known crime families. Shaking with terror, Trish closed the web page with a quick click on the x in the corner of her screen. She didn't want to see the nightmare any longer. She had just had dinner with a man who portrayed himself as normal and not the monster she was seeing him as now. She feared for herself, and questioned how to proceed. Knowing what she knew now, how many shady things had she swept under the rug in her initial perusal of their finances? Those mystery payments could be anything now, and she was afraid of what they were and if she would find out.

Deciding now was not the time to find out any additional new information about her client, Trish packed up her things and made her way to *The Brewing Bean*. With any luck, a cup of coffee would settle her nerves. If not, then she hoped Sal was still working, and they could go out for a stiff drink after she called it a day.

Instead of calling a cab, she decided to walk to help push the deranged thoughts from her head. She couldn't trust a taxi driver with herself right now. She would most likely look like a crazy woman, and they wouldn't stop anyway.

Bobby seemed reasonable and never set off my radar for creeps. What is wrong with me? The last thing I need is a psycho boyfriend who likes a little murder on the side. Trish's thoughts were all over the place. She really didn't think of Bobby as boyfriend material, but she did go to breakfast with him. *What were people who knew him thinking? Did they believe that I was his new side piece?* The last thing she wanted right now was to have any association with that kind of filth.

After a while lost in dark thoughts, Trish walked inside *The Brewing Bean* still reflecting on her logic versus reason. Nothing she had going through her head made sense. She had gone over it all enough she felt like she had slipped into an upside-down topsy-turvey world where life didn't make sense. This was the last thing she needed. Life needed to make sense. Work needed to be clear. Her life was numbers and numbers were clear, but this was far from that.

Blindly, Trish walked up to the counter. She didn't see who was serving her. Like a robot, she ordered her drink and quietly made her way to the end of the bar as they got it ready. She couldn't shake her unease and discomfort for what she had gotten herself into all for a promotion. Did her bosses know who the Castenellos family were? Were they buried deep into the crimes to the point they had to take cases without concern blindly?

"Trish? Trish?" she was startled back to the here and now by Sal trying to get her attention.

"Oh, hey. I didn't hear you." She reached for her coffee with slightly shaky hands.

"I should say. I called your name at least ten times. What has you so distracted? Not to mention a coffee trip twice in one day. You never do that."

"I ended up at work after breakfast which turned out to be more than I could handle."

"I noticed you met up with Brian outside. Did you guys have breakfast?"

Her words were accompanied by a dramatic eyeroll, "I most certainly didn't eat with Brian. I would consider that cruel torture. No, I went to breakfast with a client I bumped into outside, literally."

"Wait. You actually collided with a customer and you didn't get fired? You must be doing something right. Was he at least attractive?"

Trish didn't know how to answer that question after what she had just learned. Not wanting to bring Sal into her chaos. She opted to keep this part of the conversation short and sweet.

"He was attractive enough. I didn't suffer though breakfast." Trish assumed it was a vague enough answer to keep Sal at bay.

"I get off in an hour. I want to hear details, since you know I don't have any kind of life. I'm going to live vicariously through you."

Trish's stomach rolled with the thought of lying to her. That was the last thing she ever wanted to have to do to her friends, but could she tell her the truth? She decided she would take the next hour to think it over. Then they could go out for drinks, and she could either spill the beans or get Sal drunk enough to forget to ask again.

The next hour passed faster than Trish expected. She was distracted by her thoughts. Her mind wandered to dark places that not only worried Trish, but terrified her as well. If this family did the things that her brain conjured up from her vast knowledge of television dramas and violent movies, then she was likely in over her head. *What am I supposed to do? I don't have any real evidence, but I don't know what will happen if I up and quit for no apparent reason.* Trish was so overwhelmed that she didn't even hear Sal approach.

"Ready? I want out of here I don't care where we go, but if it doesn't smell like coffee, I'll be more than happy right now." Sal eyed her noticing Trish's demeanor was off somehow.

Swallowing down all her emotions she put on a brave face, "It's about time! A minute more and I was going to walk out on you. I'm dying to get a drink."

A smile crept onto Sal's face, "Good, maybe with enough to drink you'll be willing to spill about your gorgeous men problems."

• • • •

THE NEXT MORNING TRISH woke up to the sound of her text alert. *Who is texting me this early on a Sunday morning? Who has to work on Sunday?* Reaching blindly for her phone she felt a twinge in her head, but nothing she couldn't handle. Squinting at the brightness of the screen she read.

Bring me Tylenol and the will to live.

Trish had to look to see who this was from because it was such an off the wall message. Then she laughed out loud because it was Sal.

Why, what happened?

Trish wasn't sure what could have happened between when the cab dropped her off last night. She assumed from the near lack of light outside her bedroom window that it must be about the butt crack of dawn

YOU! YOU HAPPENED! I made the mistake of going drinking with you. You're a bully, a peer-pressuring alcohol bully!

Now Trish was full on roaring with laughter. Not just a chuckle or a snicker, she was belly laughing. A snort slipped out she didn't expect. Trish realized she hadn't laughed like that in ages. It felt good to release all that built up tension.

That's what you're complaining about? It was only fourteen shots of tequila. Grow up!

Of course, Trish was joking, but she had matched her shot for shot. There was nothing she would ever ask a friend to do that she wasn't willing to join them in. That wasn't how friendship worked.

Oh, I'm grown up alright. I get to go to work hung over like a boss!

That wasn't the response Trish was expecting. She instantly felt bad.

Why didn't you tell me you had to work today? I wouldn't have suggested shots. I could have been happy with a beer or two and some girl talk. God only knows no one needs to drink like we did last night, but it was fun in the moment.

Shooting up from her bed she quickly made a beeline for the kitchen; she kept the ingredients for her instant hangover cure on hand at all times. The least she could do was mix up some magic for Sal and run it over to her. Quickly she threw tomato juice, pickle juice, and a couple of raw eggs into her blender and flipped the switch. After a second or two, she stopped it and threw in a splash of Worcestershire and a pinch of black pepper. Pouring them into two to-go cups, she placed them in the refrigerator to chill.

She ran to the bathroom to throw herself together like she always did this early after a night out. No one cared what she looked like, and it wasn't a big deal to her to run out with yoga pants and a tank paired with a swipe of mascara a messy bun and flip-flops. Her phone chirped from her bedroom, and she quickly went to retrieve it.

It was fun and no I didn't know I was working today or I would have said something. I got called in this morning because two of the girls called in sick. Since I rank right below a manager, they think I can handle it if a rush pops and I don't have help.

Trish didn't hesitate. She fired off a message that said she would meet her at the shop with a peace offering. Not wasting another minute, she grabbed the cups and her purse and headed out the door. Sipping her drink on the way she was feeling better long before she got to the door of *The Brewing Bean*. They hadn't opened yet, but she knocked on the glass and Sal let her in. Not to be a mean friend, but Sal looked like the walking dead. Trish's heart broke for her. There is no way anyone would want to work after the night they had. Immediately, Trish thrust the second cup into Sal's hands.

"It looks gross, and I promise to tell you what is in it, but you have to take a drink first. I have one too so we can both be in the same boat. I have decided I might be inexperienced, but I'm going to stay and help you today. I can run the register while you work your coffee magic."

Sal hesitated, as she examined the glass in her hand. It looked like murky swamp water, and Trish remembered the first time she had made them. It took everything in her to drink it, and Trish resorted to plugging her nose. Not that it tasted terrible it was actually pretty good after she allowed herself to drink it. Sal just needed to get over the hump.

"Do whatever you need to get the first drink in, and you won't regret it, I promise."

With one last look of disgust, Sal tipped the cup and swallowed a mouthful. At first, she made a face. The flavors hitting her tongue rejected initially by her tastebuds. But as Trish watched, she saw Sal's contorted expressing smoothed somewhat as her taste buds adjusted.

"You're right. This as bad as I thought it would be. What's in it?" Sal took another drink, and Trish joined her taking another drink of her own cup. She ran down the ingredients for Sal and watched her nose scrunch up.

"What made you think any of those would taste good together?" That thought didn't detour her; Sal took another drink.

"I didn't. It's an old family recipe. My ancestry is Polish, and it is standard for them to use pickle juice to ward off a hangover. Somewhere along the lines it got blended in with everything else and had been deemed the magic potion."

"Well, I agree. It is magic. I'm feeling better already," Sal said as she slugged back the last mouthful.

"Perfect. I'm glad I could help. Let's continue this helping hand. Teach me how to use the register. You are going to get my assistance either way."

The next hour went by faster than Trish expected, but when the doors opened for business, she was as ready as she could be. Sal had given her a pricing cheat sheet for the most popular drinks and add-ons. This was just a tiny crutch, but it made Trish confident she could handle any rushes that might ensue.

The floodgates had opened, and within an hour they were swamped. Trish wiped her brow and wondered how Sal did this all the time. Trish wasn't even doing the bulk of the work. She glanced over at Sal flitting from machine to cup to flavor bottle and was in awe. How did she have the ability to keep a smile on her face the entire time?

When they finally had a lull, Trish was exhausted. Sal brought out coffees and a scone for each of them. Settling into a bistro table by the window, they relaxed for a moment and enjoyed the quiet.

"You love this, don't you?" Trish asked taking another sip of her coffee. She smiled, because Sal remembered her preference and brought it to her perfect as usual.

"What do you mean? Are you talking about the shop?" Trish nodded allowing Sal to continue. "I suppose I do. It doesn't seem like much for me to aspire to as an adult, but this place is like home to me. The owner treats me like family. Yeah, I get called in for the crap shifts that no one wants. In situations like today, it is no picnic. I'm sure the girls who called in were hungover this morning and not really sick, but I'm not going to complain. They are here every other day without fail, and I don't have to cover that often. If they started to make a habit out of it, then perhaps I'd say something. In the meantime, I'll take any shifts that they need me to take."

"What is your ultimate goal here?" Trish wasn't trying to question her friend's motives negatively. She was only trying to get to know her better.

Sal smiled as if in a happy dream that only she could see. Trish envied her, "I can't remember the last time I had that look on my face." That brought Sal out of her trance.

"I suppose I'd love to be a manager one day. I know that is more responsibility, but it would allow me to feel accomplished like my life isn't just floating in stagnant water."

"That is an incredible goal. I'm sure you will get there before you know it. Look how amazing you are." She held up her cup and gestured towards it. "You make the best coffee every time. No exception. Not to mention, I was watching you today. For how your morning started, no one would ever know. You had a smile for every customer and conversation for the regulars. You are beyond what everyone wants to see every morning when getting the most important drink of the day." Sal blushed at her words and Trish knew she had her, she didn't stop there, "Not to mention you are probably the prettiest barista they will ever see."

Sal turned her face but not before Trish saw a tear escape. Getting up she walked in front of her to show her that she didn't have to hide from friends.

"I'm sorry," Sal breathed and feverishly swiped at her tears. "Those were the nicest things anyone has said to me. I'm not used to it."

"Well, hanging out with me, girl, get used to it. I will tell you every day if I have to. You need to know what you mean to people. I bet your promotion is right around the corner." Trish planned to talk with the owner the first chance she got to rave about her favorite barista. Then she would have everyone in the group do the same. With enough positive feedback, the owner had to realize what an asset he had on his hands. Trish had a new project to take her mind off of the problems at hand.

Chapter 9: Brian

Patrick walked into the precinct Sunday morning at Brian's request. He told Patrick that he found something huge that would give them the springboard they needed to jumpstart their investigation. Where yesterday they had nothing to go on, now they had a name. That didn't seem like much, but in reality, they could start running down leads.

"What did you find that you had to drag me away from my beautiful wife on a relaxing Sunday morning? I was perfectly happy spending the day in bed with her all day." It was common knowledge that Grace and Patrick were talking about kids, but no one knew if they were actively trying or just in the talking phase.

"Don't speak to me about your wife in bed unless you plan on sharing details." Brian loved teasing him. Patrick was a jealous husband, and needling him was Brian's favorite pastime the past few months. Patrick didn't dignify his comment with an answer, but he could have sworn he heard the smallest growl come from Patrick's chest.

Smirking at his success, Brian continued, "I've identified our body. Even though they thought they'd covered their tracks, I got a fingerprint hit in CODIS. I figured we were up a creek until that system chimed last night."

"Well are you going to keep patting yourself on the back or are you going to tell me who he is?" Patrick was never one who liked information to be drawn out. He preferred to get to the point and move on.

"Seymore Hamilton, a local accountant that seems to have a connection to the Castenellos family. I had to do some digging to find that tidbit, and it was obscure. We will need more definitive proof before we go down that road. I figured we could start at his office and see if we can get a client list to run down for motive.

"You sure have been busy this weekend. That isn't like you at all, Brian. Did you have some trouble at the bar last night or are you developing a sleeping disorder?" Patrick teased, but he didn't know just how close he was to the truth.

"There is nothing to tell. So do you think you might want to get to work or continue prodding into my social life?" Brian wasn't in the mood to talk about what had given him such a strict work ethic with this case. That was usually Patrick's department, and Brian brought up the rear filling in wherever Patrick needed him.

Patrick chuckled and raised his hands in a defensive gesture, "Okay, killer. Back down. We can get to work, and you can tell me when you are ready. I know there is a story there."

They both got into Brian's car and made their way to Seymore's office. When they got there, it was surprising how small it was. Not at all what they were expecting.

"What are the odds the Castenellos family decided small was better for them? I would think they'd do better with an extensive corporation, like Phillips and Baker," Brian not so subtly hinted at Trish's office. He wasn't sure if he was ready to tell Patrick everything, but this was important enough for someone else to know.

"Wait. What made you think of them? Isn't that where Trish works?" Patrick didn't completely catch on, but was definitely interested and was on the defensive for the sake of his wife's best friend.

"Calm down, I don't know much yet. Trish bumped into a guy yesterday morning after getting her coffee. It turns out it was Bobby Castenellos. The icing on the cake is that he is the big client case she has been killing herself over for the promotion she wants. I'm not sure what that means, but I feel like she needs an extra set of eyes just in case there is more to it than crunching numbers."

"You know if you tell her we are going to be watching her, she will have both our balls in a vice. She is nothing like Grace in that aspect. Grace wasn't comfortable with you at first, but you've grown on her over time. Her biggest concern was new faces and taking people away from family life. Trish doesn't think she needs anything more than what she has. If she can't provide it for herself, she doesn't need it. That goes double for protection. I can't see her accepting it even if we were to prove she needed it." Patrick had been well versed in all these things. Trish and Brian got a huge dose of that reality after Trish was kidnapped, in place of Grace, by that psycho who thought Grace was his. Making Trish nothing more than a debt to be paid. Unfortunately, in this case, Patrick was also right about how Trish was going to react.

"I guess that just means I'll have to be sneaking around a bit. I've already been checking on her at night to be sure she gets home alright. Then in the mornings, I try to pop over to her office and give her some face time when I can." Brian didn't look at Patrick as he said this. The potential expression on Patrick's face scared him, just a little.

"Are you saying the one woman who actually can't stand you, my wife's best friend... you're stalking her? Are you an idiot or do you have a death wish of your own?" Brian could tell he was joking, but underlying it all was a hint of seriousness that Brian came to expect. Patrick never said something without meaning it to some degree even in a sarcastic way.

"I'm not stalking her per say. I like to think of it as bumping into one another." Brian hedged knowing he was lying, but couldn't admit to himself or Patrick the truth that was hovering just under the surface.

"Bumping into each other when one of the parties plans it and the other is unaware...that sounds like stalking, Brian. Please don't overdo it. I love spending time with my wife, and when Trish gets wound up, I lose my time. Don't make me regret siding with you for now over Trish. If my life becomes a mess because of it, I'll switch sides in a heartbeat and defend Trish myself to save face with my beautiful wife."

"Way to man up, in this situation," Brian rebutted. In his opinion, no one should have to give up their friends for a relationship. "You'd sacrifice me to make yourself look good to your wife? She knows we are friends. What happened to 'bros before hoes'?"

"Did you just call my wife a hoe?" Patrick glared menacingly at Brian causing him to turn away.

"You know I didn't mean it like that. I just thought nothing would come between us. We've been friends forever." Brian realized he sounded like the biggest chick flick storyline ever, but this was important. He couldn't lose his best friend who was supposed to have his back no matter what.

"Well when one of your hair-brained schemes is the reason I don't get laid, and you can just head down to the nearest bar to pick up another candidate for the night, I find that a bit out of balance. I will protect my own, and that includes all of me." Patrick gestured to his middle region in multiple large circles. Not that Brian wasn't already very well aware of what he was referring.

"Okay, I get it. I'd do the same just so you know. Let's just go inside and see if anyone will help us if we tell them that Seymour is no more." Brian winked at his pun and looked at Patrick expectantly.

Patrick's hand came to his face, and he groaned as he rubbed at his eyes, "That one was bad. If you are going to get punny, please do so with a little more charm."

They laughed together and made their way inside. The outside wasn't hiding anything. Seymour's offices seemed more like family-owned rather than corporate ladder. Again, this didn't align with what he was seeing the Castenellos family doing now. Brian started to second guess himself.

"Maybe I got it wrong, and the connection wasn't business related with Seymore and the Castenellos family."

"Let's start asking questions before we change our thoughts on this one. That family is very unpredictable, and even though this doesn't line up with what you see now, that doesn't mean they aren't changing the scenario to throw us off the scent. Also could be why we haven't gotten close to the family in the past."

Brian knew Patrick was right, and he nodded silently thanking him for getting him back on track. They couldn't afford to take two steps forward and one step back in every avenue of this investigation. They had to push forward if they were going to see the right person or people put away for this.

"Think they will consider more than life for this crime? It was very violent and more than just a murder. They worked this guy over and then shot. The only thing missing was the firing squad. They were kind enough to make it point blank and put the poor guy out of his misery. Is it bad that I hope they shot him because he refused to give them any information they were asking of him? I hope he frustrated the hell out of them." Brian's tone was hushed but loud enough for Patrick to hear him.

Patrick stared at him in disbelief. "First of all, I guess if you are hoping they didn't get what they wanted then it's not too crazy. However, the fact that you are discussing this with me right now with the receptionist merely feet away from us, might singal an unhealthy attachment to this case," Patrick said in a whisper, but his scolding was apparent. Brian once again bobbed his head in agreement and moved with Patrick toward the desk.

"Can I help you?" a sweet voice rose from the lips of the receptionist. If they couldn't see her with their own two eyes, they could have easily mistaken her for a child. Smiling between each other, Patrick spoke first. He usually took the lead in active investigations.

"Hello there. My name is Detective Dart, and this is my partner, detective Thomas." Patrick gestured in Brian's direction, and he smiled one of his award-winning smiles to ease the tension in the room. This was normal for him. He knew that having detectives walk up to your desk unannounced could be unsettling. Patrick continued, "Is there an owner we can speak with?"

"It seems Mr. Hamilton has decided to take a few days off. Mrs. Jane Hamilton, is in her office, and I can let her know you are here." She picked up the phone and placed a call to announce them. Patrick and Brian stepped back to exchange a few words before they were on display again.

"Days off? This could benefit us in the long run. If Mrs. Hamilton is covering for her husband, she might be willing to part with some information," Brian shared hopefully, but Patrick came in quickly with the devil's advocate perspective.

"Or she could be aware of exactly what happened and clam up because she is trying to protect herself and any family she might have. Seymore has flown under the radar enough that we had trouble pulling anything relevant about him. That could be more than a coincidence. He might have planned it to keep his wife and any children out of the middle of his problems. If he was working for the Castenellos', then he likely figured out what was going on and hid the things most precious to him."

"Seriously, why do you have to turn a positive into the biggest negative ever?" Patrick laughed at Brian's question but didn't get a chance to respond. That childlike voice caught their attention.

"Detectives? Mrs. Hamilton will see you now."

"Thank you!" they said together and followed the receptionist into an office in the back. Knocking on an office door a woman's voice that sounded a little husky spoke up, "Enter." One word, straightforward and succinct, showed the power she exuded. What they saw upon entering surprised not only Brian but Patrick as well. The latter was hard to accomplish.

Sitting at a grand mahogany desk was an older woman likely in her late seventies, not the young bride they were expecting. Mrs.

Hamilton was obviously Seymore's mother. She had her hair pulled back into a severe bun and wore a navy suit pressed pristinely. The crispness reminded Brian of a military uniform. This woman was obviously not someone to trifle with, and she knew how to own a room. From one word and the scowl on her face, Brian knew Patrick's scenario was more likely than his own. He hoped Patrick had a few tricks up his sleeve because Brian didn't have experience with the elderly side of the fairer sex. He doubted she could be won over with a smolder and a few choice words.

"Mrs. Hamilton," Patrick started to which Brian was thankful. Patrick always did have an amazing way of reading people, and he must have figured Brian was outside of his wheelhouse with this one. "Thank you for seeing us on such short notice."

"Sit, Becky please get coffee and bring it back in." Once again straight to the point and not allowing an ounce of feeling into her words.

"That sounds fantastic." Patrick waited for Becky, the receptionist, to make her way out and close the door. What they had come to discuss wasn't something to which everyone needed to be privy. "Now forgive me for getting straight to it."

"No, that is what I'd rather you do; no forgiveness is required," Mrs. Hamilton interrupted to throw in her two cents.

"Well then, I'll get right to it. Becky mentioned that Seymore was off for a few days and that was why you were in the office, to fill in for his absence. We're here to inform you that he's not just gone on vacation."

"I know. There isn't much you can tell me about my son that I don't already know. I told that blathering girl that so that she wouldn't air our dirty laundry to every potential client that walks through the door or existing ones that call." Mrs. Hamilton actually jeered when she said this, astonishing Brian. He'd heard of cantankerous old women, but this one topped the charts. He couldn't imagine working for her much less being in the same room with her for any length of time. He was hoping this interview would go smoothly and quickly so he wouldn't have to know what either felt like.

"It is our responsibility to inform you that your son was murdered. His body was found a couple of nights ago in an abandoned warehouse downtown. Is there any reason you can think of as to why he would have been there?" Patrick efficiently continued his line of questioning in a manner that Mrs. Hamilton could appreciate and that made Brian thankful, as well.

"I don't know where my son is when he is outside of the office. Besides his current cases and what bills he has left behind, I'm not the one to ask about his personal affairs. I may have been his mother, but we didn't have a close relationship."

"On that note then, can you think of a client who might have had a grudge or any reason to have wanted to kill him?" Patrick led into that question smoothly. That was the exact question they were hoping to ask, and Brian held his breath waiting for Mrs. Hamilton's response.

Consideration crossed her face as she thought through Patrick's question. She was deep in thought, and neither man dared interrupt her for fear of what she might say or do. She seemed like the type of person who would throw things at them if they displeased her. Brian took inventory of stuff within her arm's reach. A stapler. *That would hurt upon impact.* A bowl of paperclips. *While that wouldn't leave a mark, it could hurt with the right amount of force behind it.* A letter opener. *Now that could be used efficiently and create an actual laceration. A* nameplate. *Solid wood and it looks heavy. Someone could be left unconscious at the very least bruises would ensue.* Cup of pens. *When launched all at once not a very good choice for weapon, but oddly they are all the same pen.* Brian shook his head to dislodge the thoughts building. He had been in the murder industry too long if he was taking inventory of the lethality of office equipment.

While Patrick continued the interview, Brian brought himself back into the conversation. Looking at Mrs. Hamilton so he wouldn't think about office supplies any longer, he did his best to focus.

With a frown on her face, Mrs. Hamilton replied, "I'm not saying for sure, but I can't think of anyone in particular. We deal with a variety of clientele, and they range from the elite to the people only trying to prepare a will for their children in the event of their deaths. While we don't prepare the wills directly, we do help them figure out what they have to make available for their children and what it will take to make that happen."

"I know this might sound unorthodox, but would it be possible to compare your client files with our notes to see if anything matches that we could follow up on?" Brian thought it was a valid question, but didn't hold his breath for a positive outcome.

Mrs. Hamilton turned her face to look at Brian for the first time since they arrived. He realized quickly that this was the first he had spoken for the entire visit. He wasn't concerned until her frown turned to a scowl. Brian leaned back slightly in an attempt to put space between them even though the large wooden desk separated them already. *She really knows how to make a man feel small.* Brian made a mental note to see if she was married or widowed. There might be a chance to question the husband. If they could, then they'd have to do it alone to get any definitive information. If this woman was so intimidating to Brian - and he hoped Patrick too, so he wasn't alone - then chances were her husband was probably just as afraid of her.

"I'm not sure, to be honest," her face never improved. "I might be here to fill in, but I am not privy to all the information from the clients. We have a wide berth of clients."

"Okay. If you think of anything or anyone who we should be looking into, please let us know." Patrick chimed in so Brian wouldn't have to endure Mrs. Hamilton's wrath again.

Just then a knock came to the door, and the receptionist came in with their coffee. She was a little unstable, and before Brian could jump up to rescue her, Mrs. Hamilton spoke.

"Becky, you clumsy girl, you've taken too long. We have finished our meeting. Take that all back to the kitchen and get back to your desk. I don't want to have to answer the phone due to your inability to stay on task." Spittle flew from her mouth, as she literally spat the words at Becky in a tone that no one should ever take with employees.

Patrick and Brian stood up, but before they could turn to say anything to her, Becky tore from the door and ran down the hall. They could hear the china clanking in her wake.

"We'll be on our way now and let you get back to work, Mrs. Hamilton. Thank you for your time. Again, let us know if you think of anything." Patrick nodded toward the door and Brian made a break for it. The dragon lady could stay in her office, and he wanted to be as far from her as possible. As he made his way down the hall, he heard sobs coming from a door that was closed but not sealed. Through the crack in the door, Brian caught a glimpse of the back of Becky. Her shoulders bobbed up and down in rhythm with her nearly silent crying as she leaned against the counter by the coffee pot. He pressed the door open until it creaked. He stopped suddenly as the receptionist jumped and quickly turned toward the door. Seeing that it was him, she relaxed slightly. She turned away and wiped her face clean to hide the evidence of her tears.

"I'm sorry, Detective. Is there something I can do for you?" Becky said as she turned back to face Brian with reddened eyes and tear-stained cheeks. Brian's heart broke for her, and he wanted to help her in some way.

"Nothing. I just wanted to apologize for what happened back there. Unfortunately, our meeting didn't run as long as we had intended. Mrs. Hamilton is very direct and to the point. Most people we have to talk to aren't like that, and it takes longer to get the information we need." He went out on a limb and placed his hand on Becky's shoulder to reassure her, smiling to let her know it would be all right.

Becky sighed, and the corners of her mouth quirked up a little. "Actually she is a tyrant, and I hate it when she decides to come into the office. I'd have rathered her just left me a message that said Mr. Hamilton was on vacation and I needed to push all appointments until future notice. She acts as though that is too much to ask. I'm the one who's been running the day to day for years. Her son comes in when he feels like and works his own hours. I hardly schedule any in office appointments for him anymore. He just emails clients he needs to meet with and has lunch with them or something off-site. I rarely see anyone here."

This piqued Brian's interest. Now he had to figure out a way to get some information out of her without telling her that her boss was dead.

"You sound like you are devoted to your job and that you have a great work ethic."

"Ha! *Devoted*?" she raised her eyebrow in question. "That is not the word I would choose. I'm *devoted* to having a paycheck every week, and I've been paid more here than any other office has ever offered me. It probably has something to do with some of our shadier clients. He'd rather pay me more than introduce someone else to that side of things."

Brian was thanking the stars above for this turn of events. "What do you mean 'shadier clients'?"

"Oh, I probably shouldn't have said anything, especially not to a detective." Becky slapped her palm to her face in regret, but Brian didn't let it stop him.

"I'm sure there isn't anything going on behind the scenes that I'd be interested in. However, if there is someone out there that might, say, be willing to harm a person or is possibly escalating to that point, then I wouldn't mind hearing about them." Brian hoped that didn't give away too much, but he needed to get her to trust him. He topped it all off with one of his panty-dropping smiles that had never failed him.

"I don't know. There have been a few in the office that I thought seemed intimidating, but more like bodyguards than clients." Becky was hesitant, but he was getting somewhere.

"You mean your client had bodyguards when they came in for a meeting?" Brian wanted to clarify before he dug in any deeper.

"Yeah. We have some higher profile people. At least that is what I've been told. They usually come in with extra people. They act as bodyguards, so that is what I assumed they were. They never speak but look scary and angry all the time."

"Can you tell me what client has been in most recently with bodyguards?"

"Up until a week or so ago, that would have been Bobby Castenellos. He is in charge of his family's account here, and something was up. He made a visit here two or three times a week for the last month. Come to think of it, he hasn't even called in the past week. They must have gotten it sorted out, and that is why Mr. Hamilton decided he needed a vacation. Having clients breathe down your neck has to be exhausting." Becky busied herself cleaning the counter from the coffee mess she had created upon bringing back the unused tray.

That was the name Brian had hoped to hear, and he didn't even have to work very hard to get it. He had seen a news clipping while researching Seymour a picture that had Seymore in the background. At the time, he didn't know the relationship to Bobby, since he was walking behind and Bobby was facing the camera. It was an indirect image that placed them at the same event. He assumed there was more but had nothing to go on. Brian wondered if this was a meeting that Seymore was leaving and trying not to be identified with Bobby Castenellos. Either way, they now had what they needed to push harder and get some more information about the family and their activities.

"Becky, I hope your day gets better and thank you for your help. You really are good at your job; I should let you get back to it." Brian gave her another award-winning smile and made his way back out the door. As he entered the hallway, he nearly collided with Patrick who was waiting for him patiently.

"Did you get anything out of that or just her phone number?" Patrick asked with a knowing grin.

"For your information, she was crying when I got in there because we didn't get to drink her coffee. I went in to console her, and in the process, yes, I got something." Brian's words were just above a whisper, so his voice didn't carry around the office. He jerked his head to tell Patrick to follow, and they made their way out of the office.

Brian led the way out to the car. He was in a hurry, but tried to keep his stride steady. Patrick needed to know about the connection to the Castenellos family. This meant they could dig deeper, find out more about the elusive family, and perhaps finally nail them for something once and for all.

Chapter 10: Trish

The past weekend had been longer than Trish had expected and that had nothing to do with actual workload. It was more an emotional workload. Knowing what she knew now, Trish needed to decide how best to handle the situation. After a long, hot shower, Trish dressed for work in a pantsuit to portray her professional side. She didn't want them to think she wasn't capable of handling the position. Especially since she was planning on taking everything, she had learned to her bosses and hope they would understand why she didn't feel comfortable working on this case. Trish just hoped they wouldn't fire her for this.

As she approached the doors of her office, Trish's feet slowed on the sidewalk. Her body was telling her this was a bad idea. Something was off about everything, and it made her stomach roll. She hadn't eaten anything or even stopped for coffee. There was nothing she could consume that she felt would sit on her stomach without making a second appearance. Steeling herself, Trish forced herself through the doors. She had to give her bosses the information she knew.

Walking through the doors, she didn't stop at her desk as she would normally. There was a part of her brain that knew she was likely to be fired and to make her way to her desk would be a useless break in her process that morning. Stopping in front of her boss' door, she halted her steps and raised her fist to the door to knock. She paused before her hand connected with the wood. Her neck broke out in a sweat, and her face was red with worried heat. This one conversation was going to change her life either for worse or for better. She took a deep breath, lifted her long hair off her neck, and lightly lowered it. Then, Trish took a deep breath and held it as she knocked on Mr. Phillips office door.

"Come in," Mr. Phillips voice was muffled as he yelled from deep within the office.

Trish twisted the handle, and as she walked through and her boss's eyes looked up from his desk and met her, she finally released the air she was holding in anticipation. Taking a large breath, she found the nerve to speak.

"Sir, do you have a minute to talk about my project?" There was no need to elaborate because she was only actively working on one case and they were more than aware what case it was.

A broad smile stretched across Wyatt Phillips' face. He puffed his chest out of his double-breasted, heather-grey suit. He adjusted the button and sat up straighter in his leather, high back chair. Trish then took in his face. His salt-and-pepper hair was combed back pristinely, as always. When he smiled, the corners of his eyes sprayed wrinkles that gave him an endearing quality.

"Trish, for you I've got all the time you need. What can I do for you this morning?" He gestured toward the seats in front of his desk indicating she should come in and sit.

"Well, Mr. Phillips, I've been working really hard on the Castenellos file and put in a lot of hours." She had no clue how to start this conversation, and she just hoped he didn't take the beginning wrong. He didn't speak up just smiled encouragingly. So Trish continued to speak.

"I've dug in incredibly deep to figure out where they have their money tied up and what is necessary and what isn't just like I was asked to do. In the process of this, I've come across some disturbing information." With this last bit of information, a frown crossed Mr. Phillips' face and his brow deeply furrowed, but he didn't say anything. He was apparently waiting for her to continue, but her level of discomfort had just doubled upon seeing his expression change.

"Initially, I just thought there were discrepancies from amending the books from paper logs to electronic copies. After a more thorough investigation, I discovered there might be something else to explain the differences. Then, I found a payout that seemed off. They were paying way too much for cleaning services. Wanting to compare their existing services, to other options I looked up their website and found more than I bargained for." Trish explained the services she found listed on the website for *A Bloody Mess*, the cleaning company they were currently using. When Trish finished explaining her findings, she took a much-needed deep breath since she rushed through it all with minimal air to get the words out faster.

She watched as Mr. Phillips' head dipped down just slightly. Instead of speaking to her directly he reached for his phone. Trish had no idea who he was calling, but she waited as patiently as she could as he was talking to the person on the other end of the line.

"Can you come in here?" he asked the invisible person. "No, NOW!" He raised his voice slightly and emphasized the last word enough that Trish jumped in her seat, startled by his harshness. That was a tone she had never heard his voice take, and she didn't know how to handle this situation that was brewing. Mr. Phillips hung up the phone but still didn't meet her eyes. It was clear that he was avoiding her until the mystery person arrived. A sharp knock sounded on the door, and they didn't wait for a response. The doorknob turned and in walked Mr. Paul Baker, the other owner of her firm. Mr. Baker was a few years younger than Mr. Phillips, but not by much. His hair was still chocolate brown and styled short with waves flowing on top giving the illusion that if he were to let his hair grow out, he might have some curls. He had a strong square jaw that gave him an air of superiority that he didn't let go to waste. When he walked through the office, people took notice and usually scrambled to appear to be working. He was the scarier of the two employers.

"Trish here was just informing me of her findings on the Castenellos case," Mr. Phillips spoke directly to Mr. Baker and still didn't look in Trish's direction once. He just talked about her to Mr. Baker.

"Oh, is that so? What did she find and does it help or hurt our bottom line?" Mr. Baker was blunt and to the point. He never sugarcoated anything, and it was always about how much money it was would or wouldn't' make him. Nothing else mattered as much as his paycheck.

"I'm not sure yet how it will affect our finances, but I wanted you here when I realized where it was going. She has found out about their cleaning company, and it seems to have alarmed her." Mr. Phillips looked her right in the eye then, and it terrified her more than ever. The look in his eye was almost dead. As though the news of the Castenellos behind the scenes activities did not surprise him. Phillips didn't react positively or negatively. He just looked at her as though it were deeply seated in him that it didn't matter one way or another.

"That didn't take her as long as I thought it would," Mr. Baker stated flatly.

"Well, she has been putting in more hours than required trying to get to the bottom of this one sooner rather than later, it seems." Mr. Phillips look almost turned into a scowl at that. Trish was still unsure what that meant.

"How do you feel about what you have learned, Trish?" Mr. Baker asked her without the slightest hint in his voice that he actually cared.

She hesitated to answer because she was now more worried than ever as to how much her answer would change the atmosphere of the room.

"I suppose I was alarmed when I first saw that website. I'm not sure how real it all is. I met Mr. Castenellos over the weekend, and it's hard to believe after talking to him that he would be capable of such violence." That got a rise out of both men. Their eyes expanded and widened in the biggest emotional reaction she'd seen out of either of them.

"Where did you meet with Mr. Castenellos? You didn't clear that with us. All client meetings with lower level team members must go through us first." Mr. Baker's eyes flared with anger unhidden. Trish trembled and wasn't sure her voice was strong enough to respond.

Mr. Phillips slammed his hand down on his desk; the sound ricocheted around the room. Trish felt the vibration all the way to her bones. The sound jolted her out of her stupor.

"I didn't schedule the meeting. I ran into him outside my local coffee shop, and while I was apologizing for my clumsiness, he stopped me and introduced himself. When I recognized his last name, I asked if he was affiliated with the restaurant. When he said who he was, I said I was working on their file. He then took me out for breakfast. We spoke a bit about the file, but no more than how long I'd been working on it. Otherwise, he kept the topics neutral and steered clear of work-related conversations." She didn't have anything else to tell them about their meeting. She didn't think they wanted to hear how charming he was or that he was a complete gentleman and paid for everything not letting her even leave a tip.

Mr. Phillips and Mr. Baker exchanged glances. Trish didn't know what this meant as they proceeded to have what seemed like a telepathic conversation between them. Anxiously, she waited for them to speak. The men sighed at the same time and then turned back to Trish.

"I think it would be best for us to pull you from this file for now. You should send us all your findings so far. We aren't sure exactly what to make of this, and we need time to figure it out. Why don't you go back to your desk and collect everything and send us what you have saved on your computer. I'll send someone to your desk to retrieve the paper files that you were provided by the Castenellos family directly." Mr. Phillips put a smile back on his face trying to lighten the heavy feeling that had settled over the room. It was evident, though, that it was nothing more than a front.

Without argument, Trish rose from her seat and proceeded to make her way to the door. Turning back, she thanked them for their time. She then quickly slipped out of the door and took a large breath in an attempt to settle her rapidly beating heart.

Making her way back to her desk, Trish was in a daze. That meeting hadn't gone as she had expected. As far as she knew she was still employed, but she had nothing to work on at the moment. She sat down at her desk and before proceeding to do as she was instructed, Trish placed her face lightly into her hands as she rested her elbows on her desk. She fought tears and relief. It was all so surreal, and she didn't know whether to laugh or cry. Waving her hands in front of her face as if to blow away the emotions, Trish steeled herself and turned on her computer. She pulled open her drawers while the desktop booted up and proceeded to pull out all of her notes. Logging into her computer, Trish quickly located all of the files about the Castenellos case and dropped them into an email bound for both of her bosses. She wasn't sure who was going to responsible for them, so she opted for them both.

That was all finished quicker than she expected and then she was left with nothing to do and an entire work day ahead of her.

By late morning, Trish was beyond bored. She would leave if she thought she could get away with it. Then out of the blue, her desk phone started to ring. Not many people had her direct line, and this wasn't ringing from the operator. Assuming it was Grace, Trish quickly answered.

"Hello, this is Trish Montgomery. How can I help you today?" Since it was her business line, she answered it professionally out of habit.

"My dear, Trish," the voice was deep and rich. It was most certainly not Grace. "I'm so happy I caught you this morning, but I hope you aren't working too hard."

"My load has significantly been lightened. Who am I speaking to?" She didn't want to elaborate further not exactly sure who she was talking to. She had her ideas which were quickly confirmed.

The man laughed lightly on the other end of the line. It sounded husky and fit his voice perfectly. "You know who I am. It's me, Bobby Castenellos. I held off as long as I could to avoid calling you and disturbing your work today, but I couldn't get you out of my head after our unexpected meeting this weekend."

Trish's breath caught in her throat. She thought after relinquishing the file she wouldn't have any more dealings with this family. She wasn't sure exactly what all they were into, but she was sure that she didn't want a single hand in it. Since she had him on the phone, she opted for formality instead of encouraging any personal relationship he might think they had.

"Mr. Castenellos, it's a pleasure to hear from you. Unfortunately, your case was pulled from my desk just this morning and is apparently being reassigned. I won't be your financial advisor any longer." Thinking she did a good job of defusing the situation she prepared to end the call, but her caller had different ideas.

"What do you mean reassigned? That was not at my request. No one does anything with my files without informing me first." Bobby's temper flared, and she caught a glimpse of what would likely be much more terrifying in person. It was still incredibly scary over the phone. Without saying another word, Mr. Castenellos hung up violently.

Trish wasn't sure how to take what just happened, but as she replaced the receiver in the cradle, her hands were shaking. This wasn't her intention at all. She wanted him to go away peacefully like any other client whose file had been reassigned. This shouldn't be anything to get worked up about because they hadn't had any client to advisor relationship before this weekend. Even that was minimal as they didn't speak about the file hardly at all.

Deciding she should just go ahead and take her lunch break, she made her escape from the office that had given her more grief today than any night she stayed late to actually work. Upon making her way out the front doors she nearly collided with one of the last people she wanted to see, but given what she had just done that morning even Brian ranked higher than usual.

"What are you doing here?" Trish asked with her usual snarky tone, not wanting him to realize he wasn't the last person she wanted to see.

"I swung by to see if I could take you to lunch. I guess I have perfect timing if you are already leaving. It's good to see you taking a break without having to be dragged away kicking and screaming." Brian always had something sarcastic to say when he was around her, even when he was trying to help.

With a sigh of defeat and because she didn't want to be alone, "Fine, but only lunch and you drive because I don't feel like walking."

Brian lightly placed his hand against her forehead, "Are you feeling alright? I've never had you agree to anything I've suggested or offered since I've known you."

"I've had an exhausting morning after a similarly tiring weekend. There isn't much left to argue with you." Trish's shoulders slumped forward when she spotted his car and trudged toward it. She didn't have the energy to walk to lunch. This was a perfect turn of events even, if it wasn't what she would have chosen if given a choice beforehand.

Chapter 11: Brian

Brian climbed in the car after opening the door for Trish. She was acting out of sorts and almost zombie-like. Going through the motions, but not like herself. Instead of striking up a conversation in the car, he took her to the deli a couple of blocks over for a light lunch. It was still a little early, so the rush hadn't had a chance to hit yet. They had their choice of seating.

Sitting down to eat their sandwiches, Brian noticed Trish was just picking at hers and not actually taking a bite.

"Is everything okay? I know I'm not your most favorite person, but you can still talk to me."

She sat there staring at him, but he couldn't read her expression. He had never seen her seem this lost before. Deciding to give her a little space, he took a bite of his sandwich while waiting for her to speak next. It was a few minutes before she found her words.

"I'm not on the Castenellos project anymore. That should make you feel better," Trish spoke just above a whisper, and Brian almost didn't hear her. If it weren't for the nearly empty eatery, he would have missed it.

"Actually, because of circumstances you are unaware of, I'm a bit relieved to hear that news." Brian matched her tone and leaned slightly towards her, but refrained from touching her.

She looked up at him and met his gaze, but didn't speak. She just stared at him, and he noticed she was leaning slightly into him, but like Brian, she wasn't touching him. It was as though she needed human contact, but couldn't quite bring herself to touch him. He didn't wait for her to ask, he broke the silence and explained what he could even though it was an active investigation. He felt she should be aware of some of what Brian knew.

"Trish, there is some stuff I want to tell you even though I proba-bly shouldn't. This may or may not pertain to you, but even if it does a fraction, I want you to be prepared." He placed his hand on top of her hand. She looked at where they were connected and froze.

"What are you talking about, Brian?" She didn't move her hand, but she didn't lean any closer either.

Speaking softly and only to her, Brian continued, "Patrick and I are investigating a murder from a few nights ago. This is no different than any other case we have, but evidence has come to light that there is a connection with the Castenellos family. I wouldn't tell you this except the person who was killed appears to be their most recent financial advisor." Trish's eyes rounded wide with surprise.

"What do you mean most recent financial advisor?" Trish's voice shook with nervous jitters. She gripped his hand tighter and wasn't hesitant anymore.

"We had some new evidence that our current victim worked for them, and they had been making more visits to their office of late. We haven't dug down deep yet. This is the newest development in our investigation." Brian didn't release her hand realizing she needed the support.

"What happened to him?" Trish asked. Her tone was now one of disbelief, but she looked like she was accepting what he was saying and not denying.

"Details are unimportant. Just know that it seemed he was tortured before they killed him, and the scene didn't provide much information. We've been struggling for anything we can get. As of now, what I've told you is all I can without interfering with the investigation." Trish trembled her obvious terror and leaned into Brian. He put his other arm around her and embraced her attempting to comfort her.

"What do you know about the Castenellos family? Obviously, you are concerned about them, but I'm wondering about any business activities that I should be aware of." That was a question Brian wasn't expecting, and she didn't elaborate as to why she was asking.

"I don't have any real evidence supporting what I think they are into, but I will say I have my speculations." Brian didn't want to accuse them unwarranted and have her paranoid, but he wanted her to be aware and not walk blind into any potential situations.

Chapter 12: Trish

As Trish arrived back at the office, she had a lot on her mind. She had the perfect opportunity to share her findings with Brian. The fact that he didn't have any hard evidence against them was the only reason she held back. Trish knew Brian was a detective first and her friend second. So she didn't want to force him to take her information and use it for something, especially since she didn't have any real proof herself.

The moment she walked into the office, Trish was bombarded. Things were out of sorts; people were running briskly from place to place with no obvious destination. She saw Mr. Phillips and Mr. Baker standing among the crowds with a panicked look on their faces. For men who rarely showed much worry, their looks were expressive. She was immediately on alert.

Her eyes quickly scanned the rooms and hallways until her eyes landed on the culprit. Bobby Castenellos and Little Timmy were the faces she recognized, but there were three others with them. When Bobby's eyes fell on her a smile spread across his face. This wasn't a smile that made Trish feel relaxed. Instead she was more on edge than ever. What she didn't know was whether it was her gut instinct or the speculation Brian had alluded to during lunch.

"Trish, there you are. I was worried you had left for the day. We've been making some changes around here," Bobby said, but he glanced over at Mr. Phillips and Mr. Baker. They both visibly blanched. Trish worried about what that meant.

"I just went to lunch with a friend. I wasn't too busy, and after all the extra hours I put in I figured no one would mind if I ran a little long." She smiled though it didn't make it all the way to her eyes.

"Well, I hope it was a lovely lunch. You deserve only the best. While you were gone, we've rearranged some desk spaces. You are one of the people we relocated." Trish was extremely concerned now and wondered why she was moved, but Bobby kept talking and motioned for her to walk and follow him.

"The management around here has recently changed, and your desk was situated right beside mine." He led her to the office that had previously belonged to Mr. Baker. Trish didn't even walk inside. She glanced behind her to look at Mr. Baker, and his face was red with anger. She knew this wasn't by choice. Then what he said rang in her ears. Her new office was right beside his office. That means that Mr. Phillips had been booted out of his space as well. What she didn't know was whether they were demoted or fired. And how could someone do that since they co-owned the firm?

"I don't need to be moved. I'm perfectly happy where I am with the rest of the employees at my level. I'd hate to be frowned up or stir up trouble within the ranks. I like where my desk is. It is perfectly fine for me." Trish was trying to smooth things over and push off any unnecessary special treatment. Why was Bobby taking an office in the firm?

Before Trish had a chance to ask anyone that question behind Bobby's back, he spoke again.

"You will be right where I need you. My case needs special attention, and you are the only one I trust to work on it. No one consulted me before removing you from it, and I am just rectifying that minor infraction. Please escort these men from the building." Two of the unknown men with Bobby came forward and gripped the owners around their upper arms firmly and jerked them toward the door. Now Trish was even more confused. *Why are Mr. Phillips and Mr. Baker being removed from their own company?* She didn't have long to think about it. Bobby lightly pressed her into her new office followed by Little Timmy and the last unknown man.

"Trish, I believe you've met Little Timmy, but I want you to meet Mickey. These guys are my most trusted men, and I want you to know who they are. One of them or both of them is to be with you at all times when you are working, at least waiting outside your office - so you don't have any unwanted visitors. I don't want you to be alone at the office anymore. I know you've worked very hard and put in long hours on my file, but a young woman as yourself," his eyes raked over her body in a slow lingering gaze, "shouldn't be here by yourself. Not to mention, there is sensitive information I don't want to be seen by just anyone. That is why you have this office. All current files you are working on will now remain locked behind this door."

"Where will Mr. Baker be working if I'm in his office? Surely, he won't be working from my cubicle, will he?" Trish knew this question wasn't necessary. She just wanted to hear Bobby say what he had done. She had put enough of the pieces together and knew he was up to something.

"Those men won't be around anymore. They no longer own any portion of this company, and all employees now report directly to me until I hire new management. That will come in time. Today I want to get you settled and allow you more time to get a better handle on your workload.

After Bobby left the room, she turned and made a petulant face at the door and stuck out her tongue. She couldn't have looked more childish, but that was how she felt. *Mr. Bossypants wasn't what I expected when I came back from lunch.* Immediately she regretted her gesture and moved on to feeling angry. She had been thoroughly nervous in the beginning, brattiness, frustration, and now anger were next in line. She was mad that this man had jumped in and taken over so much in so little time. Her bosses had essentially been fired from their own company. Not that they were the best employers in the history of time, but they weren't unfair. They had taken the case away when she felt uncomfortable. Mr. Phillips and Mr. Baker could have easily told her to buck up and deal with it. Instead, they took the sympathetic approach and decided to investigate further. She was upset because now she seemed to be on lockdown against her will.

She would have no real privacy. Sure, it was under the guise of late night protection, but she saw right through that. He was trying to keep tabs on her.

After what Brian had told her about their previous financial advisor, she was a little on edge. Knowing what she knew and was going to learn, this job was potentially worth killing for. What had the mystery accountant done to have warranted his death? That would be essential information to prevent repeating the offense.

Deciding she couldn't do anything to change her current situation at that time, Trish decided to set up her workspace. One thing she loved was organizing and preparing her desk the way that suited her everyday work life. Knowing that a notepad or a post-it was within reach was like knowing she could pick up the phone at a moment's notice and talk to her best friend. It calmed her. Needing something to keep her hands busy to keep them from shaking, partly from rage and partly from insecurity, she got to work on putting things away.

After spending the bulk of her day trying to avoid the brute force located on the other side of her door, Trish looked at the clock and counted down the time until she could leave for the day. A moment later, a knock resounded on her door, startling her from the silence in her office. It was followed by the twisting of the knob. Not waiting for her to answer, Bobby popped his head into her space. *Apparently, I don't have privacy with the door closed either.* Trish fought an eyeroll and plastered a smile on her face hoping it looked genuine.

"Mr. Castenellos, to what do I owe the pleasure?" holding his gaze so that he wouldn't see her falter. She hadn't done any actual work today, but she didn't want him to know that.

"Please, call me Bobby. I think you and I have made it past formalities," his voice crooned, hinting at an accent that he had been hiding up until now. She knew he was trying to seduce her into believing he was a good man. Brian's revelations combined with the knowledge she had dug up herself told her she knew he was far from good.

"Now what would the rest of the team think if I started calling you by your first name, Mr. Castenellos? I'd hate for them to get any silly ideas." Trish fluttered her eyes slightly in hopes he would let it go. She didn't want to get on a first name basis with this man. She honestly just wanted him to leave her alone and forget she existed.

Taking her actions as flirting, he leaned over her desk and dropped his tone to a little huskier lilt, "I wouldn't mind stirring the rumor mill with you anytime. Just let me know when you'd like to take that plunge, or I'd be more than happy to surprise you." His strong arms flexed under his weight as he leaned in toward her. Her eyes flew to the ripple motion of their own accord. She cursed at herself for being so shallow. Unfortunately, he noticed the trail of her eyes and the corners of his mouth turned up slightly. On any other man, this entire look would have been sexy, but on him and with what she knew it came across as creepy.

"I'll let you know when that day comes, but until then the rumor mill can get their feed from other sources. With all the changes today I think I'm going to call it quits at five. Then I can gear up and be ready to get a running start on my day tomorrow. I hate starting a project in the middle of the day." Trish held her smile hoping to soften the blow she knew she was delivering.

"Now my dear, Trish, this isn't a start of a project. This is the same one you've been working on all along. Just now you have unlimited time and space to get things done." His eyes flared his annoyance, but his face didn't show it. He was putting on a good show, and she hoped never to see the vengeance she knew lurked just under the surface.

Placing her hand on his arm, Trish laid it on a little thicker hoping he would cave to her request. "I know nothing has changed with my day to day, but today was new, and I'd like to start fresh tomorrow." She added a touch of pout to her tone, hoping he had developed a soft spot for her.

Bobby took her hand and brought her fingers to his lips, "For you my dear, I will allow you this one night. First thing tomorrow, though, I want you back on top of things." More than anything Trish wanted to jerk her hand from his grasp. It felt like tiny spiders were crawling up and down her arm. His lips were soft but almost too smooth as though he spent a little too much time on his appearance. When he finally relinquished her hand, she fought the urge to wipe it instantly. Waiting instead for him to turn his back as he rose to leave. She quickly slipped her hands off the desktop and mentally tracked where she had put her hand sanitizer. She jerked when he turned back around.

"Oh and my dear Trish, I hope you don't mind planning to have lunch with me tomorrow. I'd love to go over your progress." Putting a smile back on her face hoping he didn't see the look of disgust that had momentarily replaced it.

"Certainly. That sounds like an excellent idea. Are we going out or eating in for the meeting? I'd like to plan my presentation for you accordingly." The spiders were still crawling up her arm as though her body sensed the evil that came from this man.

"Let's order in. Then, you can take as long as you need and have all your resources. I imagine that will be more comfortable for you." He licked his lips on his last statement, and that caused the spiders to travel all over her body. This wasn't the good feeling she got when she thought of an attractive man getting her alone. He gave her the heebie-jeebies.

Leaving Trish after lunch was one of the hardest things Brian had ever done. She was so vulnerable and had even tolerated being close to him. Perhaps he was wearing her down, or she was just in shock from the news. Either way, he didn't want to leave her to go back to work. At least now she had been pulled from the case that his nightmares had stemmed from recently. When he found out she was working on something for that family, his stomach rolled. Instead of letting his fears consume him, he just decided to not let anything happen to her. He had bigger plans for Trish, and they didn't involve any horrific things happening to her.

As Brian made his way back to the office, his phone rang. A glancing at the screen told him, it was Patrick.

"Are you done stalking my wife's best friend?" Patrick rumbled through the phone.

"I'm not stalking her, I'm watching out for her. She was on one of the worst projects of all time. The Castenellos had her working on something, but I'm sure it was a coverup for something else." Brian hadn't told Patrick about what Trish was working on yet, but now that she was off that project it was okay to tell Patrick without her getting upset with him further. Just like police work, Brian understood that corporate projects could be classified, as well, if they were high profile enough.

"Are you saying that she was working for our suspect and you didn't tell me before now?" Patrick's voice was getting louder, and Brian knew he needed to defuse the situation before Patrick lost it.

"They weren't our suspects until today, and as of this morning she handed the project back to her employers and informed them of some of her findings. They took the file back without question and are planning to reassign her with a case that isn't so shady."

"That doesn't change the fact that she is on their radar. What is to stop them from doing something to her now that she has been taken off their file just to keep quiet anything she might have uncovered?" Patrick's voice wasn't calming, and Brian could see the logic in what he was saying.

"That is why I'm not going to let her be alone. I'm going to head over there at the end of the day to make sure she gets home all right. I doubt she will be putting in any more long hours at least not until she gets another project. From talking to her at lunch, I don't think that day is today." Brian felt a tightness in his chest. He wasn't going to let anything happen to her, not if he could do anything to stop it.

"Let me know if you need any help. I can have her stay at our place for a few days if need be. That way they don't catch her scent, follow her home, and try anything after you leave." Patrick was calming down, but he still had an edge to his voice that said he was still unsure.

"She has a doorman who is scarier than either of us. That should deter anyone from trying to break in without being noticed. The last thing they will want is to draw unnecessary attention to themselves." Brian had met Sam, and he was like Patrick and Brian - put together and on steroids. If someone wanted past him, it would cause a ruckus in the process.

They ended the call shortly after that, and Brian made his way back to the office. He could hear more of Patrick's concerns in person while they reviewed what they had. They needed to do more research to try and put together further scenarios where Seymore and the Castenellos family were connected.

· · · ·

AFTER A LONG DAY OF research, Brian left Patrick to finish up for the day. Brian headed to try and meet Trish after work. As usual, he didn't wait in the car for her to get outside. Instead, he marched in the doors and what he saw alarmed him. Glancing in the direction of Trish's desk, he noticed it was empty. It had been cleaned out, and she was nowhere in sight. *Was she fired this afternoon for challenging a customer file? Where did she go? What if she is somewhere vulnerable?* Questions flashed through Brian's head so quickly it was hard to land on just one thought, and some went by so fast they didn't make sense. Turning abruptly, he nearly collided with a small woman. She had mousy brown hair and wouldn't stand out in a crowd.

"Excuse me. I didn't see you there." Brian gently clamped onto her arms when he stopped his forward motion. She ducked her head hiding from his view making it so he couldn't make out her face. This was an odd reaction, but he let it go.

"Out of curiosity do you know where Trish Montgomery is or where I might find her?" If all else failed, he asked the locals. It worked for him when he was on the job. He hoped she would be able to tell him what he needed to know.

Without looking up, she merely pointed in the direction of the other hallway. He hadn't been down there before in his previous visits to the office and assumed it was a different department. Perhaps that is where they held meetings or where the larger offices were.

"Thank you," Brian said as he released her and made his way in the direction she had stretched her finger. As he came through the next archway into a reception area, Brian halted in his tracks. To his surprise, he saw two of the Castenellos goons. Noticing him, they each gave him a dark scowl and crossed their arms. They were standing between two doors, and the only other door in this area was glass. Brian assumed by looking at the accompanying glass wall that it was a conference room. It was empty except for the large table and high back leather chairs surrounding it.

Before Brian could walk into the space, one of the doors the men seemed to be guarding opened. Just in case it was someone he needed to be aware of, Brian stopped and waited. He saw a lithe leg come out followed by a slim body with curves in all the right places. He knew this body better than he knew his own, well at least clothed that is. It was Trish. She had her purse strapped to her shoulder, and she was locking the door behind her. That was odd. Why was she coming out of what looked like one of the main offices?

Brian knew this company was owned by two life-long friends, Phillips and Baker, and named after them. Surely, they wouldn't just sacrifice one of their offices for her. As she turned from the door, she caught sight of him and gasped, but then immediately sighed as though she was happy to see him. Mumbling goodbye to the men at her door, she hurried over to Brian.

Without touching him, she fell into step beside him and hurried out the door.

"You have no idea how happy I am to see you." Trish was saying the exact opposite of the words she had been saying for months. Something was wrong, but Brian was going to let her get to it without pushing her. He didn't want her to get upset and shut down.

"I'm just glad your co-workers knew where to find you. When I saw your desk cleaned out, I got worried. I thought you were fired, but it looks like you got a promotion instead." He let the concern flow through his words.

Trish laughed humorlessly, "Far from it, I think it is more like a prison cell." Her words worried Brian, but she wasn't done yet.

"When I got back from lunch, Mr. Phillips and Mr. Baker were escorted from the building, and it seems I have a new employer." Trish's words were spoken low just above a whisper. It was as if she was trying to make herself believe what she was telling him. Brian had a hunch who she was talking about, but he asked anyway.

"Did Castenellos take over the company?" He led her to his car, and she didn't speak until they were both inside.

"I'm not sure if he bought it or is just holding something over their heads. I can't figure out how he could buy the entire company and take over in one morning. He was there waiting for me when I came back from lunch. He already had my office relocated and had eradicated the previous owners. Now I'm on lockdown in my office guarded by those meatheads. I don't know what I can and can't-do, but I'm betting the can't list outweighs the can side. Not that I have been given a list of either." Trish wiped at her eyes, but not before Brian noticed. He grabbed her hand as they drove out of the parking lot.

He didn't head straight for her apartment but instead headed for a bar. Trish needed a drink and quite frankly so did he after all this news. He had thought she was relatively safe but now she was under the watchful eye of a crime boss. This was not what Brian had planned, and he had to do everything in his power to fix it. As they pulled up to the bar, Trish was so lost in thought she didn't even notice where they were headed. Brian didn't see the need to tell her. She needed someone else to take care of her now. While she got her bearings, he fired off a few texts.

Climbing out of the car, Brian walked around to open Trish's door and help her out. She was still a little glassy-eyed from her emotions running amuck.

"Where are we?" her voice was still soft and sounded exhausted. Brian grabbed her hand and pulled her toward the entrance.

"Come on. After the day you've had, home isn't where you needed to be. You need a drink, and I'm buying." He smiled reassuringly. She didn't resist him and let Brian lead her to a table. He took that as a win and motioned for a waitress to come over.

"Order anything you want. I mean it. I'm buying all night, and I'm driving you home," Brian ordered himself a bottle of beer. Trish ordered the same.

A few minutes later the door to the bar opened, and their eyes moved to the motion. Brian watched as Trish's eyes lit up in recognition. Brian smiled because his plan was in motion. In walked Grace and Patrick, Abigail and Ted, and bringing up the rear was Sal. Everyone had a big smile, and all made their way to join the pair.

Brian hadn't told anyone what was happening, but as soon as Grace took in Trish's appearance, she immediately embraced her in the tightest bear hug. Brian assumed it was either women's intuition, or they had just been friends long enough to know when something was wrong.

"Why didn't you call me?" Grace spoke into Trish's hair and hadn't yet released her.

"I was just going to go home. I didn't want to bother anyone." Trish sounded defeated. Brian was sure that a lot would be said tonight. No matter what happened, he would be here to pick up any pieces.

Abigail was next to scoop up Trish, but her words weren't as sweet. "I ought to thump you for trying to do this on your own." Brian didn't realize Patrick had filled everyone in.

"When did you have time to catch everyone up? You haven't even heard the latest and greatest news yet." Brian's hushed words spoken as he leaned toward Patrick who was standing on the opposite side of the table as the girls.

"I haven't said anything to anyone. You sent the text that said get everyone to the bar. That is what I did. No one is aware of anything we spoke about today." Patrick stood in as much shock as Brian. Neither could figure out what the girls could be talking about if they were still in the dark.

Everyone sat down, and once they had their drinks Brian started, "I wanted everyone here because Trish had a horrible day, and she needed her friends to support her. I'll let her fill everyone in to whatever level she chooses." Brian leaned back and placed an arm around the back of Trish's chair to show his support. On some level, it was also because being closer to her eased the ache in his chest. She needed him, and he would be here for her no matter what.

Chapter 14: Bobby Castenellos

Leaving the office for the day was a new thing for him. It was probably good that Trish decided to leave and not stay late. He had plans that he couldn't change. He didn't want to have to worry about what she would come across while he was gone. He was trying to win her over to his side early in the game, so if she came across anything later, there wouldn't be a period of panic.

They headed out to his car. His guys climbed into the front while he was left to the back chauffeured as usual. This allowed him to conduct his business without being distracted by driving.

"Are they ready?" Bobby spoke into his phone. He was gruff, but that was how he usually was with his guys. They needed to know he was the boss at all times. If any of them thought they'd get an inch, he would have a war on his hands for power.

"Been working them over all day just waiting for you, boss," Toby spoke through the phone. His voice was raspy, because he smoked too many cigarettes. Bobby assumed it started as a way to hold up his badass image.

"Good. We are on our way, and I will take over the questioning." He said gruffly, hanging up the phone without warning. This was something his guys were used to and shouldn't ever be surprised by it. His time was valuable and every second wasted was something he could have used to work on something else more important.

The rest of the car ride was silent. His crew was never under the delusion that he was their friend, so they never attempted to strike up small talk with him. They knew their place, and he hated mindless chatter.

Approximately thirty minutes later, they arrived at their secret location. It wasn't listed under any of the family names, but one of the unknown aliases that was only used for property they needed hidden.

This property was far enough from town that when they were in the questioning phase of their meetings, no one would hear the screams of pain. His guys were thorough, and they got to the point fast. All they wanted was answers, and if given freely, no one endured much pain. However, it was very rare that someone would make it out pain-free.

Parking in the driveway, Mickey came around and opened his door as expected. If one of them didn't, then they would pay. They made their way inside, and both men flanked him knowing that there was no danger inside and any threat would be coming from behind.

As Bobby crossed the threshold, he was met with the sound of two men groaning. It was one of his favorite sounds next to screaming. He also liked it when his women screamed and writhed in his bed. That was the biggest turn on for him. Then his thoughts wandered to Trish, and he pictured her in his bed. He wondered if she would scream or fight him. A fight would only make her screams sweeter in the long run.

They passed into the kitchen, because they always handled the messy ones there. It was easier to clean up on the linoleum floor. They opted against a home with tile, because the grout would've been a bear to clean. Of course, they weren't the ones actively cleaning up the messes.

With their backs to the entry, Bobby smiled as he saw the two men strapped to chairs tied down at their feet, wrists, and throat. They could hear him enter, but couldn't turn to see him. He loved that. Bobby was like a cat and loved to play with his prey. This was a psychological game as much as a physical one. He walked in slowly. Only the sound of his shoes clicked across the floor. He noticed the guys had staggered the men, so he walked up and slipped his hands over the eyes of the first one he saw.

"Guess who." His voice was a sing-songy pitch that eluded to a lighter mood than was actually present. When the man struggled away from his grasp, Bobby recoiled and slapped him across the face impacting his nose with such force it caused his nose to bleed. The sight of this made Bobby laugh.

"You are such a weakling. You bleed from a mere slap to the face. I can't imagine how you could possibly satisfy your wife." His low voice vibrated through the room changing the atmosphere, and he laughed again.

Walking around in front to face the men, Bobby smiled as he saw Wyatt Phillips with his nose pouring blood. Paul Baker's eyes were practically swollen shut. He was proud of his hired men. Their mouths still worked, but his boys had inflicted enough pain that they should be ready to share.

"Perhaps I should take your wife into my bed and please her myself. Show her what a real man feels like." Bobby enjoyed this part most of all. When they had someone to exploit, it was so much easier. Wyatt flinched at his words and struggled to free himself.

"Leave my wife alone!" Even beaten to a pulp he still had enough vigor left to try and defend his wife. Unfortunately, his efforts were fruitless If Bobby wanted to have his wife, there would be no stopping him. He didn't always go the extra mile, but sometimes it was nice to have someone in his bed without effort. In these times, it was easy to convince them that if they pleased him it would save their husbands.

"Oh, then you have the motivation to tell me what I want to know. You took Trish off our file. Was that your decision?"

Wyatt and Paul both struggled against their bindings to no avail, but they didn't speak. So Bobby decided to target Paul.

"Paul, your wife is a known socialite. I bet she is tired of being cooped up and is bored with not having an event to plan. What if I bring her in with Wyatt's old lady and make it a party? I bet that would make her happy. She can suck my cock while Wyatt's wife licks her clit. I bet that would make her very agreeable. I could probably get her to do anything I asked."

"Don't you dare touch my wife," Paul growled through his teeth continuing to struggle against his bindings. Paul's wife was indeed a socialite and also a trophy wife. He was probably thirty years her senior and Bobby expected her to jump at the young blood without thought. The more he thought about it the more this idea was building into a beautiful plan. If he kept them away from news sources and phones, he could probably keep this scenario going for a while and get plenty out of both women. Wyatt's wife wasn't much older than Paul's, but wouldn't be considered a trophy as she was only ten years younger than Wyatt. They were both younger than Bobby and would find him a delicious morsel; he would make sure of it.

"Then, I ask you again. Did you pull her off our file on your own or was there another reason?"

Both men side-eyed each other and sighed in defeat. Neither wanted their wives molested in any way, and with luck, they figured they would make it home to their wives mostly in one piece.

"It was our choice, but she requested it," Wyatt spoke after a long minute.

"Why did she do that?" Bobby was slightly alarmed but didn't let it reflect onto his face. Outwardly he was cold as ice. No one ever saw him with his guard down.

"She has spent many hours on your file, and she is a go-getter. When she thought you were spending too much on basic things, she was going to research a way to minimize your costs," Paul answered reluctantly but was still ready to do whatever it took to save his wife.

"What did she think she found that caused her to want to bolt?" Bobby was flexing his fingers in and out of a fist mostly out of habit, but he was sure it was intimidating as well.

"Your cleaning company," Wyatt said flatly devoid of emotion.

As the words hit him, Bobby fumed. How did she figure that out so fast? It shouldn't have been something she looked at that closely. None of the others had paid any attention to the individual companies he'd chosen in the past. He was so angry that he was seething. Wyatt and Paul were only vaguely aware of a fraction of his business, and he held it over their head. Since they pulled her from the file and didn't tell him what she had uncovered, he was furious. He pulled his gun from his back and leveled it at Paul's head first since he was the closest. Not giving him a chance to react, he pulled the trigger. One shot and one of his problems went away.

Seeing as they were making decisions together, he turned and in one shot handled Wyatt as well. Unlike Paul, Wyatt was a blubbering idiot, and when it was over Bobby was happy for the silence.

Walking from that room to one of the back bedrooms, he quickly changed clothes. He always kept clothes on hand in case he ended up getting more than his hands dirty. It didn't often happen, except in cases of a major screw-up.

Bobby made his way back toward the kitchen. His guys were waiting for instruction on what to do next. *They can't figure out how to do anything on their own. They are like children.* With an exaggerated eyeroll, he walked up and surveyed the situation.

"Looks like this is going to require some finesse. Mickey, this one is going to be your pet project. I think it will be a chop and flush job. All identifying markers removed and flushed. Chop everything else and put into smaller trash bags. Then call the cleaners to come and get rid of what is left." He dusted the invisible dirt from his hands that he collected while walking into the space. He knew no one would be here looking for evidence, and the bodies would be moved to another location.

"I'll get my snips and pliers and get to work on digits and teeth. I'll have that done quickly and flushed before you even get back into town. I'll need one or two to stay and help with the chop job. I don't care who just whoever you want to leave behind. I'm sure you have a busy evening." Mickey sneered in his direction and that reminded him.

"You keep Toby. I have a pickup and delivery I need Little Timmy to make for me." Smiling at his newfound plans, he headed out the door without a backward glance.

In the car, he made the first of two phone calls.

"Mrs. Phillips, I have a proposition for you, and I think you'll find it more than fair."

"Who is this? I don't recognize this phone number." The woman didn't sound scared, more like bothered. She would soon change her tune.

"The man who is in possession of your husband. Unless you do exactly as I ask, you and your husband will regret it." She gasped into her end of the phone but didn't speak. "I'm sending a car over to you shortly, and you will get in the car peacefully if you ever want to see your husband again." He didn't wait for her to respond. He knew she would listen. She was a good girl and would do anything to save her precious husband.

He immediately dialed Mrs. Baker and had a similar conversation with her.

"Drive to pick up Mrs. Phillips first and then we'll head to Mrs. Baker's house. You will go and get them both and bring them down to me. Then off to my place for a fun evening." He instructed Little Timmy from his seat in the back. This was a Town Car and would easily hold the three of them comfortably in the backseat.

Soon they were all seated in his car, and he informed them of his plan in detail.

"I have come into a situation that resulted in my need to acquire both of your husbands. I am in need of payment on your end to sort this all out.

Both women were practically trembling at the knowledge that their husbands were being held captive.

"Wh..what do you want?" Mrs. Phillips finally dared to ask.

"I want both of you on your knees for me," Bobby said simply without a hint of humor. He was dead serious.

Their mouths opened in shock, and Mrs. Baker squeaked slightly.

"Oh good. You are practicing. We will be at my condo shortly, and you can each have your turn. I think I'd like to see you, Mrs. Phillips, pleasure Mrs. Baker. That would make me very happy, and I think her as well."

Mrs. Baker blushed but didn't shy away. Bobby knew this was going to be an entertaining night. His eyes were alight with mischief, and he was looking forward to these women. Neither was hard to look at and having both at his disposal would be more than enjoyable. It had been too long since he'd had two women at once.

• • • •

GETTING THE WOMEN UP to his room was no trouble. They moved in front of him and did as instructed. Manipulating them was almost too easy. They had no idea their husbands were already gone. That just made this more fun for him.

"Go into my bedroom at the end of the hall. I want you to undress each other while I watch. I don't want to hear any complaining or whining. Make it sexy and get each other ready." The women were walking slower now that they had a final destination, and they kept side glancing at each other attempting to gauge each other's reaction.

Upon cresting the bedroom threshold, they nearly stopped. Bobby nudged them inside and made his way to the bed to prepare himself for the naked bodies he was about to see.

Trish felt the love of her friends instantly as soon as they walked in the door. Brian was right; this was what she needed after the day that she had. Now he was leaving the ball in her court. She could tell them as much or as little as she wanted.

"I've had a horrible day, well a month. You all know how many hours I've been putting in at work lately. I was assigned a high-profile case, and I thought it was going to be my break to get off the bottom of the pile. What I didn't realize is it might be more than that." Trish was so overwhelmed with emotions her tears were escaping before she could stop them.

Grace was sitting next to her. She squeezed her hand, but what caught Trish by surprise was Brian. His hand had been resting on her chair, and he slowly moved his hand to rest on her back and rubbed slow, soothing circles. He was becoming more than a nuisance lately. It was more like he was her rock. Always there like he sensed she would need him before she knew that it was necessary. Steeling herself, she took a deep breath and continued.

"After digging into the customer files, I started noticing discrepancies and some things that didn't add up. It turned out to be more terrifying than it was worth. I asked my bosses to relieve me of that file and reassign me. I knew I was at risk of getting fired or missing the promotion, but at the time I felt it was necessary. After I got back from lunch today, my bosses had been removed from the building and the business that they owned and built from nothing. They've been replaced by my client. Now I'm back in charge of their file. I guess I got a promotion, but it feels more like a prison sentence."

Brian's hand stopped moving instantly, "You are back on their file? I thought they took you off and reassigned you."

"They hadn't reassigned me yet. When my bosses were escorted out of the building, I'm pretty sure that means the torch was passed on to my customer somehow." Trish sighed and placed her head on top of her hands stacked on the table.

"It sounds like there was a hostile takeover that caused a power shift. That would be the quickest one I've ever seen, but with the right amount of money you can get anything done quickly," Ted chimed in. Since he owned his own business, he was the only one at the table with insider knowledge of such things.

"Well, money wouldn't be an issue for that family," Patrick offered his two cents.

"Not according to their finances. I haven't shown any substantial evidence of liquid assets. They have money from the restaurant, but no other business income or personal income to the family as a whole. Just some strange transactions that seem to cover payroll for some off the books employees. I haven't dug deep enough yet to figure out what those employees do." Trish absentmindedly spoke not paying attention and not bothering to lift her head from her hands. She was much too depressed for that. She thought she had put this behind her, but now it was right back in her lap. Trish didn't know how she was going to handle this file and her new work situation.

Brian's ears perked up at this and glanced over at Patrick. A knowing looked crossed Patrick's face, but he subtly shook his head to keep Brian from speaking about it then. Sal who had been quiet up until now decided to get up quietly. Grace and Abigail watched her leave but didn't say anything. Their focus was on Trish at the moment.

Grace leaned over and stroked Trish's hair back, "Does this mean you are going back to long hours and no available weekends?"

"I'm not sure yet. I have guards posted at my door through the day now and anytime I'm working. I'm not sure what is so sensitive in their files that they now need to be under lock and key. When I left today at five o'clock, Mr. Castenellos seemed disappointed since he knew how many hours I'd put into it before. Me leaving early wasn't what he was expecting, I guess." Trish had lifted her head, but her tone was still dry with depression.

"That's not fair. No employer can require you to work that many hours unless they are adequately compensating you. I can't imagine you are making enough money to cover the time lost in your personal life." Abigail was starting to sound like she was applying for a union representative position. Too bad that wasn't what Trish needed.

Just then Sal made her way back to the table. Everyone turned to her in surprise as she lowered the tray to the center of the table between them all.

"What is this?" Trish said sounding confused.

"What does it look like? This night has had enough drama. We are moving on to better things. Shots all around!" Sal reached down and grabbed one for herself and motioned for everyone else to follow suit. When Trish didn't grab hers, Brian handed it to her.

"Sal is right. We need to cheer you up, so no more talk about work or any problems. Let's enjoy the rest of our night. Then I'll take you home, and you can get some rest before your day starts again tomorrow." Resigned to her friends and not wanting to fight or think anymore, Trish accepted the drink. Everyone raised theirs and Trish did the same.

"Here's to friends and family and nothing in between!" Brian toasted. Cheers and clinking of the glasses rang out from the rest of the table.

The rest of the evening was perfect. Everyone shared stories of embarrassing moments while the remainder of the table joined in the laughter. No one was singled out and this cemented the bond between them all the more.

• • • •

BRIAN DROVE TRISH HOME as promised. She was pleasantly buzzed and no longer wallowing in her misery, at least for now. Brian had been nothing but supportive all night. Somehow, she wasn't annoyed by him once through the course of the evening. He even stopped on the way to her apartment to grab takeout. Since he hadn't eaten either she invited him up to eat with her. It was the least she could do.

Walking into her living room, Brian followed closely. He closed the door and secured the deadbolt and the chain.

"Paranoid much?" Trish glanced over her shoulder at him when she heard the click of the locks.

"Habit. I don't even think about it anymore. It has become second nature." Brian's cheeks heated slightly, and Trish giggled. She hadn't ever seen him act this vulnerable and had never seen him blush. *Did guys really do that?* Covering her mouth, she tried to hide her reaction.

"I have a doorman who is way scarier than you. I have those locks, but when I'm in here, they are usually just for show." She made her way into the kitchen, and Brian carried the food behind her.

"Do you want to eat at the table or is the living room okay with you?" Trish gestured toward the sofa and hoped he sided with her sense of comfort. She wasn't planning to eat a lot, but she needed to appease him now that he bought so much food. Chinese was her favorite splurge food, but she had indulged enough today. The last thing she needed was to add more food to that. Her body would rebel in the morning for sure.

"I'm a sofa man. I stopped using my kitchen table at home unless my mom comes to visit. Her last visit was a while ago." His eyebrows shot up to emphasize his point. She could relate. As much as Trish loved her mother, she didn't jump for joy when her mother made a trip to stay with her.

"Thank God! I didn't want to have to sit in those uncomfortable chairs on account of formalities." They worked together to unpack the food and between the two of them hustled it into the living room. She dropped onto the sofa like a sack of potatoes. Immediately her body relaxed into familiarity; she hadn't realized how truly stiff her muscles had gotten today. Unintentionally, a sigh escaped her lips.

"You work too hard, Trish. You need to take care of yourself. I'd hate for you to get sick or something because your body can't keep up with how far you are stretching yourself." Instead of reaching for food he bent down and scooped up her foot by the ankle. He slipped her shoe off and started rubbing her sole slowly. Trish began to protest, but he found a particularly tight knot and pressed a little harder. She let out a small moan instead. Realizing what she had done her eyes flew open in surprise, and she jerked her foot away from Brian's hand. She reached for a container of food at random and started stuffing food into her mouth.

Brian watched Trish cram mass amounts of food in her mouth to avoid talking to him about what had just transpired. He couldn't help but laugh.

"What's so funny?" Trish asked him with her mouth still full.

"You are! It was just a foot rub, but you are acting like I proposed marriage on our first date." Brian was laughing so hard he barely was able to get the words out.

Trish couldn't help it. His laughter was contagious. She started to giggle herself. Before she knew it, her sides hurt, and then she did the unthinkable, she snorted. Her hand flew to her mouth, and she cringed. *Maybe he didn't notice.* The twinkle in his eye told her she was wrong.

She covered her face with her hands, dying from embarrassment. His hand came up and touched her shoulder, and she jumped from the unexpected caress.

"Don't hide from me," Brian said in a whisper. "Please." The last word he spoke is what got to her attention. Trish looked up stunned, but she didn't know what to say. His hand brushed the hair out of her face. *When did he get this close to me? I never noticed that his eyes had little flecks of green deep in the ocean blue color. That is incredibly sexy.* Before she realized what was happening, they were leaning into each other, and Brian grasped the back of her neck to pull her the remainder of the distance. He closed the gap. Their lips met in a soft kiss. Trish's mind was lost in oblivion.

Brian's free hand came up to cup her cheek, and his thumb stroked her jaw. Nothing else existed besides this kiss. Trish made the next move and deepened the kiss. One nip at Brian's lower lip was all it took, and he opened for her. This wasn't a battle for control. They were equally taking what they needed. She wrapped her arms around his neck and pulled him closer. He lifted her and placed her across his lap. Trish wanted to get closer. She pressed her body against his.

Brian tangled his hand into her hair at her hairline and tightened his grip turning her head so he could get better access to her mouth. Trish released another moan into his mouth. This time no embarrassment followed. He swallowed her mewling and laid her down on the sofa. Trish moved her hands to his chest and stroked every muscle she could reach. No words needed to be exchanged. At that moment all that mattered was that they were together. This moment had been building up for a while. Trish knew that even though there had been fighting between them, she wanted nothing more than to live out every fantasy she'd ever had with Brian as the leading male. Right then.

When Trish stood up, Brian looked at her like he had lost the best gift ever granted to him. Until she reached her hand down to his, he grasped it. She dragged him up to his feet and down the hall to her bedroom.

Sitting at his desk the next morning, Brian recalled last night's turn of events. Kissing Trish wasn't planned, but it also wasn't a regret. She was perfect. Everything about her drew him in, even that little snort when she laughed too hard. Brian knew he had brought out a side of her she hadn't felt in a while. He couldn't remember at any of their shared group nights a time when she let loose that much. She needed to let go sometimes.

He might have kissed her, but Trish took the next step and pulled him into the bedroom. He wouldn't lie. Even though it wasn't planned, that didn't mean he hadn't thought about it every chance he got. Then to have her fulfill that fantasy was mind-blowing. It had been too long since he was satisfied by a woman. They all just didn't quite do it for him anymore. Not Trish though. She was everything he wanted and more. As his thoughts moved through the timeline, he realized it was perfect. The best night he'd had in ages.

Patrick made his way in not long after that, "Did Trish make it home alright?"

"Yeah, I stopped and got takeout since I took her straight from work to the bar for drinks." Brian left out that they didn't eat any of the food until it had long gone cold. They also might not have had as many clothes on either. He could still see her draped in only the sheet eating her Moo Goo Gui Pan right out of the carton. Patrick must have noticed his daydream.

"Don't tell me what happened. Just say it was mutual and not alcohol induced. I don't want to deal with the aftermath of that shit storm."

Groaning Brian nodded his head in affirmation. "Of course, it was mutual, and I didn't even run off afterward. We enjoyed a post-coital moment and each other's company. I slept in my own bed, and she was alone in hers." Brian didn't share anything else with him because that wasn't for Patrick. Trish had spoken to him as though they were longtime friends, and Brian will always cherish her for it.

"Okay enough about your sex life. With what Trish said last night, I feel like we need to figure out this case sooner or later before she gets in any deeper with these mobsters."

A chill ran over Brian's spine. The last thing he wanted was for Trish to come to harm. "How did you do it?" Brian asked vaguely without looking up at Patrick.

Knowing exactly what he meant Patrick answered, "A lot of sleepless nights and extra effort. I kept Grace as close as she would let me. I remember feeling like I was crazy, because I was acting like an overprotective psycho." Patrick's rough demeanor always lightened when he spoke about Grace and her attack. Brian knew he still felt like he failed her by letting her get taken and attacked a second time.

"At least it proved worth it. Had you not been around so much it could have been worse. I just can't explain how angry and scared I am. It's the worst mix of emotions I've ever experienced. I don't know how to process them to get a handle long enough to function day to day. All I can think about is what if Seymore was Trish. Then I see red and lose, what is left, of my sanity. I don't know how to get through this case." Brian looked down and realized he was clenching his fists so tight his knuckles were completely white.

"It sounds like you are taking this too personally. Maybe I should take point on this one?" Patrick asked sympathetically, but Brian slammed his tight fists on the top of the desk, knocking over the pen cup.

"There is no way you are taking this away from me. I need to protect her. How would you feel if I had taken Grace's case away from you?" Brian practically growled out the words. He realized his mind had gone someplace primal. He needed to calm down, but at that particular moment was nearly impossible.

Patrick held up his hands to ward off Brian's wrath, "Whoa! Back off, killer! I was just offering a suggestion. All you had to say was no." Brian could see the laughter in Patrick's eyes and softened instantly.

"I'm sorry bro, I don't know where that came from." Brian released his fists and lowered his head slightly embarrassed by his reaction.

"I do, and now you have my full support. You are right where I was a few months ago, and I know how you feel." Patrick's knowing smile concerned Brian more than anything. He didn't know what it meant, but he was smart enough to be worried.

"Let's get back to work. The sooner we crack this case, the sooner I can take a few days off and figure out all this other stuff." Brian switched his attention to his computer and his list of what they knew.

"Well, it looks like we now have new things to add to that list. Have you added that it seems they own more businesses than we initially knew? Perhaps we need to talk to the secretary again and see if there was a power struggle we don't know about." Patrick was looking at the same list through their shared file.

"I agree. I wonder if that is something these lowlifes have done in the past even if not with Seymore's office. If not, this is a new turn of events and that means they are escalating their process. We will need to figure out why. Maybe we need to talk to Trish's former employers." He did a quick search and pulled up contact information for Wyatt and Baker's former fearless leaders.

"Do you want me to call their home numbers while you do a city record search for all property owned by anyone in the Castenellos family? I feel like they use different names, and that is why we've missed some along the way." Patrick's suggestions usually revolved around Brian doing any tech related things seeing as Patrick wasn't the most computer friendly of their duo.

"Is that all I am to you, a glorified nerd?" Brian smirked at him, and Patrick laughed.

"No, you are *my* nerd. No one else can have you." Patrick always joked about that, and it never got old. They had been together too long to consider ever being separated. They worked best together and closed more cases than anyone else in the department.

"If I'm your nerd, then you are my meathead." Patrick was very brawny. Not that Brian couldn't hold his own, but it was always nice to know that Patrick had his back.

Brian got to work on the property search. This would take some time, because they had so many family members. He would have to dig a bit to find the obscure ones that aren't in the public eye.

Patrick, on the other hand, had the easier job, as usual. Hanging up the phone his face showed a puzzled expression.

"What's up?" Brian knew all of Patrick's hidden looks and this one was more than obvious.

"No one was home at either address, but the housekeeper at both homes answered. It seems that both the Phillips family and the Baker family have taken an extended vacation. When I pressed them further explaining I was a detective, they informed me it was to Barbados. Could Castenellos paid them enough for their family-owned business that they just decided to go on a beach vacation?" Patrick's confusion was apparent and made perfect sense to Brian.

"Maybe rich people are backward thinkers. All they care about is money, not the mini-empire they were in the process of building. Didn't Trish say they looked angry when they were escorted from the building?" Brian was putting some pieces together but ran another search.

"Well, I just ran a search for flights out yesterday, and they bought tickets and checked in for their flight to Barbados. I guess they weren't as heartbroken as most would have been." Brian was now on the same confused plane as Patrick. This case keeps getting more and more confusing by the minute.

Waking up from the best sleep she had in ages, Trish stretched lazily in her bed knowing she still had to go to work.She tried to soak up as much of this feeling as she could. Brian was perfect last night. Every aspect of the evening was just what she needed from the moment he woke her up to when he left for the evening.

It had been so long since she had taken a guy to her bedroom, but with Brian she wasn't even nervous. It was as though it were meant to be. She was better off for it even that morning. She rolled over to check her phone and smiled seeing a text from Brian.

Good morning, beautiful. I didn't want to wake you, and I went into work early. Text me when you get safely tucked away in your new plush office.

Trish couldn't wipe the smile off her face. It was like it was now a permanent expression and strangely that didn't bother her. She had always been drawn to Brian even though most of the time he was the most annoying creation on the planet. Perhaps this change was because there were more frustrating people in her life now. Brian didn't quite rank as high on that list allowing her to see his attractive side freely again.

She hurried through her routine to get ready for work. Seeing as she had a larger office now and essentially a promotion, Trish felt she needed to try a little harder in her workplace attire. She pulled a fitted tan dress out of the back of her closet. She didn't find occasion to wear it that often. It was too nice for a night at the bar with the girls, but not formal enough for, say, one of Abigail's galas. That thought reminded Trish that she and the girls needed to find time for a shopping trip soon. They had to find the perfect dresses for a night of charity. Now that she and Brian had taken a new step in their relationship, even though they weren't dating yet, Trish wanted to find a dress that would knock his socks off. Smiling maliciously, Trish finished getting ready and spun her hair into a very professional French twist. Applying light makeup to complete her look, she quickly made her way out the door. She had taken too much time and now wouldn't be able to make a stop for coffee.

Rushing to the office, she arrived with mere minutes to spare. Thing One and Thing Two were already stationed outside her office. The thought of being guarded for any reason didn't sit well with her. Perhaps she could get Mr. Castenellos to agree that a door lock, while she was inside, would be sufficient.

Squaring her shoulders so they wouldn't know how intimidated she was by them she offered a friendly greeting, "Good morning gentlemen." Trish smiled brightly, sashayed into her office, and closed the door. Immediately her smile faltered knowing she would be stuck in there all day if she didn't want to deal with the guards.

Resigning herself to the facts of her new life, Trish quickly sat down and booted her computer up. While it was loading, she slid open a drawer and pulled her notebook out and started to get a handle on where she left off, as if she could ever truly forget. *A Bloody Mess* was the last thing she discovered in their files which had immediately shut down her research.

Deciding to put that aside, for now, she chose to dig a little deeper into properties owned by the business and the family. She could figure out if there was any equity or need to refinance to have funds made available to include in the inheritance.

Doing a quick search through the boxes scattered around her office, she was thankful they were in some sort of order. There was a box half filled with property deeds and information. She spent the next few hours listing out property details in a new spreadsheet. She had them sorted by style, location, and value. When she finished, she had found multiple properties scattered across town that varied in size and location. Some were small homes in suburbia that she decided where probably their residences. Others were warehouses located in the industrial district, and she could only imagine for what purpose they had those. The total amount of property was in the millions, but she was still confused as to how they were able to liquidate so much money to purchase her firm.

Adding her findings to her official report, she was slowly starting to build a profile of her client, but she needed to have something to present to Mr. Castenellos later. He would explain anything that seemed awry.

"There are just so many boxes it is hard to figure out where to go next," Trish mumbled to herself as she surveyed the room. Boxes were covering all floor space surrounding the room. Just then she realized she never texted Brian. He was probably sick with worry given the fact that he had spent every morning and evening checking on her for the past week or more. Quickly she tore her phone from her purse tucked safely away under her desk.

I'm so sorry that I have been here for about thirty minutes, and I forgot to text. Don't be mad at me, please.

His reply came back to her within seconds. She was right. he was worried. He was watching his phone waiting to hear from her.

How could I be mad at you when you simply forgot? I'm just glad you are safe and sound.

Trish's heart melted. She had never seen this side of Brian and wondered if it was too good to be true.

Yes, I'm locked safely in my office guarded by Tweedle Dee and Tweedle Dum. I only wish I would have had time to stop for coffee.

Trish set her phone down and got back to work. After about an hour she was dragging. It was becoming a detriment that she hadn't gotten up early enough and had missed her coffee run. Just then a knock sounded at her door.

"Come in. It's open," Trish yelled at the mystery guest. A moment later one of her hulking goons was standing in her doorway holding a cup of coffee.

"This was just delivered for you," he said in his gruff tone. His voice wasn't as deep as she expected given his sheer mass. He set it down on her desk and turned to walk away.

"Who delivered it?" She noticed it was from *The Brewing Bean,* she didn't realize they delivered.

"Some girl, but she didn't leave a name just the coffee with your name on it. We assumed you ordered it." Then his expression changed to something fiercer and slightly afraid, which was an odd combination Trish didn't understand. "You didn't order it?"

Knowing it came from her favorite coffee shop and was likely made by her favorite barista, Trish decided to calm him. "No, I ordered it. Don't worry about it." Seemingly placated, he continued his way outside.

Taking the lid off Trish took a giant whiff and instantly smiled. The delivery person must have been Sal, because this was Trish's favorite. She reached for her phone to send her a thank you, but it chimed in her fingers.

Did you get your delivery?

The message scrolled across her alert bar, and she was startled at first. That is until she opened the message and realized it was from Brian. *He must have called or run down and asked Sal to put together a cup of my favorite coffee. Could he be any sweeter?*

Yes, and it is outstanding. I had no idea The Brewing Bean delivered.

Taking a life-giving sip of her brew, Trish closed her eyes and let it soak into her body. With a sigh, the corners of Trish's mouth quirked up slightly.

I have the best connections. You can do anything when you know the right people. Hope it helps your day go a little smoother.

I could kiss that man. He is truly the most considerate guy ever! Trish let her thoughts wander a bit longer about Brian and their activities from the previous evening. Memories of the way his hand traveled over her bare skin were enough to keep her lost in her dream world all day.

Another knock at the door jolted her out of her fantasies. Before she could speak, the knob turned and in walked Bobby Castenellos. He had a brilliant smile plastered on his face. Trish fought the urge to wither under his watchful eye.

"Good morning, my dear. I trust you had a pleasant evening." Mr. Castenellos was obviously a morning person, and that gave Trish one more thing to dislike about him. She may work all hours sometimes, but that didn't mean she had to enjoy the morning hours.

"Good morning. Yes, I had an absolutely relaxing evening. It was just what I needed after all this extra work I've been putting in." She thought if she hinted about the toll on her body after so many hours that he might not make her continue with them at all. The way he spoke last night was a bit disconcerting.

"I'm looking forward to our lunch today. I'll send the boys out for whatever you want. Just let them know in the next hour or so that way they have time to get it back for us. I hear you had a delivery this morning." His face remained steady, but she caught a slight thinning of his eyes. He remedied it quickly so, she thought she might have imagined it.

Laughing slightly, Trish realized it sounded a little nervous and quivered a bit, "Oh, my coffee. A friend of mine sent it over knowing I didn't get over to pick one up this morning. I have a wonderful group of friends, always looking out for me."

"Well, in the future just send one of the boys over. There is no sense in you going without because you ran out of time." Did Trish imagine things or was he trying to discourage visitors? What kind of a workplace didn't allow your friends or family to make deliveries or stop by and say hi even if just for a few minutes? She was starting to get concerned.

"Of course. Hopefully in the future, I won't be running so far behind. I guess I forgot to set my alarm. I made it with just a few minutes to spare." She habitually ran her hands over her dress to smooth out the invisible wrinkles.

Mr. Castenellos perused her from head to toe meticulously, slowly roving her eyes over her more intimate areas. She felt goosebumps crawling over her skin and not the good ones like when Brian did something similar. These felt like thousands of spiders running a marathon over her entire body.

"I don't think you missed anything in your morning preparations. Coffee is something we can make happen once you get to work. If you need to take extra time in order to look as delicious as you do right now, I don't see an issue with you coming in late. So long as you make it up to me once you are here." Trish had no idea what he meant by that, but the words didn't sound like something she would want to experience.

Mental note: don't be late to work for fear of what making it up to him might involve.

"I just wanted you to know I was in my office when you were ready. I'll let you get back to it. I'm sure you are very busy with my file. If you have any questions, then make a note of them. We will go over them after you present your findings so far at lunch." Without another word to her, he left her office.

"What is with him?" Trish mumbled to herself so as not to be overheard by the minions on the other side of her door. The last thing she wanted was for them to run and tattle on her. Then Trish had a horrible thought. *What if they bugged the room?*

She spent the remainder of the morning in silence, but slipped out and gave Bert and Ernie outside the door her lunch selection. Just before she was supposed to go to her meeting, she fired off a text to Brian.

About to go into a meeting, but is there a way to inconspicuously sweep for bugs?

She was sure this would light up all of Brian's freak out alerts, but she had to ask in order to alleviate her nerves. Trish gathered her notes and made her way to the office next door. Smiling sweetly at the Lone Ranger in front of her office, she knocked lightly on Mr. Castenellos door. His only response was a scowl. Trish couldn't tell if his disdain was for her or for the job he was given.

The door opened startling her. Filling the doorway and her vision was Mr. Castenellos giving her what looked to be bedroom eyes as he leaned against the frame.

"My dear, Trish, no need to wait out here, I was waiting for you, and besides, my door is always open for you for anything you might require." He ushered her inside and gave the guard a pointed stare as if to say no one comes in. Nodding his understanding and moving between the doors, Mr. Castenellos shut the door behind them.

"Please have a seat, Trish, and make yourself comfortable. When our lunch arrives, Travis will bring it in." Trish assumed that was the name of the missing barricade. As Mr. Castenellos walked past her, he seemed to slow down and peer down her neckline. She felt overly exposed and uncomfortable, but there was nothing to be done in this particular moment to rectify that problem. She wished she had opted for a burlap sack that morning. Instead of letting him control the situation and bring her level of comfort even lower, she decided to begin.

"Well, my findings are still in the preliminary stage. I have gone through your payroll system, and it seems you have many contracted employees that appear to be paid under the table. That can be accounted for by use of ten ninety-nines and still allow you to write off the funds. From what I can tell, you are still spending as much or close to what you are bringing in. Your profit levels aren't apparent, and I was hoping that was one area you could enlighten me on. Perhaps there is a field I missed." Trish knew she was speaking very fast, but she had an ulterior motive. If she could get through this and eat quickly, she wouldn't be required to stay any longer than that.

"Then, I looked into your spending to see if I could see if anything was exceeding your means. I didn't find anything per se there, but haven't concluded that search and listed all my findings yet." She was not about to tell him what she knew. The last thing she needed was to have him upset with her for any reason. This is just a progress update and the first one at that. She could be a little vague. That might not work down the road, but today it shouldn't be an issue. She chose that moment to glance up at Mr. Castenellos. He was smirking slightly, and she had no idea why. Deciding against giving him a chance to chime in just yet she pressed on.

"Today I decided to focus on properties and any investments that are tied up. I'm looking for ways to show liquidatable funds that can be listed as assets, but if too much money is tied up, it isn't available funds. I found many properties listed under family names amongst the boxes brought over. You have quite the varieties of buildings and homes titled under the family as a whole. When I get further along, I'm sure there will be more questions and probably a few properties that will require some attention. It might be in your best interest to not have them on the family as a whole and list them under individual members of the family. I won't know until I have completed my research. Also, properties that don't serve a purpose might be better to be liquidated now to free up funds. I will be giving you a complete list of properties at the end of the day for you to list purposes if known. Then, we can discuss that further." Taking a deep breath, she had exhausted all of her notes and even backhandedly asked questions without asking them outright. Raising her eyes from her notes as she closed the notepad, she gave him a clue that she was finished.

Instead of just speaking he rose, walked over to the window, and looked out in silence. Trish wondered when he would speak. After a few moments, he turned and faced her, his eyes looking intense. His gaze took her breath away. No one had worried her in this way, and she didn't know how to react. Still he didn't speak. Trish shifted uncomfortably in her seat. Mr. Castenellos surprised her then. He came and stood in front of her, reaching down he held out his hand to her. She hesitated, but in the end accepted it. He helped her to her feet quickly. She was off balance and wobbled on her heels. He steadied her by grasping her hip with his other hand. Trish stiffened under his touch because it sent those spiders skittering over her skin radiating from his hand like magic.

"Come and sit on the sofa. Those chairs look uncomfortable. I will have to have them replaced. They are awful.

Trish settled slightly seeing he was attempting to help, but there was still a tingle across her skin that didn't go away. Following her to the more intimate seat, he joined her as she sat, a little closer than she expected.

"Now, Trish, my dear." His endearment was always consistent, and she didn't understand. She hadn't heard him use such a personal name for anyone else. "I want to talk to you about what I actually expect of you. I waited until now, because I wanted you to have a handle on our file before we had this conversation. Our family is different. We control more funds and power in this city than most are aware of. The longer you are working with me and with our finances, you will notice more things. I just need to ensure I have your discretion. We are a quiet family, and I don't like drama, or our business, waved around. Every family has skeletons in their closet. Isn't that right, my dear?" He gave her a knowing look. *What does he think he knows?* Trish watched him glance at her again and lingered on her stomach. He then took that a step further, reaching to her. She jumped slightly, but willed herself to calm unsure what his intentions were. Then she felt his hand skim up her arm. Bobby placed his hand on her shoulder. Resting it there, he leaned in and continued to speak in a hushed tone closer to her ear.

"You have your secrets, my dear, even from your friends. I have one for you. I didn't place the lunch order for you. I know you don't want it." Trish looked up into his eyes, her own wide with shock. How could he possibly know that? Shame spread across her face. No one knew that, not even her mother. She leaned away from him, but he didn't let her get far. Reaching across to her far hip, he slid her back into him, "I'll keep your secret if you keep mine." With that, he pressed a forceful kiss to the corner of her mouth. Leaping up from the sofa, Trish raced out the door and back to the quiet of her office.

Rereading Trish's text, Brian gripped his phone tightly, "What could she need a scanner for?" Patrick looked up from his project befuddled.

"Who needs to scan what?" Patrick's statement made Brian realize his question was incomplete.

"Trish, she just texted to see if there was a bug scanner that wouldn't be noticed. Why would she ask me such a thing?" Brian started looking through his resources to see what he had available because even if he didn't understand her request, he wouldn't deny her.

Patrick's brow furrowed, and he slid his chair back, "I have no idea, but if she is asking there is a damn good reason and now I'm worried. I'll text Grace and see if she has heard from her. Maybe she can enlighten us."

"Good because she went into a meeting and I can't get an answer out of her, but if she has a bug I hope they aren't tracking other things. I want to get her some apps for her phone to block them from getting to that information as well." Brian stood from his chair and began pacing unable to sit still any longer. Patrick typed furiously on his phone and Brian impatiently waited for his answer. When the alert sounded Brian almost pounced on Patrick, if it weren't for the death glare then he may have succeeded.

"Grace says that she hasn't spoken to Trish since last night. That means we are going to be in the dark until Trish can text you back. In the meantime, I guess we should get with the tech team and see what secret stuff they have available that a novice can use." Brian tucked his phone into his pocket, and the two of them made their way to the tech department.

Not even a full hour had passed before Brian's phone chirped. He snatched it so fast that he fumbled it and nearly dropped it. This is why he never made quarterback in high school.

Don't worry, but something was said, and the thought crossed my mind. I'm not even sure if it is validated, but after the meeting I just had I think it might be a necessary precaution.

Brian relayed the message to Patrick and had to restrain himself from throwing his phone given it was his only way to communicate with Trish. It seemed she needed it more than ever.

"What the hell does this mean? What happened in that meeting that she now doesn't feel safe?" Brian was pacing again. They had spent about thirty minutes in the tech department, and they gave them two different models that should work for what Trish needed. They would just have to give her a crash course and see which one suited her style better and which she could keep hidden better.

Brian tried to work for a few more hours not getting much done. His mind was wandering to all the worst scenarios for what could be happening to Trish. He couldn't wait any longer. Grabbing his keys, he headed for the door.

"Where are you going?" Patrick asked him. Brian decided to use his words against him.

"Out, without you," Patrick smirked at him recognizing that he had said the same thing to Brian a few months prior when he was working on Grace, his now wife's case. Without another word, Brian walked out to his car with the equipment hidden in his pockets.

Brian struggled to keep his speed near the speed limit. He didn't know what he would find since he hadn't heard anything else out of Trish all day. He knew if he didn't know for sure, he would concoct numerous wild ideas that would soon drive him mad.

The day crawled on once Trish had sealed herself inside her office, it felt more prison-like by the hour. After she answered Brian's text upon returning to her phone after her lunch meeting Brian said he would find her something and that was the last they had spoken. Trish's body had been crawling with spiders since she left Mr. Castenellos' office. She had never had arachnophobia, but she feared after the past few encounters with her new boss, it would be manifesting itself regularly.

Deciding there was nothing to be done, but her job, Trish proceeded to comb through files. Now knowing there were things the Castenellos needed to keep hidden she feared more and more about her involvement with them. Even though she was being forced to participate, she was still human and possessed free will. Unfortunately, her will was also very aware of her need for self-preservation. That would inhibit her decision-making skills.

Just when she thought she would pass out from the conflicts in her brain not wanting her to process any more information that could potentially harm her, there was a commotion outside her door. Raised voices and she heard Buzz and Woody's voices gruff and slightly raised, but another unknown voice became louder with each passing phrase. Trish hesitated but decided to go to the door. If nothing else she could stop the assailing voices by making her presence known.

Opening the door, Trish was surprised to find Brian in the hall being restrained by her office guards.

"What is going on?" Everyone froze at the sound of Trish's voice. Beyond the chaos, no one heard her door open and were all surprised to find her looking on. Mike and Ike were holding Brian by the arms trying to keep him out of the space, and the entire scene angered Trish. They were about to see a side of her that was almost unheard of.

"Get your meat grabbers off of him. What do you think you are doing?"

The two enforcers looked between each other and the one she figured out was Travis decided to speak.

"We were told to keep anyone besides you out of that office. There is sensitive information that the boss wants to keep under wraps." He spoke a little softer so his voice wouldn't carry, but Trish heard the intonation of his words.

"This is my friend, in the future just make me aware that he is here and I will come out. If he's not allowed in my office, such is life, but you will not manhandle friends because they are attempting to visit me at work." She put a scowl on her own face, and though it probably wasn't very intimidating, she wanted him to know she meant every word. Brian was then released, and she turned back to her office.

"I'll just get my purse, and we can take a walk. I could use a coffee anyway." This, of course, was just an excuse to leave the office, and she was more than thankful Brian was there. She scooped up her phone and purse quickly and nearly ran back out the door.

"With you two standing her keeping watch do you want me to lock the door? I'll be back in less than an hour." They glanced at each other and just shrugged. Trish took that as their blessing and left the door alone. She figured they probably had a second key to get in if they wanted anyway.

Making their way out of the office, Brian kept quiet reading her mood, and she appreciated it more than he knew. As soon as they got outside, he captured her hand.

"My car, we aren't walking I want to talk to you somewhere and not have to worry about who might be following or listening." He dragged her to his car and opened the passenger door. Before they took off, he pulled something out of his pocket and ran it over her and her purse.

"Why did you do that?" Trish asked not realizing exactly what he had done.

Before he spoke, he looked at the device in his hand, "I just scanned you for any bugs. If you are worried about your office, there is no reason why they wouldn't put something on your actual person or in your purse. You're clean, so we can talk here." He leaned over and placed a chaste kiss on her lips and pressed his forehead to hers. "Please tell me what is going on I have been worried sick all afternoon. I've imagined the worst." Trish's heart squeezed. She never intended for him to worry. She was just trying to weigh her options.

"Today has been a strange day, and I don't feel one hundred percent comfortable at work right now, but due to unforeseen circumstances I'm not sure leaving is the best course of action." Trish's words were spoken in a defeated tone. She proceeded to tell him about her day leaving out her new boss' threat against her but eluded to the possibility.

"So, I gathered that they weren't letting people in to see you, but now you're telling me that you feel like they are watching you as well. I can understand your resistance to trust them. I'd be the same way. Now what we need to do is figure out which one of these is easier for you to use and read. Then we can conceal it in your purse. Whenever you go into your office, you can check for new devices. Then you will know how much can be said behind closed doors. Now let's get back to what happened in your meeting. You said he told you to keep his secrets, but did he say what he may or may not have on you to make you believe him?" Trish hesitated and felt her neck get hot. Instead of voicing the lie she merely shook her head as an answer. Brian paused studying her face and response. If he doubted her, Brian didn't express it. He just drove on and reached over and clasped his hand with hers resting on her leg. He held on as though if he were to let go, he might lose her.

Sooner than Trish hoped they pulled up to Brian's apartment. She hadn't been here, but since it wasn't hers and she didn't recognize it, she assumed. He parked and quickly came to open her door for her. Taking his hand, he helped her out of the car and into a tight embrace. It was one of those moments now that she didn't want ever to see end.

"Come inside with me, and we can talk. I didn't find any devices in your purse, but do you mind if we leave it in the car just in case?" Brian smoothed his hand over her forehead and across her hair. He spoke just a few inches from her face not releasing his hold on her.

"Will it be safe? I don't want anyone to steal your car or break into it." Trish was trembling slightly, the events of the day were taking a toll on her emotions.

"It will be as safe as my backup weapons and gear. Remember, I am a detective. I have to be prepared just like a regular officer, even if my car isn't a regular issue patrol car." He popped the trunk and Trish understood. When most people had a spare tire and a tire iron, he had a mini arsenal ready for any situation. She lowered her purse inside, and Brian secured the lid. With the click of a button, he activated the car alarm.

"Not only is that safe and now under the protection of an alarm, my neighbors know who I am and what I do. There isn't one of them who would cross that line. This is a tame area, and there is minimal crime here. The people here just don't try to commit crimes so close to someone who could bust them. I hope that eases your concerns." She nodded silently and followed him inside.

Brian unlocked the door to his apartment and escorted her inside. "Can I get you something to drink?"

"I'd ask what you have, but the only thing I want is frowned upon since I have to go back to work," Trish smirked, but it didn't reach her eyes. Brian instantly felt his heart clench. He wanted her to be happy and back to normal. The last thing he wanted was for her to suffer through this.

"Well, how about you drink a beer and I'll drive you back no harm done. It will help you relax." Not waiting for her to answer he went to the refrigerator to grab her a cold one.

"Ok, now let's get down to brass tacks. I will show you the scanners, and you will use them. I brought a listening device so you can see what they will do upon finding something. Then you can have all your facts before you decide." He handed her the beer as he walked back into the room.

"Thank you." Trish simply said softly.

"You don't have to thank me. I'm here for you no matter what. I don't want anything bad to happen to you. I will do everything in my power to protect you."

"I don't want you to protect me. I can take care of myself. I just needed a little help along the way." Trish squared her shoulders as the lilt in her voice went up slightly. Brian smiled, her bravado was endearing. He adored women with a backbone, but he also wasn't going to let her go through this alone.

"Ok Tiger, I'll let you handle it for now, but know that I'll still be there for you in the background if you need me. Now take a long swig of that beer and let's get to work." Trish pressed the bottle to her lips, and Brian got distracted watching the way her throat worked to swallow the liquid. The length of her neck was begging to be touched. Brian fisted his hands to keep them from acting on his mental image. Instead, he got up and retrieved the bug from his pocket. He walked into the kitchen and placed it on top of the microwave then walked back to the sofa. Trish was sitting with one of the scanners in her hand looking it over.

"This one is small it fits in my hand, but I have no clue what to do with it." Trish flipped it back and forth looking for the power button. Brian took it out of her hands and pressed the screen make the device come to life.

"It's all touchscreen, and it is very easy to use. Once you turn it on it will walk you through the steps and tell you what it is doing." He showed her the screen, and the message read 'Begin Scan, ' and Brian touched the button. He handed the machine to Trish so she could get a feel for it.

"Well this seems easy enough," the beeping was quiet and consistent rhythm. She moved through the room and the closer she got to the kitchen the sound grew louder and faster. When she got into the kitchen, the sound was nearly piercing. It echoed in the space, and the sound was horrible. When she got to the microwave, it had become constant.

"This will not work at all!" Trish said fumbling with the tiny banshee. "If I use this at work they will come barreling into my office before I get anywhere. Let's try the other one; I hope it is quieter than before."

After Brian looked over the other one, he realized it had a vibrate setting. It was a tad bit larger, but he was confident she could make it work.

"I've made an adjustment to this one, and it should just buzz in your hand, give it a try." Their fingers touched as they passed it between sending a jolt of static from their feet shuffling across the floor as they followed the beeping around. Trish jumped slightly, and they almost dropped the scanner. Brian's quick hands were the only thing that saved it. They both erupted into a fit of laughter. It was the most beautiful sound Brian had heard in ages. She had the laugh that made others smile and want to join in. It was perfect. Once they got control of themselves, Brian placed the machine securely in her hands.

"Think you could hang onto it this time?" Brian's mouth quirked up at the corners, and a bubble of giggles escaped Trish, but she reigned them in quickly.

"I'll do my best. This one is a bit off balance with its oblong shape. Why would anyone design this in a way that doesn't fit comfortably in your hand?" Trish started to walk around the room slowly bracing the larger side with her other hand to avoid dropping it.

"I think it is designed to be used with a secondary system, but will work on its own as well. That is why that one has more software features. They are both touchscreen though, so that simplifies things." They moved toward the kitchen, and the low hum increased. They were making their way to the bug, and Trish nearly dropped the device again.

"Holy Moses! That thing is a better vibrator than mine at home," when she realized what she said she froze and her eyes were as big as saucers. Apparently embarrassed she turned away from Brian swiftly and moved back toward the living room. He gave her a minute to compose herself and then headed in; he was only so much of a gentleman.

"I hope after last night you won't have as much of a need for it. I can't say I think I will put it out of commission because I know how you ladies are with your toys," winking at her he took the scanner from her and placed it beside the other one. It was significantly larger, but with the vibrating feature, it was by far the better choice.

"You presume to know my bedroom habits after one night?" Trish feigned offense, but Brian knew better than that. They had been bickering for months for real, and this wasn't the same passion she usually put into her words.

"I don't presume to know. I was there and I saw how you attacked me." He gave her one what he knew to be a panty dropping smile running his hand down his body to insinuate his irresistible muscle tone. He wasn't as buff as say Patrick, but he had enough definition to make most women drool. His six-pack was defined and hinting at a couple more cans. His pecks were visible without the need to flex. Then there was the "v" that all the women would kill each other to touch. He never understood the obsession with that one in particular other than it created an arrow directly to where he wanted them most.

"You are so sure of yourself, and yet up until last night you had never seen the inside of my bedroom, and until today I've never been to your apartment. I find that interesting, don't you?" She loved to get him riled up, and he wasn't one to disappoint a woman. He always took the bait. This time would be no different.

"If I weren't a gentleman, I could have had you anytime I wanted. I just enjoy the chase a little more than you realize. Yeah, those women in bars are easy for a night here or there, but with you, I was playing my long game. And last night you realized exactly how long it was." He pumped his hips to get her attention, and she didn't disappoint. Her eyes flicked toward the motion, and she licked her lips. It was perfect, but she snapped out of the trance almost the same instant. He would have to work a little harder to get her to climb onto his train. His mental revelry made him chuckle under his breath.

"You think you have me all figured out, don't you? Well, I'll tell you something bucko, you have to work a little harder now. You have had a taste, but I won't fall so quickly every time. I need to be wined and dined. After the last time, you tried that I'm not sure you will be capable. I'm not some dime store hooker. You will have to win me over to keep me around. I have plenty of options, and you might not be the right person for me. You might just be some guy I slept with once." Crossing her arms, she huffed her satisfaction for telling him off, but he had other ideas. Brian made a sound in his throat that sounded a lot like a growl and flew over her, and his lips crashed into hers claiming them in a bruising kiss. His tongue licked hers begging for entrance. She tried to fight him, but when his hand slipped behind her head to press her against him, she gasped. That allowed him to push further and he swooped into her mouth and their tongues danced. After what felt like an eternity Brian broke the kiss, and they both sagged, breathing heavily from the exertion.

"I will win your heart and no other man will have you. I have wanted you from the first moment I saw you and no one would stand between me and what I want."

Trish laid back on the sofa. Her head unable to move she was thoroughly ravished and still breathless. He knew she wouldn't be able to go if she tried because of the glazed look in her eye. If nothing else she now knew his intentions, and he fully intended to live up to them.

When Trish arrived back at the office, she was still in a sort of daze. The words Brian spoke were a declaration she never expected out of him. After the date they had she figured he was just hoping for a few rolls in the hay. She hadn't intended to get him that riled up with the mention of dating someone else. Never in her life had she had someone stand up for her, let alone in that way.

Walking back to her office, Timon and Pumba were waiting at her door as expected. She didn't even offer them a smile or a word of greeting. She brushed past them and into her office. After the way they had treated Brian she wasn't about to make friends with them.

Settling into her chair, she rifled through her purse, not wasting another minute she pulled out the scanner. Brian had shown her how to adjust it but had left it on the silent setting. Turning it on she made sure nothing had changed, and she initiated the scan. Since her office was just one room unlike Brian's apartment which he had put the bug in a different room, it started vibrating dramatically the moment it came on. Trish nearly lost her grip on it in her surprise. She gasped slightly, reigning it in quickly so as not to draw unnecessary attention knowing Frog and Toad were right outside her door.

As she moved around the room, the vibrations changed. She and Brian hadn't discussed the fine tuning for it being such a small space. Since it didn't gradually work its way up, she had to walk around a little to get a feel for it. Realizing quickly that a few areas of the room were stronger than others not knowing what to do she texted Brian.

I think there are a few in here, but I'm not sure. It lit up as soon as it came on and I almost lost it.

She didn't have to wait long for a reply.

You can't remove them, or they will know you found them. I'll talk to Patrick and see if the tech team has a jammer we can put in your purse or tape to the inside of your desk.

Trish breathed a sigh of relief. While Brian might not be allowed in here, she would have options. She was strong-willed and knew that whatever came at her she could handle, but these were things out of her control and feeling like a prisoner in her own workspace wasn't something she wanted to deal with at all.

Trish spent the rest of her workday attempting to be as quiet as possible. She didn't receive many calls, so that wasn't an issue. Her text alerts went off periodically, but they weren't anything urgent. She worried about what else they would have access to given the reach these men seemed to have. They knew how to take over an entire company in one afternoon and essentially had it on lockdown.

Working through her files actually felt like work for the first time in her life. She loved her job, loved how the numbers relaxed her. The order and purpose of doing the calculations soothed her. Throwing her notepad across her desk, Trish growled in frustration.

How dare they take this away from me. I don't have much that makes me happy, and now it's been ripped away like a band-aid on a wound that was still healing.

Running her fingers through her hair, Trish leaned back in her chair attempting to reign in her frustration, when the door burst open. Startled, Trish looked toward the commotion and saw one of the Jolly Green Giants filling the doorway with a questioning look on his face.

"Is there something I can help you with?" Trish raised her eyebrows as a false sense of calm settled over her.

"I heard a crash and thought I should check on you when I heard you holler." He was a direct person, and she wasn't sure yet if his concern was sincere or if he was just doing his job.

"I'm fine I just got a little frustrated. This is the most complex file I've ever worked on." She smoothly lied because there was some truth in it. This one was challenging, but in reality, it wasn't the direct reason for her outburst.

"Do you need anything? You've been locked up in here all afternoon it is well past five. One of us can get you some food or coffee if you need it." His tone surprised her, but she wasn't going to be baited. Trish's concern now was that they were trying to earn her trust. The last thing she wanted was for them to lure her in and get her to reveal something with a slip of the tongue. She had more secrets now, most of which revolved around the workplace. Luckily, she had a lifetime to hone her skills at being a verbal safe.

That was why when Bobby noted that he knew her biggest secret, Trish was instantly terrified. She had kept that from all of her friends and family. Grace didn't even know, and they lived together all through school until Grace left after her attack.

"No, I think I'm good. I'll put in a little longer, than I will head home for the night." Not that she would go straight back to avoid anyone following her even though she was sure they all knew exactly where she lived, seeing as it was in her employee file. The beast nodded and silently shut the door behind him.

True to her word, Trish finished up the spreadsheet she was working on, still trying to get all the properties detailed and listed. Her goal was to finish one project today after everything she had been through; it was the least she could do. It felt normal to have a task, no matter how daunting it might be. Baby steps and she would be back on track before she knew it.

Upon leaving the building, she fired off a text to Brian.

I know you can't come to the office anymore, but I wanted you to know I was off work. I'm not sure where to go.

Brian surprised her by pulling up in front of the building instead of sending a reply.

"I might not be allowed inside, but they can't police the parking lot. I just wanted to be sure when you left you weren't alone."

Trish's heart swelled, while she hated to be treated anything less than anyone else. This made her feel special like someone cared enough to be there for her even if she didn't need it, she wanted it.

"Thank you, where can we go? I don't want to go home right away, and I think them following us to your place isn't wise either."

"There is always the bar." Wagging his eyebrows at her in his signature move that was becoming endearing rather than annoying, Brian opened the car door for her.

"I don't want to make a habit of going to the bar every night. I might like to party I don't prefer to drink my sorrows away." He closed the door and ran around to settle into the driver's seat. Trish waited for him to respond.

"Then don't drink. Let's go to dinner. You are already dressed up, and I can pass for decent in my work clothes. Let's grab a meal and just talk. Somewhere where we don't have to worry about who is listening."

Trish thought that was a much better idea and she would just order something light, maybe a salad. She could blame her nerves, and her secret would still be safe. Nodding her agreement, Brian tore out of the parking lot. Trish was forced to grab the handle above her head.

"Easy Lightning McQueen, we aren't in a hurry. The longer we take, the less likely I will have to worry about any visitors at home." The last part was spoken softer because it was a fear she wasn't planning on voicing.

"You have told me time, and again, you have a doorman to screen your visitors. While I haven't tried to get in without your permission, Sam seems to be the right amount of scary and straightforward. Chances are even those goons won't get past him. I drive my car like this any chance I can get because I feel like she doesn't get to stretch her abilities very often." Brian gave her a smug look, and she couldn't help but smile. He was growing on her, and there wasn't anything she could do to stop it.

Because of Brian inherent need to drive faster than he should, they arrived at the restaurant in record time. *Maybe it's because he is a police officer he can get away with it.*

"Have you eaten here before? Brian questioned, and Trish glanced out of the window for the first time in miles. She had kept her eyes locked on the floorboard while they were driving to avoid car sickness. He had brought her to a little-known Italian place, *Squisito.*

"Nope haven't had the pleasure." Trish didn't go to many restaurants because there was always a chance she would lose herself and binge. That was something she always regretted, and the thought alone was terrifying.

"Then you are in for a real treat. Patrick and I helped the owner a few years back, and it has become my absolute favorite place to eat. You're going to love it." Trish instantly felt horrible for agreeing to dinner. He brought her to a place that meant something to him, and she wasn't planning on eating much food.

Trish didn't look too thrilled to be there, but Brian just chalked it up to a long day. Knowing she didn't want to go home, he chose a place that would be as far out of the Castenellos inner circle as possible. Knowing the owner personally made him feel that much more comfortable with his decision. He held the door for her and was instantly greeted by Mrs. Capitani met them and encircled Brian in a hug.

"It has been too long, detective. Why have you waited so long?" She yelled toward the kitchen for her husband to come out. This was a family restaurant, and it was always loud with family love and expression, something Brian envied.

"Brian. We aren't formal anymore, you know that. I've been busy with work, and I haven't made it over here." She smiled, but had tuned him out and was now solely focused on Trish. She had stayed behind him and barely a step into the building Trish was clearly out of her element.

Mr. Capitani made his way out of the kitchen wiping his hands on the white apron at his waist. He was always in the kitchen cooking while his wife greeted the guests. They were the perfect team; Brian envied them.

"Eh!!! You are back, Brian. It makes me so glad to see you." They had an unmistakable Italian accent, but they had been in the states long enough that they both weren't impaired by it. They spoke English as clearly as any American would. After a brief, but warm hug Mr. Capitani was entranced just like his wife.

"Who is this delicate flower you have brought with you?" He never beat around the bush and unlike his wife called attention instead of just silent wonder.

Laughing at his forwardness, "This is Trish, she is a close friend, and she has never been treated to the delectable food you serve here."

Placing her hand out to them in greeting, Trish smiled. Brian knew it was a nervous one, but she was trying. Outside of her element and her close friends, her independent, forward personality took a backseat. What she didn't know was the Capitanis were as close as family, a handshake would never do.

Slapping her hand away, Mr. Capitani, tugged her close for a friendly hug. Trish stood stiff unsure of what exactly was happening and what to do. When she was released it was short-lived, Mrs. Capitani mimicked her husband's gesture. With all the hugs passed around, Brian led the way to his usual spot that was saved and always kept open for the customers who were special in their own right. In Brian's case, it was because he had helped return the Capitani's daughter to them unharmed after an abduction case. Something they didn't talk about anymore for the painful memories, it brought back, but it was the unspoken gesture that was respected nonetheless.

Seated Trish still hadn't relaxed, "Can you bring us a bottle of vino? House special is fine, just something to ease the day's tensions." Brian didn't elaborate, but he was sure a drink would take some of the pressure of off her.

"Of course, I'll bring out only the best for you and your...*friend.*" The lilt in her voice said she was sure that Trish was more to him, but she wasn't going to push it, for which he was thankful. Brian had exhausted a lot of time and energy to get her to this point, the last thing he wanted was to run her off because people were nosey.

"Do you have a favorite Italian food or one you have always wanted to try?" Brian knew this was the best food she was ever going to eat and was willing to recommend his favorites for her to try. He would order every item on the menu so that she could have a sampling if she couldn't decide.

"I'm not really that hungry. I think I'd just like to have a salad." Trish's voice was small and unsure, and that piqued his interest. His detective instincts flared to life, though he tried to tamp them down.

This wasn't a case, this was Trish, and she was more important to him than anything else.

"What do you mean you're not hungry. This is the best food in town, and it is the perfect comfort food if there ever was one. You have to try something at least, anyone can make a salad, but they have the best pasta because it is homemade here daily. They have the most savory bread that Mrs. Capitani and her daughter bake every morning. They get up at the crack of dawn so it will be perfect for everyone who comes in." He knew he sounded like a fanatic, but it was all true to form. He was aware that their food no matter what she chose would far surpass anything she had ever eaten.

"I've just had too much going on today with everything. I know I need to eat, but I'm afraid if I order something heavy it won't sit well on my already tight stomach." He knew she wasn't referring to her workout habits so he took pity on her knowing that she was probably right. The last thing he wanted was for her to have her first *Squisito* experience end so badly. He finally conceded to her and nodded his understanding. What surprised him was her palpable sigh of what seemed to be relief. *Did she really think I would force her to eat something on a twisted stomach? Did she think I am so bullheaded I wouldn't listen to her or is there something else?* Brian was watching her face closely. Time slowed as he took in every inch of her and noticed a slight sheen of sweat across her brow. Her breathing had increased just a hair. Not enough to pick it up unless you were looking for certain signs. After a moment, Brian realized she was hiding something. Now he had to figure out a way to get her to open up without her noticing.

Instead of coming right out and asking her he started up some mild small talk to clear the air. Soon their wine arrived, and they had placed their orders. Brian watched Trish swirl her glass, closing her eyes she inhaled the rich scent of the blood red liquid inside before lifting the glass to her lips and swallowing the flavor.

"I could watch you do that all day. You are a vision indeed." Brian's voice was one of awe, and he didn't try to hide it. That was the most enticing thing he had ever seen, and it wasn't even intended that way. Watching her throat bob as she swallowed was the perfect torture. Although it seemed his words surprised her out of her haze and a drop of wine escaped her mouth and dribbled down her chin. Her hand shot out to catch it.

"Seriously? Now I have to watch how I drink around you. You are such a creeper." He could tell she was playing, but the banter was what they were good at more than anything. Seeing that she was lowering her guard was a good sign, he'd take it.

"I can watch enough for the both of us. No need for you to take on more work. I'm happy to bear the burden." He just stared at her and awaited her response.

Instead of speaking she simply burst into a fit of giggles. Unable to control himself he succumbed and joined her with a small chuckle. It felt right to be in this moment with her. He couldn't think of a place he would rather be.

When their meals arrived, he dove in with a vigor. It had been over a month since he'd been in and as soon as the flavors hit his tongue, it was as if Brian were transported to another place. Their food could do that with one bite. You would easily feel as though you were truly in Italy enjoying the local cuisine.

After a little bit of silent eating, he looked up from his plate and saw Trish cutting her salad and eating tiny bites. He thought she was trying to keep her stomach in check, so he didn't comment about that. In an effort to kill the silence he decided on another plan of attack.

"How is your salad?" It sounded lame ringing in his own ears, but he had to do something to break the quiet.

"It's lovely, I have always been a fan of romaine lettuce." Her words were vague, and he realized that she hadn't eaten much of anything. The closer he looked, she was really just cutting up her food into smaller pieces and moving it around the plate. She took a bite ever so often, but not actually eating anything substantial.

The silence descended again as they both ate. He observed her and quickly realized that something was wrong. He took in the rest of Trish's outward appearance that up until now he had overlooked. Her body was thin, and she never wore terribly fitted clothes, though her clothes all looked nice and appropriate to the moment. Taking in her arms, he realized that her arms were hairless as though she either had it removed or shaved. This was odd, and he put all the pieces together. He thought more about how to broach the topic but realized bluntness was probably his best course of action.

"How long have you suffered from an eating disorder?" His voice was pitched low so as not to be overheard by the other guests. This was a conversation for just the two of them.

Chapter 23: Trish

What did he say? Surely, I heard him wrong. Trish questioned herself before voicing her thoughts out loud. This was the last thing she expected Brian to ask.

"Pardon?" She opted for naivety and questioned him in return.

"I asked how long you have you suffered from an eating disorder." He didn't elaborate but left the question hanging again and ringing in her ears. There was no way he knew. This was two people in one day who had called her out on it.

"I'm not sure I know what you're talking about." Trish had been keeping this secret so long that she didn't know she knew how to own it and admit it to someone.

"You do realize I can tell when you're lying? I have been through hours upon hours of training for just that. Besides I've seen the signs before do I need to list them for you?" She stared him down in challenge and hoped he would let it go without her having to answer, but she was disappointed.

"First of all you barely eat anything when we are together. I thought that was odd, but I just chalked it up to girls not eating in front of guys. I hate that by the way. We all know you eat, so don't try to hide it. Second, you shave your arms. I've only ever met one other person who does that, and there was a reason for it. People with an eating disorder grow extra hair to help heat the body where the natural fat is missing. Third, you never seem to gain anything, and I noticed you don't wear clothes that are all that tight. I think you don't want anyone to see just how thin you really are, even though now that I look closely you show signs of being more gaunt than classically slim." He wore a look of satisfaction that he didn't deserve because she still hadn't given him a response. She merely sat and stewed in her chair and wondered what she could say. After holding his gaze for what felt like an eternity, he never once caved. He held her stare the entire time, challenging her. She knew then she was going to have to admit everything. With a sign, Trish's shoulders dropped in defeat.

"Fine, I've been struggling with it since I was a kid. Something you might not know about me is I come from a family in society. My mother is the biggest socialite and expected me to be the same. When I was supposed to have my coming out ball as a debutante. Yes, don't laugh I was a deb." Trish said with a dramatic eyeroll, but Brian only smiled and let her continue.

"My mother expected me to do whatever it took to be the perfect daughter and socialite just like her. I realized as the day got closer I wasn't going to be able to fit into my dress and displeasing my mother wasn't an option. So, I started purging I thought it would just be long enough to get into the dress, but when it worked so well, my mother just said to continue doing whatever I was doing because it was working. She never asked, and I never told as long as I fit into her cookie cutter mold. I've been doing it so long now it is second nature for me. Stopping never crossed my mind; my body is just so used to it now if I try to do anything different it just rejects it anyway. Food no matter how good it tastes would be begging for release within an hour or two anyway."

"Why do you hide this from everyone? You realize with everyone helping you this could have just been a distant memory by now. I hate that you are killing yourself because of food.

"I hide it because it's easier than explaining it to everyone," Trish said indignantly.

"You don't think they would understand?" Brian's tone was calm and in direct contradiction to her tone. Trish was defensive and expected to have to defend her actions.

"What do you care anyway?" When Trish couldn't pick a fight with him, she resorted to childish arguments.

"Because I care about you and I only want the best for you. I can't believe you hid this from Grace as long as you have. Your mother makes sense because she sounds like she is a very self-centered person, no offense."

"None taken, she can be a big pill to swallow and at times very overbearing. I think on some level I wanted her to find out, so I knew she cared enough to pay attention. When she didn't, I just figured I wasn't hurting anyone except myself."

"Trish, I'm so sorry you had such a difficult childhood. I'm here for you now, and I noticed. It might have taken me some time to put the pieces together, but now that I know I am willing to do whatever it takes to help you overcome this battle. The first thing I'm going to do is make you eat a bite of this amazing pasta." The corners of her mouth tilted up slightly. She had been enduring the smells in here, and it wasn't going to take much to convince her to take a bite. Not to mention, the one things she had wanted her entire life was for someone to care enough to notice what she was doing. Brian was the last person she thought that would figure it out.

Brian scooped up a mouthful of noodles and made sure to cover them in the sauce before bringing them to her mouth. Trish tried to resist, but the smells were wafting so close to her nose her stomach actually growled. That didn't happen too often, and Trish took it as a sign and opened her mouth.

Closing her eyes, she allowed the flavors to play across her tongue. They danced and moved around allowing Trish to realize quickly that Brian was right. This was the best things she had ever eaten in her life.

"Mmhhh," she moaned in a way that was pure pleasure. She chewed and chewed until there was nothing left to do, but swallow. She hesitated because her gut instinct was to grab her napkin and spit it out. The best of both worlds, chewing for flavor and living in the ecstasy of the moment, then spitting it out so she wouldn't have to relive it in the worst way later. Looking up into Brian's waiting eyes, Trish made the decision. She couldn't disappoint him not again she would do this if not for herself, but for Brian, with that, she swallowed the bite of food heaven.

"I'd ask how it was, but I'm pretty sure you were on the verge of an orgasm. I had no idea food could produce such a reaction." Brian's smart answer should have embarrassed her, but with him it was different. He made her comfortable in a way no man ever had before. He waved over the waitress and ordered another bottle of wine, but then did something Trish didn't expect.

"Since we aren't in a hurry tonight, do you mind fixing the lovely Trish here a sample platter. She won't be able to eat everything, but I would love for her to try a little of everything." Trish opened her mouth to object, but before a sound could come out, Mrs. Capitani smiled and bustled away.

"What are you doing? I tell you I don't eat and you order everything on the menu. I will be so sick tonight I won't be able to sleep." Trish couldn't grasp what was going through his mind, and she most certainly didn't want to consume so much food it required her to sleep on the bathroom floor.

"Listen, I know your stomach won't hold much, but I just want you to taste them. I'll box your leftovers, and either you can take them home or I will. No pressure, baby steps and I'll be here the entire time." The look of compassion in Brian's eyes melted her resolve. Trish nodded because she couldn't formulate words anymore.

"While we wait let's talk about work. I know we've been dancing around that subject and more or less avoiding it. I don't like that you found listening devices in your office. That means they are watching you too closely. The goons were bad enough, but understandable given who we are dealing with. Do you realize what I'm talking about?"

"I get the gravity of it if that is what you're asking. I'm not in a good position, but I can't quit. Not that it matters now since you know, but Mr. Castenellos is looking for things to hold over me. He knew about my eating disorder and threatened to tell everyone I was hiding it from. I'm not sure it is relevant now that you know, but I still don't know that I'm ready for everyone to know." She started twisting the napkin nervously in her hands. Brian reached across and took it from her.

"If you tell them then he has nothing on you. Did you ever consider that?" Brian kept his hand on top of hers in a reassuring gesture.

"Yes, but if he doesn't have that what is to prevent him from using something else. Who knows how he figured this out? We only spent one other meal together and I ate just to be polite given he was my client. There is no way he should have known. If he can find out that what else could he hold over me?"

"You can't live your life on what ifs. Take a risk and tell the most important people they might surprise you."

"I'll consider it. Now let's move on, did you find anything with your tech department?" Trish was hopeful that he would take the hint and move the topic along.

"Yes, I have a device that is a little tricky, and I want to give you a crash course, but I can't do it here. Let's go to my place after dinner, and we can avoid yours a little longer."

"I think I can make that work," Trish said with a hint of seduction purposely trying to distract him from the topic at hand.

"Don't start that, we are in no place that any of that talk is appropriate and don't think you can distract me from the food that is coming out shortly." His laugh rumbled in his chest, and Trish joined him. She had to try, didn't she?

"Well you can't blame a girl for trying, can you?" Trish shrugged and refocused her attention away from her ulterior motives.

Unlocking the door to his apartment, Trish stumbled slightly behind him. While he hadn't gotten her to eat much, she did eat, and for that, he was extremely proud of her. Unfortunately, for every bite he got her to take, it proceeded copious amounts of wine. She kept spouting on about liquid courage. Brian would just smile and let her have her methods without any shame. Never again would he allow her to feel unappreciated or unworthy. Food was a necessity of life and with that, life was given in return. He told her "Everything we do during our time here is about balance. We just need to find yours.'

He turned to right her back to her feet, and she leaned on him. Giggling she said, "I'm sorry. I never get this bad on a workday."

"I'd say with the past few days you've had; an exception can be made." He reassured her and helped her into the apartment. Setting her on the sofa, she immediately leaned over onto the second cushion.

"I'm just going to lay here while you get what you need." Closing her eyes in that moment, Brian smiled. He needed to go over the scrambler, but it seemed she needed coffee more.

"While I can't make coffee like Sal, can I go make a pot before we start going over what I brought from Tech?" When she didn't respond, he worried she had fallen asleep. He didn't have the heart to wake her so he walked back and leaned down to pick her up and relocate her to the bedroom where she would be more comfortable.

"Uhhh," she moaned something inaudible.

He smiled into her hair, "I'm going to carry you to my bedroom. You'll be more comfortable." Wrenching her head back so she could face him. Brian struggled to hold her thrashing body, as she tried to break free from his hold.

"I said, I'm not tired. I'll have a double." Her eyes were clearly open, but still, she didn't make complete sense.

"Why don't you let me put you to bed?" Brian chuckled low in his chest.

"No, you make the coffee, and we will get to work. I have to learn this stuff tonight and then I have to get home. If they are watching my house, the last thing I want is for them to think I'm not staying in my own home. What if they go looking for my friends? I don't want them to find you since you've been to the office, what is to stop them from starting here? What if they find out about Grace? She doesn't need any more nightmares showing up on her doorstep." The alcohol while it wasn't making her as tired as he thought, was making her lips loose. Brian was sure she wouldn't have voiced those fears otherwise. He pressed his lips to her forehead to soothe her and placed her back on the sofa; then he sat down beside her.

"Don't worry about me; I can handle anything that comes knocking on my door." He was using his police tone that didn't waver, even in times of genuine fear. Nothing broke through that persona, and he wasn't about to let it start now. She needed to know that he didn't fear for himself, but only for her. "Until we prove what all those devices are picking up in your office, there is no need to think they are going to find out about Grace before me. Not to mention, she has Patrick to watch out for her. I will make him very aware of the situation tomorrow at work, so he is on high alert for anything out of the ordinary. Besides they are further out of town and Wes installed that fancy-schmancy security system as a first defense. Patrick would never take any chances with Grace's life ever again. He took care of her before it was entirely necessary it was a choice. Nothing will ever change his choice. Just like mine will never change either. I will protect you even when you are stubborn and won't let me. I'll still be in the shadows keeping you safe." Brian made his declaration without thought or concern as to how she would take it. She needed to know he would always be here for her, no exceptions.

Trish didn't speak at first, and Brian didn't know if that was good or bad until he looked up and realized a single tear had escaped. Before she could brush it away and allow her to close herself off to him again, he reached up and swiped it away with his thumb. Then not planning on it, he looked in her eyes and got lost in the swirls like clouds brewing, then he placed his thumb into his mouth and licked the tear clean. He watched her eyes grow in surprise at his actions. Leaning forward, he captured her mouth in a kiss full of emotion. He didn't know how she took his words, but he needed her to feel them. He poured everything he was feeling into that kiss. His anger at the men putting her through this and his passion for keeping her safe. He wanted her to know that she was the only thing that mattered and that he would die to keep her from harm. Nothing and no one would be able to get past him in order to get to her. He needed her to feel this the way he did so he gave it all to her.

When the kiss broke, they were both breathless. Neither of them spoke or could if they wanted to. So much emotion had passed between them. She had kissed him back, and he felt her fear and drive. He knew she wouldn't let anyone use her friends to get to her. She would put herself in harm's way first. It was just the kind of person she was. He knew he would have to stay close to prevent her sacrifice. Unlike Grace who had to watch her friend be beaten to turn herself in, Trish wouldn't let it come to that. Brian knew she would sacrifice herself in a heartbeat all they had to do was ask, and she would come no matter what other options were available to her.

"So how about that coffee now? I think that has become necessary and is hovering just outside of my brain fog." Trish smiled, and Brian laughed because she just derailed the entire mood lingering in the room. She had a way of changing the situation to her liking no matter what was happening. It was like her superpower.

"Care to join me in the kitchen? I don't trust you not to fall asleep in my absence." Trish gasped in mock offense pressing her hand to her chest to emphasize the point.

"Me? Fall asleep? I don't know what you're talking about. I am wide awake." Trish yawned deeply proving Brian's point, and he grabbed her hand and yanked her up off the sofa.

"Come on Sleeping Beauty, let's put some coffee into your system.

• • • •

AFTER SPENDING THE next three hours with Trish going over the scrambler and enjoying the entire pot of coffee, Brian was torn. He didn't want to take her home, but he also didn't want to upset her by trying to get her to stay again. She was pretty adamant that she needed to protect him, no matter how ludicrous Brian thought the idea was. Instead of overthinking it and pushing the issue, Brian caved, and they were en route to her apartment. Her coffee was starting to fade, and it was well after midnight. Brian was watching her as he drove and she was drifting in and out of sleep. The street lights flashing overhead created a glowing effect on her face. She didn't know he was watching her and he kept quiet allowing her to wilt slowly in her seat. She was a vision in monochrome. The greys of the night were reflecting off of her skin. If he didn't have to drive her home, he would have been happy just to watch her sleep. Sooner than he had hoped, he pulled up to her building. The stopping of the car caused Trish to jump, startled out of her dreamy haze.

"Oh, I'm sorry I didn't mean to fall asleep. I guess my sleep habits or lack thereof the past couple days caught up with me. I feel like we just got I the car. Were you driving erratically again?" Trish was visibly still lost in her faded reality. She had no idea that she had her eyes closed the majority of the drive and only towards the end did she give in and relax her bobbing head to the headrest.

"No, I just remained quiet and allowed you to rest a bit. You have to get up for work tomorrow, and I've kept you out late enough. Would you like me to walk you in just to be safe?" Brian's voice was soft in the quiet car, with her just waking up there was no need to be loud or overly direct.

"No, I think it's late, and I need to get to bed. You have to work tomorrow as well, and I'd hate for you to be more tired than necessary or late because of me." With that, she leaned across the console and kissed him on the cheek.

"I will see you tomorrow. I'll text you in the morning to check on you." Brian reached for her before she could get out of the car and gave her a proper goodnight kiss. When they separated, she was frozen in place. Brian had succeeded in kissing her senseless or at least close. She shook her head slightly, and they said their goodbye. Trish disappeared into the building, and he waved at Sam as he held the door to the building for her. True to form, Sam just scowled at him making Brian smile all the more. He liked that guy more and more every day.

Chapter 25: Trish

Trish walked blindly into her apartment and headed straight for her bed. With a full stomach from dinner and all the wine. Thankfully Brian had made coffee, or she wouldn't have made it this late. Her lifestyle was catching up with her, all the hours she had put in at the office and the lack of sleep from the last few days of stress and worry. Now all she wanted was a long date with her bed and to wrap her arms around her pillow.

• • • •

AFTER A RESTFUL NIGHT, Trish woke up feeling refreshed and surprisingly no sudden urges to run to the bathroom. Brian had encouraged her to eat so much food, yet he didn't force her, nor require her to eat entire helpings, but she did taste everything and somethings even had a second bite.

Her head did hurt from the consumption of wine to gain enough courage to eat whatever he put in front of her one bite at a time. He never looked at her with anything but care and compassion. It was as though he understood her struggle and while he wasn't going to harp on the issue he wanted her to agree on her own to take each bite.

Now that she had time to rest she was of a clear mind she knew she what needed to do. They had spent a lot of time going over her options for the disrupting device; Brian had brought her from the tech team. He was very patient with her and helped her understand how to operate it as well as the best ways to conceal it.

The machine was silent but worked over a wide area. That meant her entire office would be safe to speak in again and send text messages. She had begun to fear that her messages might have been intercepted. After talking to Brian last night, he said the only way that could have happened is if they cloned her phone. She couldn't think of a time she had left it unattended in her office, but she didn't know for sure. He said he would look into options of how they could go about it, but didn't think they had escalated to that point yet, no matter how much they wanted to keep tabs on their minions. That gave Trish a little bit of breathing room, and she was thankful for it. Since all of this had begun, her mind was running wild.

After her meeting with Mr. Castenellos yesterday, Trish wasn't going to give him any room to work with at all. She opted for a pantsuit and a conservative blouse. Doing everything in her power, Trish created an image that portrayed no sex appeal. At this point, she wouldn't put anything past him.

• • • •

THE OFFICE WAS QUIET when she arrived, but as usual Scooby and Shaggy were waiting in the lobby for her outside her door. Deciding to be polite if for no other reason, but to throw them off, Trish flashed them a beaming smile.

"Good morning, boys! I'm sorry I didn't grab you guys a coffee while I was out, I didn't know your preference." Feeling proud of herself for extending an olive branch she didn't know how heartfelt it really was, but she had said it nonetheless.

They merely shrugged and grunted their good mornings and responses. No real words were exchanged, and Trish wasn't sure how she felt about two basically silent goons hovering over her all the time.

"I guess I'll have to get you guys a book about conversations or exchanging pleasantries. No worries I'll get you hooked up." With that, she sauntered into the office and clicked the door securely shut. She even considered locking it but thought better of it since they could easily get in if that were the case. She also didn't want to appear to be hiding anything, even if in reality she was hiding a lot.

Busying herself around the office allowing the sounds of her settling in to float through the space. She didn't want to get down to business if they were intently listening as she thought they were. Trish only wished she knew who exactly was listening on the other end of the devices.

Sitting down to her desk she logged onto her computer and pulled out her notes from yesterday. She had finished up the properties and needed a new area of focus. With a job this big, it needed to be broken down not to be overwhelmed by it. Trish flipped through the files. Her eyes landed on one labeled spending. Without much thought Trish decided she would track spending habits next. As she pulled out files, she worried how far the rabbit hole this project would take her. She had to do this right, or she would be lost in the chaos that seemed to be attracted to this family.

After about an hour of clicking away at her keyboard, Trish decided it was time to put their plan into action. Reaching into her purse, Trish removed the small box and looked around the room at all the places she knew the bugs were located. *Why did they need so many? Wouldn't they interfere with each other?* These were questions Trish didn't know how to answer. She didn't know if she would get away with this, but if nothing else she was going to try.

She pulled out her desk chair, squatting down she looked for the best place to secure the device. Then Trish saw it, the best place ever. There was a small ledge underneath her desk that ran behind the drawers and across the entire back just wide enough to hold it and keep it hidden. Placing it behind her drawers concealed it and allowed her to close them still.

Feeling pretty proud of herself, she turned it on and returned to her seat, pulling out her phone she shot Brian a text.

All taken care of, will I see you tonight?

She was deliberately being vague because she still didn't know if they had done anything to her phone. True to form, Brian returned her message quickly.

Perfect. I'm not sure for how long. Patrick and I haven't lined out our day yet.

A pang of disappointment rang out in her chest. She didn't know exactly when, but whereas she used to rejoice in not seeing him, now she was planning her evenings around if and when she would see him next.

Feeling a bit distant from her work, she thought about her now previous employers. Knowing that they probably hadn't jumped into any new endeavors in such a short time. She picked up the phone to call Mr. Phillip's wife.

The housekeeper answered, "I'm sorry the lady of the house has been gone for a few days."

"Oh alright, did she and Mr. Phillips leave for a vacation?" Trish thought in light of everything that had happened, it might have been a good idea to take a few days to get away and clear their heads.

"I'm not sure. The lady left after a messenger came to get her and never returned. I never prepared her luggage, but that doesn't mean the Mr. didn't take her away for a surprise."

Trish was thankful for the openness of the housekeeper but was also surprised. Something niggled at the back of her brain and Trish thanked her. Immediately she picked up the phone and called the Baker residence, only to be answered by their staff as well.

"This is Trish Montgomery from Phillips and Baker I was hoping to speak with Mrs. Baker to offer my condolences."

"I'm sorry the Baker's aren't home and haven't been home for days." This was starting to sound oddly familiar, and Trish was concerned.

"Oh, did they get away for a little vacation and probably dodging the reporters?" Trish was probing hoping this lady would be as forthcoming as the Phillips housekeeper.

"I'm not sure ma'am. I was working the day a messenger requested Mrs. Baker, and she left immediately. I didn't pack her anything nor did she take anything with her. I haven't seen either of the Bakers since, but I assume they will be back soon. They don't stay gone for too long, Mr. Baker doesn't like to leave work for too long." Without realizing it, the staff member gave Trish a lot of information. She was very concerned but thanked her for her time and help. Upon ending the calls, he needed to send another message to Brian.

Can you check on something for me? It will require you to tap into your particular set of skills.

Still not letting in the entire purpose of her conversation, she hoped he would understand what she was getting at and was choosing to be as coy.

I'm part superhero; I can do anything.

Trish had to stifle a laugh that came bubbling up out of her. She was starting to love his playful side when just a few short days ago it drove her mad.

Trish turned on some music on her desktop and cranked the volume slightly. She was going to call Brian next but didn't want to be overheard. Glancing toward the door to see if anyone was going to burst through when no movement followed Trish grabbed the desk phone.

"Hello?" Brian answered obviously confused by the unknown number.

"It's me, sorry still shy about using my cell here." Her voice was more of a stage whisper so as not to be heard over the music.

"You realized that phone could still be tapped?" Trish met Brian's words with silence on the other end of the line.

"Hello? Are you there?" Brian queried again.

Trish realized what he was saying and regretted the call.

"I'm here, sorry I'm an idiot. How am I supposed to talk to you while I'm at work? I feel like I'm always looking over my shoulder." Trish's voice sounded defeated, and she didn't know what else to do.

"Meet me for a coffee break I'll be at *The Brewing Bean* in fifteen minutes." Brian ended the call without another word. He knew she wouldn't deny him if it were this important.

Trish saved and logged out of her computer. She hightailed it outside her office and right into the backs of Fred and Barney. Halting in her track, she realized they weren't moving.

"Excuse me boys, but I have a date with another cup of coffee. If I don't get away from those numbers, I'm going to go insane." Trying to get them to sympathize with her was her only plan. Sounding nonchalant she smiled at them and leaned over the place where their shoulders met.

There was no one in the lobby, so there was no reason for them to be on high alert. When they chose not to move and appeared to be ignoring her, she shoved her way through.

"I don't know if you guys realize this, but I'm not a prisoner of this office. You are here to protect those files, so while I run and get myself a fresh cup of motivation, you boys hang out here and guard those boxes with your lives. You never know when they might try and scoot to accelerate their escape plan." Sarcasm was her fallback when things weren't going as planned. When they didn't try to stop her, she made her way toward the parking lot.

In ten minutes, she was safely ensconced inside her favorite coffee shop. Trish inhaled the delicious smells and sighed relaxing into a safe place. She walked up to the counter and Sal smiled at her.

"Wow twice in one day, to what do I owe the honor?" The greeting by the barista was one she was expecting. Trish didn't usually get to make two trips in there a day, and today it was a necessity.

"Long story, but could I ask a huge favor?" Trish reached into her purse and latched onto her cell.

"Of course, you anything you need." Sal was always accommodating and was becoming a great friend.

"Can you stash this in the back office for a bit? I'll grab it when I'm finished." Handing her the phone Sal took it with a grin.

"Are you avoiding a call? Wow, this is pretty drastic, but sure I'll run it back now and then come out and start your regular. Have a seat I'll bring it out to you." Sal ran to the back with Trish's phone. Trish took that time to reach in and pull out some cash. Laying it on the counter by the register, she made sure to include a nice tip for Sal as thanks.

Brian walked in a little while later, Trish seated by the window glanced up and caught his eye. He waved and headed to the counter. When he made it to the table, he carried two cups.

"Sal said you already ordered and I offered to deliver it to you." Brian placed her coffee in front of her and on the table. Trish removed the lid to accelerate the cooling. Brian mimicked her and rested his coffee in front of him taking a seat opposite her.

"Now that you're here, I gave my cell to Sal to stash in the back. There should be no chance of being overheard. I'm sitting here because I wanted to make sure my shadows weren't on the prowl today."

"Smart move with the phone, now what particular set of skills were you wanting to utilize?" Brian was doing a pretty darn good impersonation of Liam Neeson making Trish smile, but she couldn't quite laugh given her situation.

"Do you have the ability to trace a person's whereabouts based off when they were last seen?" She had watched enough cop shows to hope she was on the right track and not grasping at straws.

"Depends on how big of a footprint they make. Who am I tracking?" Brian looked intrigued but remained calm.

"My previous employers and their wives. I called to offer my apologies for the situation at hand even though I know it isn't my doing I still felt bad for them and their families." Brian nodded at her story but didn't interrupt, so she continued.

"After speaking with both households, I learned that they seem to have both disappeared without notifying their staff. Right now, the staff is assuming a quick surprise vacation, but the wives were summoned via messenger and left without warning or packing."

"So, you are worried something else is going on?" Brian scratched his jaw deep in thought. "I can check airports to see if they have purchased tickets and credit card activity on both the wives and husbands." Brian was making notes now, and they were drinking their coffee as the conversation volleyed back and forth. Trish instantly relaxed by the flavor of her signature brew.

"That is what I wanted, if for some reason something else is going on I think we know who is behind it. The last people to see Phillips and Baker were Mr. Castenellos' staff. This is all starting to seem a bit suspect and more than a little coincidental." Trish was gulping the last of her coffee to keep her calm. This conversation was causing her blood pressure to rise. She needed to relax.

Brian spent the next few minutes making notes and thinking to himself. Trish was content to know he was on her side and working to figure out this conundrum. She was a numbers girl, and if it was outside her realm of calculations, then she was consistently edgy.

Dropping Trish off back at the office was one of the hardest things Brian had ever done. He was determined to keep her safe, and it was a bit challenging for him to send her back into the lion's den without anything to protect her. He just had to trust she would keep him in the loop. As of now, she has kept her work and private life separate, and they have tried to keep things that will set off the devil to a minimum.

Now that she had brought to light the strange disappearance of her previous bosses, Brian was even more concerned with her safety. After a quick text to Patrick, he had voiced his concerns about the situation. Now sitting in his chair and going through the airport security feeds, he was beginning to hate life.

"Why do we do this manually, again?" Patrick grinned at Brian from across their adjoined desks. He was going through a different day, and different terminal feeds.

"Because if we wait for the team to get back after they have used facial recognition, we could be waiting until next week. They are doing it simultaneously with us. We are just hoping to catch something before they get back to us." Patrick returned to his screen without another word.

"Well after the credit card trace came back as a dead end, I'm a little amped up. I want to find something because the alternative isn't something I want to consider." Brian put his head in his hands; his brain was so wired he was having a hard time focusing. He had so much going on that he could hardly keep it all straight.

"How is she holding up?" Patrick glanced up from his computer just for a second to let Brian know he was listening.

"She seems to be alright. It is a lot for her to take but she is taking it in stride. It was Trish who figured out this situation with the Phillips and Bakers. She is so smart and has a brain that works in a way I've never seen before. She didn't panic or jump to conclusions, but took what the households said and worked out possible scenarios and hoped for the most rational one. Instead of freaking out she called me to see what I could do to confirm. It all made sense, and I agreed we needed to check it out. She is also the one who concluded that there were bugs in her office. There wasn't even anything that directly spoke to it she just had a feeling. Her intuition seems to be spot on." Brian's eyes had almost glazed over talking about this woman who had consumed his life. His every waking breath was spent thinking of her, and his non-waking breaths were spent dreaming of the things he wanted to do to her.

Patrick noticed, "So she has you completely captivated, then doesn't she? I noticed she hasn't been calling to complain about you to Grace lately. Actually, she hasn't called Grace much at all."

Brian knew why, but he had promised not to say anything to Grace. "I think she is trying to keep all the chaos that is her life right now away from your happily ever after." He spoke without taking his eyes off the screen not wanting to lie to Patrick, but he couldn't tell him the complete truth.

"I can see that, with everything that Grace has been through but just know that I'll do anything to help. This is a screwed-up situation, and I want Trish out of it sooner rather than later." Patrick raised his hand over the top of their desks and Brian met him in the middle, and they bumped fists sealing their brotherly bond.

A few minutes later, a file clerk brought a file and set it on the edge of Brian's desk. Picking it up and glancing through it quickly, Brian's eyes lit up with excitement.

"What is it?" Patrick noticed the intrigue in Brian's eyes and leaned over the desk to try and sneak a peek at who sent the file.

"This is from the team, looks like tickets were purchased in each couple's name first class and left out two nights ago for Barbados. It seems like they were taking a beach vacation after the challenges that they were going through with the business." Brian was still flipping through the pages of the report.

"That makes sense, but I know I don't have as much money as they do, but if I had an office that I built from the ground up and I wasn't actively trying to sell it, I wouldn't fly off on vacation the day it happened. Something still feels off to me." Patrick's feelings weren't something trifle with, and Brian wasn't about to just brush it off.

"Then let's dig deeper and check the airlines checking cameras and see if each couple arrived as it says. Since we didn't see the tickets on their credit card traces, you could very well be correct.

Scrolling through the videos the airport sent over, Brian found the right airline and day. Patrick stood behind him and with two sets of eyes armed with driver's license photos of each of the couple they got to work. Diligently scanning the screen for any sign of our couples as the videos came to an end, quickly due to the speed they were playing it; they were disappointed not to see them in the boarding line.

"Does the file say anything or can we get the records for who was missing on the flight. If they had tickets, then they should either show up as missing or checked in, right?" Brian was scanning again trying to find a tiny tidbit that he missed. When he couldn't see anything, he handed the file to Patrick to scan for anything Brian might have missed. Brian knew he was burning the candle at both ends and it was entirely possible that he could have missed a valuable piece of information.

Patrick was more of a reader than a scanner, and he spent the next few minutes browsing every line. If anyone would find what they were missing it was Brian. He had an incredible eye for detail.

They made a great team, having been through hundreds of cases over their years together, they each knew the strong suits of the other and played to them without even thinking anymore. While Brian waited, he returned to the beginning of the video looking for any faces that stood out as familiar or unexpected.

"Looks like they checked in according to the manifest, but now I'm confused because they can check in unless they went to the main desk. This camera covers the entire desk, and we didn't see any of them." Patrick was looking over Brian's shoulder again.

"If we can't find them the next best thing to do is to go through the manifest and pull driver's license photos for all the passengers that show checked in. Then we can just check them off as we see them. It will be a process and definitely the long way, but I want to figure this out tonight. I'm not leaving until I know who checked into this flight. The team might not get it to ping a name until tomorrow or later. After we have pictures, we can have them work on identifying our mystery guests." Nodding Patrick showed his agreement and sat down back on his side and started searching names on the manifest looking for pictures. Brian took another copy and worked from the bottom to speed up the process.

Once they had all the pictures laid out like a line up on the whiteboard, Brian started the video again. Each photo showed the name of the passenger below it to save time. It didn't take long before nearly every name was checked off. Brian was getting frustrated because he was sure this was the best way to narrow down the list. Just then a pair of couples came up to the desk at the same time. Checked in by opposite guest aides, nothing had thrown any red flags before. Only this time their faces weren't matching any names or pictures on their board. A quick screenshot and Brian clicked print on the keyboard.

"That is them, whoever these people are checked in as the Phillips and Baker couples. They must have had fake IDs made up, and no one was the wiser." Brian taped the mystery guests up on the board with question marks written below them.

"They aren't faces I recognize, but that doesn't mean that isn't why they were chosen. They probably didn't want us to recognize them. Could have just been a pair of couples they paid off with a free vacation. If we can figure out who they are, we can track their bank accounts and look for anything that doesn't fit. They will need spending money while they're there." Patrick was already on his computer emailing the images to the tech team. The sooner it was in their possession the quicker they would get an answer.

By the time they had exhausted everything they could, Brian had needed to meet Trish. Even though he said he didn't know if two of them would be able to spend long together, the last thing he wanted was to leave her to walk home alone. Especially since she had a new set of shadows that seemed to be getting more protective if what she said about leaving for coffee was anything to take seriously.

When he pulled into the parking lot, he sent her a text in their new cryptic style.

Your chariot awaits m'lady.

He smiled at his own choice of words. He always thought Old English was a fun way to tease women but didn't do it that often because it required too much thought.

Let me vanquish my dragons, and I'll come hither.

She must be in a good mood if she is playing along. Even though they spoke in code, it wasn't like it wasn't obvious who she was talking about, but after his run-in with them the other day no one should be surprised by her turn of phrase.

It took her more than a few minutes and then he saw her practically running from the building. He rushed to open her door and get her settled inside.

"Can't wait to see me, babe?" Brian was keeping the mood light, but he waited anxiously for her response.

"Tom and Jerry in there must think I need to move into that office. Getting away for anything requires too much effort, and I'm starting to lose it. We might need to look into how hard it would be to scale the windows of this office building. I mean it's not that high off the ground, right?" They both looked over at the twelve-story building and Brian turned back to her with a questioning expression.

"Ok, so maybe that is a terrible idea, but I'm at the point where I'd actually consider it. Anything is better than dealing with them another second. They are just so moronic and don't say enough words to be considered sentences." Trish sighed as she leaned back into the seat. Brian could tell she was completely drained. At that moment, he had the perfect plan.

With a quick detour, he made a stop, "Stay here, but first sweet or dry?" Trish looked around puzzled, and Brian just smiled. She realized they had stopped at the liquor store and all the thoughts clicked into place.

"Sweet and red." Trish knew what he was getting, she just didn't know why and Brian wanted to keep her in the dark.

He ran inside and went straight to the clerk, "I need to know what your best sweet red wine is with high alcohol content. The attendant directed him to a local port wine.

"You should really pair that with dark chocolate, and the flavors will pop!" the clerk suggested before walking away.

Taking the bottle to the counter, Brian saw a selection of chocolates, and he selected the darkest chocolate he could find. Not being a connoisseur, he grabbed two or three options. Checking out quickly he ran back out to the car and placed the bag in the back seat away from Trish's keen eye. She was intrigued, and he wasn't finished yet.

One more stop was in order, he stopped at the corner drug store and ran inside. Again, making a stop at the clerk and asked, "I need relaxing bath products. Anything to soothe aching muscles and relieve tension." With a look of confusion, the clerk walked him back to the bathroom section and pointed out some bath bombs and salts and bubbles. Brian had no clue what Trish would want so he picked up one of each that listed calming and relaxing properties. Checking out in a hurry, he placed the bag behind Trish's seat again and took off. Finally, Trish couldn't take in any longer; she actually lasted longer than Brian expected.

"What is going on? You are being very mysterious." Smirking at her Brian considered what he wanted to say because he wasn't going to tell her what was in the bags.

"I told you I might not be able to spend the night with you again, but I wanted you to have a night to remember. I had to make a couple stops to make it happen, that is all." He didn't slow his driving and made his way to her apartment. He knew he wasn't going to be able to go up with her, so he pulled up to the circle drive. Reaching behind the seats, he grabbed the bags and handed them to her with his hand gripping them closed.

"Promise me you'll use what is in these bags tonight and think of me, but also that you won't look in them until you get to your apartment." Trish looked at him in surprise. Brian made a mental note that Trish was going to be fun for birthdays and holidays because she wouldn't want to wait for the inevitable surprise of gift giving. Brian was notorious for giving clues without giving anything away. The person always was left in a more confused state. He looked at her more pointed and almost glared until she submitted.

"Fine, but it better be worth it because I've had a long day and I can't take much more." With a perfect pout on her lips, she took the bags from him, and he helped her out of the car.

Chapter 27: Trish

Against her better judgment, Trish true to her word waited until she was in her apartment, one full step. Shuffling the bags around in her arms she opened them. As expected she found a bottle of wine, and surprisingly a lot of chocolate in the first bag. The second bag contained a mass amount of bath products and then she realized what he had planned for her.

While he couldn't stay and spend the evening with her to keep her company, he planned a relaxing bath and glass of wine. Upon closer inspection, she noticed it was a Port wine, and she smiled. Getting excited she realized that one glass would likely put on the train to happy land very quickly.

. . . .

TRISH LAY IN THE HOT bath soaking and drinking her problems away. It was the perfect ending to a horrible day. Just as planned, her thoughts were on Brian. She had no idea he could be so considerate with her limited knowledge of him.

Trish stayed in the water until it got too tepid to withstand any longer. Goosebumps had started to form on her exposed areas. It was late, and she knew work tomorrow wouldn't be any better so she should get some rest. Thanks to the port wine Brian had picked out she would be on her way to pleasant dreams without any trouble.

Before she fell asleep, Trish fired off a text to Brian.

That was the most perfect gift you could have given me tonight. Thank you!

Still wrapped in a towel, Trish dug out something comfortable to sleep in while she waited to see if Brian would answer her. *Ah, this is perfect.* Trish pulled out a long-forgotten cotton t-shirt that would hang just above her knees. It was an old college shirt, but it was so worn that it had become the softest shirt she owned. Trish pulled the shirt over her head, letting the wet towel fall from her body. As she was putting it on her phone chimed, and in her light-hearted state, Trish nearly fell over, startled in the deafening quiet of the room. Laughing at her own ridiculous behavior, Trish pulled the shirt on correctly and grabbed her phone.

I only wish I could have been there to pamper you further. I'm so glad you enjoyed it.

Smiling at his note, Trish felt a sense of longing for Brian. He was the sweetest man she'd ever known and every day he did something new to endear her all the more to him.

I'm off to bed to bask in my relaxed environment. Another fun filled day tomorrow.

Trish made her way to her bed in a fog of happiness. It didn't take long for her to doze off and her dreams filled with one handsome face, Brian.

• • • •

THE CLOSING OF A DOOR startled Trish awake. *Did I just imagine that or was that real?* Trish wondered but didn't feel comfortable getting out of her bed. She sat up ramrod straight and listened as one would to the sounds of wildlife in the distant woods. Wondering if someone was lurking outside her bedroom door in the darkness. Trish's mind was running faster than she could keep up, then she froze. *If someone is in my apartment, then where is Sam?* The doors to the building locked after a certain time. Allowing Sam to use the restroom on his overnight shift, but no one without a keycard could get in without being let in. All of the tenants in her building were extra cautious and wouldn't let anyone in that didn't live here. They even had a directory for people to recognize faces if need be for those who weren't great with name association.

A small crash came from what sounded like the living room. "Please don't let it be my antique table from my grandmother," Trish whispered to herself but realized in an instant that her grandmother's table was the least of her worries.

Resolving not to be a wilting flower in her bed, Trish crept from the sheets and leaned off the bed in an attempt to keep the noise to a minimum. Tiptoeing across the hardwood floor, she silently thanked the landlord for talking her into that upgraded option. Her feet practically slid across the ground the only thing that would have improved that situation would have been socks. Then she could have silently slipped from her bed to the door, and it would have been much faster.

Reaching the door, Trish placed her ear gently against the wood. What she wouldn't give for a water glass right then. The house was silent once again, but she knew she hadn't imagined the crash. While it wasn't a significant noise, it had happened. Feeling a false sense of bravery, Trish forced herself to turn the knob. She opened the bedroom door and peeked her head out into the hallway. It was hard to see in the darkness, but Trish thought she saw shadows moving in the dark. *Who could be in here?* Without letting her fear consume her, she proceeded into the hallway and padded toward the living room to see what had caused the noise.

The closer she got, Trish slowed her progress. She was scared, but she also needed to know who it was. Approaching the doorway to the common areas of the house, Trish regretted not sending Brian a text to let him know about the noise. There wasn't much he could do, but in the event of a bigger emergency, he would have an idea of what might have happened.

Peering around the edge of the door frame, Trish looked on with disbelief. Standing in the middle of the room was one of her dynamic duo. He was looking at her picture wall with an unexplained interest. Before Trish could control it, she gasped, audibly. Her hand flew to cover her mouth, but it was too late. He turned around and smiled a smile that immediately sent chills up her spine. Turning to run back to her bedroom, Trish ran smack into a solid mass, that was his partner's chest. She bounced off and landed flat on her ass.

Not allowing this to stop her, Trish scrambled to gain traction and tried to crawl down the hallway. She halted when the back of her shirt grew taut and stopped her escape. Trish glanced over her shoulder and saw the first man holding her back.

"So nice of you to join us Ms. Montgomery," he said with a sneer.

"Someone asked us to come and see if you were home. You have a meeting that we are supposed to bring you to." The second man spoke from behind her. In the darkness, their size was more than imposing, and Trish knew she wouldn't be able to fight them both off.

"You couldn't call? I could have made myself presentable and come to the meeting. Who needs to meet with me in the middle of the night, anyway?" Trish was proud that her voice stayed steady and didn't waver at all.

"I think you are as presentable as you need to be for this meeting, the boss will probably give us a bonus for it." The first man spoke again still holding the bottom of her shirt and tilted his head slightly taking in more of her exposed skin. Trish jerked the fabric back towards her out of his hand and curled her legs up under her shirt to protect her modesty. The feel of their eyes roving over her was enough to make her vomit. Trish started mental calculations on how to contact anyone or leave a message if for some reason this was an actual abduction.

"My doorman will think something is up if I leave her in my nightshirt. Please let me change." This was the last ditch effort to stall. If she could get alone in her room to change she could also send a text to Brian if not, then Sam would know something was wrong and try to stop them or call someone.

Without warning, the second man grabbed her by the arms and hauled her up. The other man steadied her but didn't stop the second man from manhandling her. She was jerked and shuffled until she was in a position he could control her with her arms restrained behind her back.

"I said you look fine the way you are. The doorman is of no concern of yours. If he were, do you think we would be in here now? We can do this the easy way or the hard way; it's up to you." Trish realized they must have done something awful to Sam and now she feared for what they would do to her. Standing on her own two feet, she stopped struggling, and the man released her.

"Well if you are going to make me go out like this, then let's get it over with. Am I allowed to grab my purse?" Noticing her resignation, the men didn't answer her they just smiled maliciously and guided her toward the door of her apartment.

Making their way downstairs Trish prepared herself for a disastrous scene, but when she arrived, she was surprised to find everything in perfect order what surprised her the most was, Sam, sitting peacefully behind his desk.

"Goodnight big guy," the man in front of her guiding her outside said to Sam. Trish was in shock, *what did he just say? They know each other?* She couldn't speak she just stared at Sam in disbelief. Sam looked at her with an expression she had never seen on his face before. It was almost a look of indifference. He didn't care that she was being escorted from the building by two strange men in such a state of undress. Sam just nodded his agreement to these imposing men, and they walked right out the door without another word.

Chapter 28: Bobby Castenellos

He hadn't received a transmission from Trish's office all day. He had Travis monitoring her in his earpiece that if you didn't know what it was, you'd think he just had a serious attachment to his cell phone. He was standing outside her door and barely heard anything even a whisper coming from her office.

Bobby had been alerted after she left to take a coffee break and surprised her guards. They usually heard her coming before she even attempted to open the door. That was when they knew something was up. After that call, Bobby had to have the guys get him a replacement cell because he had launched his across the room in anger. They kept a close eye on her the rest of the afternoon and even had the door cracked so she couldn't hide anything since while she was gone, they checked all the listening devices and everything was still in place and active.

They couldn't figure out how what had happened, but they weren't stupid enough to believe she didn't have something to do with it. That night after she left to head home for the day, Bobby ordered the guys to search the rest of the space. There had to be something interfering with the signal.

• • • •

A KNOCK SOUNDED AT his condo door; Bobby stood to answer it, even though it wasn't necessary. A slow smile spread across his face at what he saw.

"Ah Trish my dear, I'm so glad you decided to dress for the occasion." He licked his lips imagining the taste of her. He could picture it clearly, and his groin got tight at the thought.

Trish pressed past him not waiting for him to invite her in. He loved her tenacity and didn't try to stop her. She sat down on the sofa and pulled her tempting legs up underneath her, staring at him. She sat in silence waiting for him to continue.

"I'm sorry I woke you, but we had some urgent business to discuss. It seems there has been some tampering in your office." He remained vague hoping she would slip and admit something. Instead, she squared her shoulders and sat up a little straighter before she spoke.

"How is that possible? Your linebackers are always outside my door when I'm in it, and I lock it at the end of the day." Trish held her ground, and Bobby found it incredibly sexy.

"I'm not sure, but the item we found caused us some alarm." He walked around behind her and picked up something and placed it in her lap. Trish released an almost silent gasp, and he knew he had her.

"What is this?" Trish said with a confusion plastered on her face.

"Ha! Ha! You almost could have made me believe you, but I know better. That was found underneath your desk and slipped behind your drawers. Did you think we wouldn't find it? You are smart, but not that smart." He moved around and sat beside her and rest his hand on her knee. It was barely peeking out from her shirt. He felt her stiffen, but he pressed his advance and moved a bit further under her shirt and up her leg enjoying the softness of her skin.

"Get your hands off me!" She pushed him back, but he grabbed her leg tighter not allowing his hand to be just brushed away.

"No! You are at my mercy, and I will take whatever I want from you." His fingers pressed into her skin hard enough to bruise her tender flesh. His eyes lit with the power that she was giving him.

"What do you want?" Tears ran down her face, and she started to shake. What she didn't know was Bobby fed off of her fear. He was raised to see fear as a weakness and that men like him should consume all weakness and turn it into strength. He was strong because everyone else was weak.

"I want you to do everything I ask. I gave you a chance to follow instructions and do what you needed to in order to keep your job, but that box says you have friends in high places. You must have told someone something to get that kind of gear. Now I want you to tell me who or I'm going to take it out on you." Bobby ran his free hand across the front of her body and roughly accosted her breasts. "I will take it out on all of you."

He watched her cringe under his touch, and it just fueled his fire all the more. The only thing he wanted was to watch her pain cross her face and enjoy the way her body tensed under his caress. Her tears we unstopping and he just let them flow.

"I'm going to enjoy breaking you."

Brian's mind drifted to Trish while he sat at his desk. She seemed so happy after their last few texts that Brian just wished he hadn't had to work so long that he couldn't see her tonight.

Unexpectedly his phone chimed startling him. Who was texting him this late? Blindly hoping it was Trish he reached for the device.

You need to come to Trish's apartment, now!

The message came from an unknown number, but the mention of Trish's name he went on high alert. Patrick had long since gone home, so Brian was alone in the office. He was spending the extra time figuring out who had apparently pretended to be the Phillips and Bakers. He hadn't gotten far but dug up a few leads. Now, this text had his full attention.

Who is this?

Brian fired off another text trying to get more information before he ran off half-cocked. Trish said she was going to sleep hours ago, but now someone had him worried. Unfortunately, the mystery number didn't feel the need to respond. Brian had wasted enough time, he grabbed his keys and sprinted to his car.

• • • •

PULLING UP TO TRISH'S building, he didn't even bother to park in the lot. Brian only pulled up to the door. Sam was there waiting for him, and Brian didn't even have to knock.

"Sam, I'm so glad you let me know. What is going on? I got a text saying I needed to get over here, but it wasn't from Trish. Do you know who would have sent that message?"

Sam held up Trish's phone and Brian wrinkled his brow in confusion. He went from panicked to angry in seconds.

"What are you doing with Trish's phone?" He lunged for the phone, but Sam just pulled it back out of reach.

"Stop playing, son. You don't have time for that. I'm the one who sent you that message. I went up to her apartment after they left to get her phone. I knew with what she was wearing they didn't let her take it." Sam set her phone down and let his words sink in for Brian.

"Wait, who left and what was she wearing that she couldn't take her phone?" Sam smiled realizing that Brian had caught on.

"I shouldn't have messaged you. The boss will have my head unless you can stop him. I have never agreed with the violence, but I turn a blind eye. Then he sent the guys after Trish, and I couldn't take it. I've grown rather fond of that girl." He hung his head, ashamed of the things he was saying, and Brian was just as confused as ever.

"Okay, slow down. I'm trying to make sense of everything. You know who took her and you didn't stop them. Isn't that your job to guard the front desk? You could have at least called the police." Brian was ranting now, and he knew it, but he couldn't get a grasp on what was happening.

"I called you, aren't you the police?" Sam said dryly raising his eyebrow at Brian.

"How long has it been since they left? You told me you knew who they were, do you have any idea where they took her?" Brian was talking faster trying to get as much information crammed into a short period of time. This entire situation was messed up and spinning out of control faster than he could stop it.

"They left a couple of hours ago, and yes I know who they are. I work for them, on some level. They just recently bought the building, but I've worked for them for years, in name only. They are practically my only family, but they would never mention that to anyone. I was adopted and brought up in the middle of their lifestyles. I don't agree with them most of the time, but I've learned not to stop them or contradict them. I had to convince myself that I could do something this time and it would matter. I like Trish; she is like the kid sister I never had. I always watch out for her. After you started coming around, I was worried for her until I realized you were doing the same thing from the outside of these doors." Sam had enough intelligence to look guilty. Brian could tell he was being honest and he was beating himself up about it all. Even though he was strapped for time, he let him finish, but if he didn't hurry up Brian was going to speed up the process.

"I wasn't sure what to do at first, but then it just clicked. They hauled her out of here with just her sleep shirt on; she was covered man, but just barely." He added that when he saw the feral look that Brian knew crossed his face. He felt it in his gut and knew the emotions wouldn't stay restrained there. "The building gives me emergency access to the resident spaces in case they need security for something. It is a trusted responsibility, and I don't use it lightly. I went upstairs and hoped to find her cell phone. She had mentioned your name once, and I prayed her cell wasn't locked so I could get you down here. When I went upstairs, I realized they had broken into her place, and her door wasn't secure when they left. I've secured it now as best I can to protect her stuff, and I'm here to block out all others." Brian nodded and took a second before he spoke.

"Ok, we are definitely coming back to a lot of what you said, but most of it isn't relevant to this conversation. I promise we will be talking, but for now, do you have any idea where they might take her? I'm in the dark, and at this point, Trish was who I would have called to figure this out any other time. She has become the resident guru on the Castenellos family. You must be buried deep because she never came across you. I also didn't know they had acquired this building. It must have been a new development like the office because Trish never mentioned finding it in her notes."

"I'm not sure the best place to look. They have warehouses all over and a few little-known houses on the outskirts. I'm not even sure the reason they picked her up, but I do know that this late and the fact that they were seen they probably stayed close. Even though it was me, they only use the secret locations if they have time to get there. They are used more for holding rather than live meetings. She was walking on her own out of here, so I imagine they expect her to be an easy mark and not a fighter. IF she plays along, it will buy her some time. I feel bad that I never talked to her about my family, but until today I didn't realize what all the connections were telling me." Sam's shoulders sagged in defeat and Brian was thankful for his help, so he decided to throw him a bone.

"Don't beat yourself up; we've been trying to pin something on these people for years. They are the epitome of cloak and dagger. They make us look one way and do the exact opposite. You just fell into their trap it's nothing to beat yourself up over. I'll find Trish and bring her home. With a little luck or a team of hackers, I'll even bring down the Castenellos family as well. I'll leave your name out of it since you've been taking care of my girl, up until your one infraction tonight." Smirking at him in a show of awareness, "What? I told you I wasn't letting that go just yet. Right now I have more important things to deal with." With that, Brian stormed out of the building already calling Patrick as he got back in his car.

"After much consideration, I think I have a pretty good deal for you. I want you to tell me who provided you with this device and what you have told them about our little family financial situation. I'm sure you are aware that you are the one person who is handed copious amounts of information and trusted to keep it to yourself." Bobby snarled at her. "Our personal life isn't printed in the tabloids or newspapers for a reason; it is personal. What we do isn't of anyone else's concern. It is our right to decide what we do and how we do it." Trish tried to push him off, but he was too strong and held her down on the sofa effortlessly.

"Please just let me go, I promise no one knows anything about your extra-curricular activities. I just got nervous about the space and went out and found something to help myself feel better about being locked in my office." Trish was sobbing because she was terrified of what Bobby was going to do to her. She knew he was capable of so much and none of it was anything she would want him to do. Her imagination was running wild.

"Why do you insist on lying to me?" With that Bobby slapped her across the face leaving it stinging in the wake of his hand. If she hadn't already been crying the impact would have made her eyes water at the very least.

"I'm not lying!" Trish was trying to hold on to some of her dignity and strength. *If I can just get him on my side, maybe it will save my life.*

"Ok, I guess since we seem to be at an impasse, I'll move forward with my plan." Grabbing her by the arm roughly, Bobby jerked her from the sofa. His goons stayed vigilant by the front door. Trish didn't know if they were guarding against entry or exit. All she could think about was that she wanted to vomit. Dragging her down the hallway, Bobby didn't let up. She could only guess where he was taking her and Trish fought him the entire way. The last thing she wanted was to be put into a situation where they were alone, and she was even more vulnerable.

Bobby forced her into a room at the end of the hall, tripping she fell to her knees trying to save herself from exposing more of herself to this awful man. Raising her head, she wasn't surprised that she was in a bedroom. What was surprising were two women lying on his bed in nothing by their underwear. Their bodies exposed unabashedly, but their eyes spoke volumes. These women were familiar to her, but she couldn't figure out how. Trish knew these women were broken, while they didn't cover their nakedness, skin, and breasts exposed they were ashamed of their behavior. Trish felt instantly sorry for them but didn't understand why they chose not to cover themselves.

"Trish my dear, I would like to introduce you to Mrs. Phillips and Mrs. Baker, your former employer's wives." His smile was taunting, and she could feel pure evil vibrating from him. Trish felt her mouth go open in utter shock. *Why are they here? What is going on?*

"Phase one of my deal for you, ladies you look lovely as usual." His look was purely carnal as he leered at them across the room. The women shifted uncomfortably but didn't move to cover themselves once again. "Please, would you come over here so we can talk?" They scrambled off the bed and over in front of Bobby without hesitation. Trish was baffled by their behavior. Where were their husbands and what is keeping them here? Trish looked closely and saw no restraints or marks of them previously. Trish remained silent since she had no idea what was happening.

"Now you beautiful ladies have been wonderful the past few days, Trish here needs to understand how serious I am. So instead of carrying this on any longer, I'll let you in on my little secret. While you have performed beyond what I expected from you so that you could see your husbands again, I lied. Both of your husbands were dead before I came to each of your homes to retrieve you. They were killed by my own hand." He paused to let that thought simmer and Trish felt her stomach roll. Her bosses were both dead, and their wives were used as some sort of sex slaves in an attempt to save them. *What kind of monster is this man?* The sound of screams silenced Trish's thoughts. Both women were exhausting the air in their lungs with their sounds of agony. These women had been through the worst kind of hell and Trish could feel their pain.

Unfortunately, this wasn't the end of the nightmare. As though in slow motion, Trish watched Bobby pull a gun from his back waistband and fire two shots, one in each woman's head. The screams silenced from the now dead women but transferred to Trish, but her screams were out of terror. *He just killed two women in front of me. I'm a witness; he's going to kill me. There can't be witnesses; I'm dead.* Her thoughts swam through her head so fast it was hard to make sense of them. As Bobby carelessly turned back to her, Trish's eyes grew in fear.

"Now that we are on the same page, care to answer my question now?" Bobby laughed maliciously, and Trish knew she was dealing with a psychopath. If she told him that Brian had supplied the equipment and then realized he was investigating another murder that now Trish was sure was a result of Bobby's disposition. That moment of realization was daunting. She had been in a sense of denial up until now. Could she really sacrifice Brian to this man just to save her own skin? What kind of person would that make her? *What kind of person am I, that I'm actually considering this now?*

Trish reigned in her wild thoughts and decided to trust her heart. Sliding her feet underneath of her she rose slowly from the floor Trish squared her shoulders and raised her chin in defiance. If she could just keep him talking perhaps, she could buy herself some more time.

"What happened to my predecessor?" Trish was taking a risk diverting the conversation, but she was hoping that his natural instinct to talk about his conquests would take over. Just as she had thought, the question threw him for a loop, but the confusion didn't last long. His natural air of confidence swooped in and took over.

"Are you referring to Mr. Hamilton?" Trish shrugged and didn't respond seeing as she should know she had to have replaced someone else.

"Yes, Mr. Hamilton became restless in his position. The money we paid him for his silence wasn't enough, and after a lengthy discussion of worth, I made sure he knew that he was worth more to me in the County Morgue with not one trace back to me or my family. See what you don't realize is I love the efficiency of having people do things for me, but things must be done first hand in order to ensure they are done correctly."

"How are you going to get away without a trace on this one? You bought the company from Phillips and Baker, and now they end up dead along with their wives?" Trish was pressing her luck, but he seemed more than calm talking about his plans. She knew that should make her worried because being given all of this information had nothing to with trust and everything to do with pirates. *Dead men tell no tales.*

"That is the perfect part of operating the way that I do, dear Trish. You just believed that I bought the business, no one asked or confirmed or did any research. I came in took over and forcibly removed the actual owners from the equation. You would think someone in the building would have caught on as smart as you all believe that you are, but not even a little. You all just took what I said as gold. Now there isn't a paper trail or a person trail asking questions because they have an alibi. Two sets of one-way tickets were purchased for the Phillips and Baker couples for Barbados. So as far as anyone knows they are happily basking in the sale of their legacy." Bobby laughed at his cleverness.

Then Trish realized that if there was no paper trail than would they connect him to her? How would anyone know to look for her or where to start. She was abducted in the middle of the night. Anyone who cared about her wouldn't come looking until well into tomorrow morning. Brian knew she would be getting up for work, but if she didn't answer right away, he'd assume she was running late and text or call later. Could she really hang on that long? How many more distracting questions could she ask. When would Bobby say enough is enough and just eliminate the problem, her.

Bobby took a few steps closer to her; he was close enough she could feel his breath touch her skin. The spiders were crawling all over her body with him standing that close. She always knew something was off about him, but now she knew what it was.

"You didn't listen to me that day in my office, I'm a very resourceful man, and I found out something about you that your own family doesn't know. Why would you try and cross me? I'm not a man to be trifled with." He piercing grey eyes were crazed with his anger. Trish didn't know what to say, but that look said she better answer him.

"I'm not afraid of what you can do to me. I"ll never betray anyone." She was hoping he wouldn't call her bluff. She was petrified of what he could do to her, but she wasn't lying about her protective instincts. Trish may not have had the training of her friends, but her heart more than made up for it. Trish resolved that no matter what this deranged man was planning she would stand her ground.

"Perfect, I was hoping you would say that. I'll find more pleasure drawing out every last scream from your body. Then if you still refuse, I'll end it and send each of your family members a piece to treasure." Pausing for a moment and looking her over, "I think I'll send you stomach to your mother. It is your littlest used organ, and she will be able to keep it longer. I might even attach a little note, so she knows exactly how disappointing her little debutant actually was.

Not her perfect little princess after all." He leered at her running his tongue across his teeth letting all those ideas sink in.

Trish considered her options, realizing aside from running for the door, even if she did make it out of the bedroom there was little chance of her getting past the thugs and out the front door. With a deep breath, she owned her fate. If she were to die that day it was what was meant to be. Her mother would just have to come to terms with whatever she thought of Trish's disorder. Never having wanted it to define her, Trish realized that is exactly what it was. This disease was the definition of what Trish never aspired to be. If she could go back and change things, that would be number one.

With her affairs mentally locked away, Trish lifted her eyes to this crazed man standing before her. Without another word, she accepted her fate. He found her eyes and must have seen the change because he held up the hand that held his gun and with a motion quicker than Trish could track, the butt of the gun came smashing into the side of her face. Stars blinked in her eyes as she tried to retain her consciousness.

Just then a commotion sounded out in the front room. Trish was still fighting her body to remain in control, but she knew this was going to be her only chance. Bobby was distracted by whatever had begun outside the bedroom door. He marched angrily toward her and hauled her up by her hair. Trish screamed in pain from the unexpected jolt. Bobby threw her to the bed, and a rope appeared from somewhere out of sight. Trish knew that if whatever was happening outside those doors didn't make it back to the bedroom; she was dead.

After tying her up, Bobby shoved a towel in her mouth, from the ensuite bathroom, to silence her. Making his way to the door, he turned, "stay here, or I will shoot you." His eyes moved to the women laying lifeless on the floor, and Trish followed his line of sight. She nodded almost imperceptibly, and Bobby left the room.

Trish sat in silence listening to the scuffle outside the room. She had no idea what was happening or who was involved. She just hoped they were there for her and not another deal gone wrong. Mere moments past and Trish heard a sound coming closer to the bedroom. She stiffened not knowing if it was Bobby returning.

As the door opened, a lock of blonde hair was all she saw first, knowing it wasn't Bobby, she sat a little straighter hoping it was who she thought. When the door fully opened, Brian walked through looking a little worse for wear.

"Trish, oh my God, are you ok?" he rushed to the bedside and gently pulled the towel from her mouth and began untying her. All along cooing and spouting apologies for not being there.

"I'm all right, at least I'm better than them." Trish jerked her head toward Mrs. Phillips and Mrs. Baker on the floor. Only then did Brian notice them and reacted with shock and anger.

"We need to get you out of here, and I need to call this in." At that moment Bobby came in looking like someone had broken his nose. "I thought I told you to stay down." Brian scowled at him showing him not an inch of mercy.

"You have no right to be here. How did you even find me?" Bobby's words laced with venom. He knew he was beaten, but he was still between them and the door. Brian motioned for Trish to stay put.

"Oh, you didn't notice my tour guide? You must not have made it all the way to the living room to see him." Trish had no idea what Brian was talking about, but it didn't' matter. All she cared about right now was getting out of this cursed room.

Brian kept her to his back at all times, never looking away from Bobby. Brian had his gun pointed right at his head, but then so did Bobby. They were just taunting each other. Trish waited for someone to make a move. She knew this was going to end in a physical fight.

Just when Trish thought the stare down was going to last all night, Brian got tired and lunged at Bobby. Instantly, Bobby's gun fired and Trish screamed. The one person she was trying to protect was Brian. Now he was in the line of fire, and she couldn't do anything.

The force of Brian's body in flight was enough to knock Bobby to the ground. It was like a bad car accident, no matter how much Trish wanted to she couldn't look away. Brian was hit she could see the blood, but she didn't know where. What she did know was it wasn't stopping him. Upon impact, Brian knocked Bobby's gun away, but the force of the blow disarmed him as well. Just as Trish predicted, punches were being thrown.

Brian was a fighter; nothing was going to stop him from winning this fight except death. Now that they were down to caveman fighting skills, the only hindrance he had was his wound, wherever it was.

Time slowed, and Trish saw every punch impact and heard every bone crack. They were destroying each other one hit at a time. Neither man was going to give up easily. What felt like an eternity later, Trish's body was so tense she was sure it would be in this position forever or need to be surgically broken free. She had watched them beat each other to a pulp. It was hard to tell who had the upper hand as it switched as quickly as it transferred between them.

Then out of nowhere, Trish heard a sickening snap. She immediately saw Bobby's body relax and slump forward; the fight had left him. Brian had gotten the upper hand and had gotten behind him somehow and broke his neck. The thought made Trish want to throw up, but by the same token, a feeling of relief washed over her. She was free, Brian was safe, and she could go home.

Rushing to her side, Brian swept her up in an embrace. Her emotions got the better of her, and when he leaned back, tears were streaming down her face. Wiping them with his hand, Brian picked her up not allowing her to walk. Trish was okay; Brian looked like he had gone a few rounds with Floyd Mayweather. She struggled to get him to put her down.

"Hush now, I'm carrying you because I thought I had lost you tonight. You will not be out of my sight for a while. I just need to hold you, feel you and know that you are alive and safe." Brian's voice told her not to argue. Instead, she did the only thing she could think to do.

"Thank you!" She leaned over and kissed his bloodied lips without regard for his appearance. Then she snuggled into the crook of his neck, relishing in the safety that was his hold on her.

When they made it out of the room, Trish took in the struggle that was obvious. *How did he take out all three men alone?* Trish was starting to gain a whole new appreciation for her man, yes, HER MAN. She was going to claim him openly from now on. After this nothing would come between them again. Then something moved over near the sofa. Trish saw a familiar looking man sitting with his bloodied hands cradling his head. She didn't need to see his face to know who it was.

"Sam! What the hell are you doing here?" His face shot up looking her square in the eyes, and she struggled out of Brian's arms, but he held fast.

"He's the reason I made it here. While I have some things to discuss with him later if it weren't for him who knows what would have happened." Brian's words took the fight out of her. While she knew Sam had left her to the mercy of these men, if he was the reason she survived then she owed him her life.

"Trish, I'm so glad you're, ok. I'm so sorry I couldn't stop them. I would have if I could've." Brian interrupted Sam stopping him from continuing.

"That is a story for another day. I need to call an ambulance and the team to get down here and clean this mess up."

Trish looked around the room and realized that the two men guarding the door were laying crumbled over each other. She didn't know if they were dead or just knocked out, but she didn't care. All she wanted was to go home and wash off the spiders that still lingered on her skin.

Epilogue

T wo months later:
   Trish -

The night of the charity ball had come. The girls were all in Grace's house getting ready. Abigail was already at the venue putting the last finishing touches on the event.

"Sal, that dress is stunning. You are going to have all the men drooling over you. Anyone, in particular, you want us to keep at bay or are you just planning to take anyone who comes along?" Grace had come out of her shell over the past year. She and Patrick were the happily ever after they all wanted.

"Very funny, I think we all have the best dresses money can buy, thanks to Trish's amazing eye." Sal was never one to take a compliment, and Trish knew it, but she did look breathtakingly beautiful. Dressed in an emerald hip-hugging gown, she looked like she belonged at the end of the yellow brick road. That dress was made for her.

As girls busied themselves getting ready, Sal leaned over the sofa and plucked that day's newspaper from the seat. "Trish, you really have outdone yourself." She proceeded to read the article aloud.

After tragic circumstances left Philips and Baker Financial Company without any corporate structure, their team has been forced to rethink their structure. With the help of an anonymous donor, the company has now established a new Employee Stock Ownership Plan. This will allow a board to run the day to day, but the employees have taken over the ownership completely. A process that was thought to have gone by the wayside in this day and age, has been revived to bring this company back together and strengthen the family within.

Sal finished reading and looked up from the page. Grace spoke up before she could begin again, "I'm am so proud of you Trish. I knew you cared about people, but this is a step above even that. All those people were facing losing their job, but you saved not only yourself, but all of them as well. You went above and beyond in this case. For the first time since I've known you, you actually used your trust fund."

Coming out from the bathroom Trish turned to face them, "It was nothing. I was never going to use that money for me. At least this way using it helped people. The best part is, we all get to keep our jobs. With the board in place we can all work together to create policies that suit the way we want to run things. The board will be there to make sure the ideas don't completely bankrupt the company.

Trish put the finishing touches on her hair, deciding leaving it down would cover the lingering bruises across her neck. That asshole had hit her harder than she thought and fractured her cheekbone. The doctor said a couple more months and she would be back to normal. Makeup was her lifeline now to avoid unwanted questions.

Stepping out into the group a hush fell over the girls it was Sal who spoke up first, "Are you channeling Marilyn Monroe? That white dress with your hair makes you look like a fifties pinup girl, all you are missing is her mole." She and Grace stared at Trish awestruck. With a wave of her hand, Trish dismissed it without another word.

Grace was dressed in a red number but wasn't as fitted as the rest. Grace said she was struggling with some stuff and felt like a looser fitting gown was just the ticket. So hers was more of a sheer overlay fabric stitched to the darker layer of black beneath, with a slit that ran up her thigh almost to the point of inappropriate. Trish had told her she was a married woman, but men could look and dream. Grace had an amazing body, and she needed to show it off, if for no one else, but for Patrick. He would thank her later.

Grace came up and lightly brushed the lingering bruising on Trish's cheek, "I'm so glad you're here." Tears welling in Grace's eyes, Trish shut them down with her usual snark.

"Now don't start that, we are now sisters to the extreme. If you start, I'll start. Then if Sal doesn't start, I'll be forced to punch her and make her cry. I don't want to cry or break a nail so enough of that." Grace laughed and dabbed at her eyes, just as Trish intended.

The plan was to make an entrance, so the girls ordered their dates to go on ahead of them. That and Sal was going stag, so they didn't want her to feel off balance. If they all showed up alone, then she could make the entrance and catch a few eyes. In doing so, her dance card could start to fill up from the first second they arrived.

• • • •

BRIAN –

Standing at the open bar with Patrick, Brian's arm was still in a sling. After the fight with Castenellos, Brian got checked by the first responders. He had been shot in the right shoulder and aggravated it further by carrying Trish out of the building. He knew she was capable of walking, but he wouldn't have changed what he did even now having to endure this pain in the ass sling for an extra three months.

He loved her and nothing would change that. They were openly dating now, and nothing made Brian happier. She was his world, and he was going to hang onto her forever.

That moment, a stir in the crowd drew everyone's attention to the door. Patrick and Brian followed suit, and Brian felt his breath catch. Three women walked through the door, one in red, another in green and the last in white. He knew his woman in an instant. His entire body was drawn to her like a magnet.

To his left he noticed his partner, Patrick was also pulled along with him, but not toward Trish. Patrick was headed straight for his wife. She stood out in the crowd in her red dress, and the look in Patrick's eye was a feral one. He was going to claim her in front of everyone before anyone got any ideas. In fact, that idea didn't sound so bad to Brian. So, he made his way to Trish to do just that.

"You look enchanting, my love." Brian leaned in before she could respond and claimed her mouth in a deep kiss that he knew would take a minute for her to recover from before she could speak. When they broke, she stood in front of him breathlessly. As expected she had to take a moment.

"You don't look that bad yourself, Slugger." This was his new pet name, and he didn't ever deny it. It came down to fits and blows for him to protect her and he stood by that decision. She was everything to him, and he would do anything all over again to keep her safe.

Once the greetings had been made, Grace and Patrick pulled in close, and Brian did the same with Trish around Sal. Grace had a look in her eye, and everyone knew something was up. Trish didn't wait on decorum as usual.

"Spill girl, you look like if you don't, you will explode." With a look at Patrick and a nod from him, Grace did indeed blow.

"We're pregnant!"

Brian was taken back by this as Patrick hadn't even hinted at anything. Not letting that stop him, he rapped Patrick on the back.

"Congratulations, man! I had no idea. You don't usually hide anything from me." Brian gave him a side look as if to say, 'what else are you hiding?'

"No, we told Ted and Abigail last week, but wanted to tell all of you at once. You are like family, and no one deserves top billing." Brian's heart swelled hearing that and nodded because he didn't know what to say to that. He had always thought of Patrick as family and now he realized, their inner circle was the closest family he had.

There was more screaming and jumping going on and a lot less civilized conversation when they looked over at the girls.

"When are you due? I have a lot of shopping to do!" Trish was battering her with questions and plans. Sal was just as excited.

"You are going to be a great mom, and I will spoil him or her rotten. Wait! Do you know what you're having?"

The evening was off to a perfect start, his friends were expanding their family, and he had the love of his life at his side.

• • • •

THE NIGHT WAS COMING to a close and Brian looked at Trish. They had agreed that tonight was when she would share her biggest secret. No matter what happened, he told her he would be there for her. Brian had no doubt it was hard for her to do this, but it was necessary for her to heal.

"Guys, I have something I need to tell you. It's not as big or as exciting as Grace's news, and I hope it doesn't spoil her announcement. Brian and I had planned this before we knew." She looked at him in distress, but that wasn't going to work.

"I'm not going to let her back down guys. She needs this. So take it as you will even if it slams the night from sixty to zero." Brian related to car analogies and couldn't help but use it now. With a sigh, Trish continued.

"For many years now, I've had a problem that I've kept hidden from you." Pausing and calculating her words, Brian rubbed her back for encouragement. "I'm a recovering bulimic. Brian has been fantastic, and I've been doing outpatient therapy. I'm on the road to better health, but it is a long road. I didn't want to lie to you all anymore it's not fair to any of you." Everyone was silent as they processed this news. No one expected it any more than Brian had when he figured it out months ago. Either way, he still loved her and would be her crutch through it all. A chair slid out from the table, followed by another and then another. Soon they were all out of their seats and walking toward Trish. Within just a few seconds she was wrapped in the arms of her friends, no her Family.

THE END

First Chapter of 3rd installment of the Dangerous Series:

With sleep still in her eyes, Sal made her way to the shop to open for another day of customers in desperate need of caffeine. Four in the morning was early even for her even after doing this for so long and in with the temperatures beginning to drop it only made it that much harder.

She had been doing it for years, but she never grew accustom to it. All she wanted was a large cup of her own coffee, but before she could get it she had to get inside and start the daily chores.

Unlocking the door to The Brewing Bean, Sal blindly fumbled with her keys dropping them twice in the process. *One of these mornings I'd like to say I got inside with the keys still in my hand.* Reaching through the doorway she flipped the main light switch. It only turned on a few lights to get her to the counter without stumbling over tables and chairs. In her current state, the light was only so helpful. Walking as though she were a blind woman, Sal felt her way to the counter. Locking her purse beneath the register she turned to start her day.

First things first, Sal needed her own cup to fire the synapses in her brain. She almost needed an IV hooked up in order to function from day to day. Fumbling around to brew the first pot of coffee she worked more from memory than from actual awareness.

Scooping the beans from the container, Sal poured them slowly and methodically into the grinder not dropping one bean. Taking her time, she pressed the grind button letting it run until the grounds were fine and even. Inhaling as the beans were broken the aroma assaulted her senses allowing her to wake up a fraction. Sal turned off the machine and took a second breath allowing the beans to rouse her that much more. She reached to the shelf just above the coffee pot and to find a filter. She had done this for years and most everything on her morning list was done out of habit and without much thought. In what felt like no time at all, Sal poured her first cup of coffee that day.

Inhaling the warm liquid, Sal took her first sip and felt it roll down her throat. Smiling Sal let it work though her body giving her the much-needed life to push through the rest of her morning. With that she worked to put together the remaining steps of the routine to open the shop. Once everything was ready in the front she made her way to the back to make herself presentable.

Since she worked in a coffee shop, Sal only made coffee at home when she had a day off and even then, she typically came in to get another cup at some point. Her addiction was only fueled by her schedule and her habit of picking up shifts even on her days off.

Since she opened more often than not she chose to get up a little earlier than necessary, but not get ready at home. Throwing on clothes, but leaving her hair and makeup until she had consumed her first cup of coffee. The bathroom at work wasn't large, but since she was the only one there wouldn't be a line.

Brushing her brown hair back, Sal opted for a tight loop to hold her thick hair in place all day. She never liked wearing hair nets, so up was always a better option. She wore a lot of messy buns and ponytails, that it was easier to keep a stash hiding in a drawer by the register in case of emergency. She had been known to break a hair tie on occasion with as much as she worked and used them it was easier to have a backup on hand.

Her clothes were kept simple, comfortable jeans that wouldn't slip down her trim hip line forcing her to spend the day tugging on them. While she wasn't the skinny as a rail she was trim. She had always struggled with finding pants to fit her tiny frame and not having wider hips to hold them up. With fall in full swing, she had chosen a pair with skinny legs and a pair of flat brown boots that climbed up her leg in a fashionable functionality that she loved. To top off her outfit, she wore a long-sleeved tunic. She preferred to dress conservatively as much as possible to detour men from checking her out and making a scene in the shop.

She had become gun shy after her customer, Wes Bowman, asked her out and that date didn't go at all as planned. She decided to sleep with him after what she thought was a pleasant date. The next day he threw her for a loop and ignored her as though they had never met. Now she didn't know how to act when a customer hit on her or asked her out.

Now that she looked presentable, Sal made her way to the walk-in freezer. She didn't need to restock anything, but this is where they kept their cash drawers and the safe. It was an unobtrusive way to store the excess that hadn't been taken to the bank. Most people wouldn't think to look inside the large freezer for money, but they decided it was better to freeze their most profitable assets.

Keying in her passcode she got into the safe. Unfortunately, for her she had to make sure she got everything out that she needed to avoid the safety feature. Each time the vault was sealed it remained that way for thirty minutes. This avoided any tampering or unauthorize entry. While it was great in theory, for a business that hadn't had any issues with robbery the employees found it unnecessary and overkill.

Sal grabbed the drawer for the morning and quickly glanced at it. Shivering from the freezing temperatures she just hoped that the night closer followed procedure and prepared the drawer for the morning shift. Slamming the door on the safe, Sal made her way out of the frozen enclosure and into the blessed warmth of the shop. With a sigh of pleasure Sal paused for a moment to absorb a little heat back into her skin allowing it to unthaw her bones.

Making her way back to the counter, Sal had only a couple minutes left before they were set to open. The first hour or so wasn't usually busy so no one would come into help her until closer to seven or seven thirty. Penny was on shift today and hated mornings, she was more than likely going to be late. Sal would just do her best until she made her appearance.

Fifteen minutes later, Sal flipped the sign to open and unlocked the door. They weren't they type of shop that usually had a line waiting to get in, but she knew within five minutes someone would walk through the door begging for some scalding coffee to break them from their sleeping fog. It wasn't always the same person so she wasn't sure who it would be.

It could be Trent. He always gets a large dark roast with a single shot of espresso. He is a nice guy but very predictable. Sort of like, Nancy who always comes in for her Mocha Frappuccino with light decaf. She gave up caffeine three years ago, but still couldn't let go of her coffee addiction.

Her other favorite was "Quad Expresso over ice in an extra-large cup extra whip" also known as, Collin. The guy, bless his heart, was as sweet as they come and just as gay. Not that one could tell from his outward appearance. He was six-foot-tall and built like a brick wall. He obviously had an obsession with the gym and frequented there a little too often. Sal realized that was more because he liked to check out the other men that made it a regular stop as well. His blonde locks were styled in a fashionably messy way. Sal wondered if it was on purpose or just because his morning was just beginning and he couldn't see as clearly in the mirror.

Her favorite pastime was watching any girls in line fawn over him. Giggling their approval of his appearance only to be sorely disappointed when he reached the front and placed his order. While his body said strong heterosexual male, but once he started speaking it was obvious he was anything but.

The door chimed indicating her first customer had drug themselves from their warm bed on this chilly fall morning. Pasting a smile on her face, Sal readied herself to greet her first customer. Quickly her smile fell as she saw the last person she wanted to see, Wes Bowman.

Forcing the smile back onto her face she greeted him, "Good morning, welcome to the Brewing Bean. What can I get you today?"

Hesitating before he replied, "I'd like a 'Dead Eye' large, please." Wes was all professional, but this was an order that Sal knew very well. He only ordered this after a long night followed by an early morning. Never one to ask questions, she immediately rang him up.

"That will be three-fifty, will you be paying with cash or card this morning?" Sal chose not to address the obvious and attempted to avoid conversation. While she was nursing her second cup of the morning, she wasn't up for any potential words with this man.

"Cash. It's quiet this morning, am I your first customer today?" Wes was apparently trying to be a bigger person today and given the lack of other baristas to distract him or the occasional other customer to throw at her, he was attempting to talk to Sal instead.

Taking the five dollars that Wes presented to her, Sal sighed, "You have managed to be the first customer of the day. Too bad they don't offer a prize for that or something. There is always the chance your barista hasn't had enough coffee to brew, measure and pour properly, yet." Her attempt at humor was lame at best. Sal handed Wes his change back, but he just directed her toward the tip jar that was always located beside the register. They split the cash at the end of each shift to avoid the openers not getting their fair share of the tips.

Making her way over she began to brew the espresso for his coffee. She already had the coffee brewed and the shots of espresso would take the time. Mindlessly she measured out the beans and ground them, inhaling the fresh scent. The tapping of the grounds in the basket, drew Wes' attention was back to her. He made his way down the counter to follow her through the process.

"Maybe you should do something about that. I think a comment box would be useful. I'd be happy to leave that comment in there. Then your customers wouldn't get subpar coffee so early in the morning, everyone is prone to mistakes when not fully awake." Wes didn't sound hateful, but he was a business man himself, he owned Five Alarm Security. So he was always looking for the right marketing strategy. She didn't fault him for this, but agreeing with her joke was a bit hurtful. To think that she would actually serve a substandard cup of coffee was unthinkable. It made her heart hurt just to think about it. Coffee was her passion and her life. She spent countless hours perfecting each brew to taste the upmost of satisfaction. Without showing him how much that comment had stung she squared her shoulders and pulled her first shot for twenty-nine seconds. It took her months to get this right when she first started here. Now she go from grind to pull without much thought. She repeated the process to get the desired shot for his large coffee and was thankful he was taking it to go. She would be finishing this cup of coffee and pouring herself a new one.

Each shot she poured went straight into his cup without delay. When the espresso was finished she grabbed the pot of regular drip coffee and poured to top it all off. She didn't mean to block out Wes, but sometimes she just got into her head while pouring coffee. It was such a simple thing on so many levels, but it was hers and she always put her heart and soul into it. Placing a lid on top, Sal handed the cup to Wes with anther smile out of habit.

"Here you go, I'll consider running the box by the owner. It's a good idea, because the customers are who keep this place running. Without you guys we'd all be out of a job."

Nodding his head Wes turned to the door. "Have a good one."

"Have a nice day, Wes. I hope that coffee does its job for you today." Sal waved at him and he left the shop, once again leaving her alone, just the way she wanted to be right then.

Now for something a little different, this is the first chapter of my new Romantic Comedy coming out Winter of 2017/2018, Disaster in Love

"You really need to find a man, Samantha," her mother repeated her usual sentiment when Sam came over for their weekly dinner. There wasn't a better topic than her fading youth and shriveling eggs. Reality was her mother wanted grandchildren, while she was still young enough to keep up, and have fun with them. "At this rate, I'm going to be antient before you have out any kids for me to spoil." Right on time, her mother never missed a beat.

"Mom, I'll get married and have kids when I find the right guy." She defended herself so often with her mother, it was easier to avoid her mom throughout the week and save it up for these special dinner nights.

"You aren't dating enough. Why don't you let me fix you up? I know a great guy you are just going to love him. Christopher is sweet guy. He's Jillian's son, you know she is from my book club." She certainly knew Jillian, she was the biggest gossip of their group. She is the one who convinced my mother that people were really streaking through the town square after midnight on the full moon.

"Mom, Jillian is like 75, how old does that makes her son?" Samantha knew he had to be older because she didn't go to school with him. He wasn't even an upper classman to her. So that meant he had to be at least 40.

"Oh dear, he's not that much older than you. Besides they say age is just a number these days. Mature only means they are more stable." Well, that meant she was definitely going on a date with a much older man.

In order to placate her mother, Samantha agreed to go on this date, but she knew she was going to regret it.

• • • •

DATE NIGHT, SAMANTHA's least favorite night of the week. Which is why she usually limited the days of the week with that title. She didn't date much, but being single was getting old.

Since this was essentially a blind date, she wanted to meet on neutral territory. She chose her favorite haunt, Joe's bar. It wasn't exactly a hole-in-the-wall, but it wasn't a super classy joint either. It just made her feel comfortable.

She got there a bit early in hopes of calming her nerves a little. *Why did I agree to this? This was a stupid idea. I should have at least seen a picture of him before agreeing,* she thought as she sat alone at her table.

The waitress came over at that moment to take her order. "You read my mind, I need a beer. Miller Light, or whatever is cold and on tap is fine with me."

Leaving Sam to her thoughts again, the waitress quickly ran to put her drink order in. Just then a man walked in the door. He was sort of rough around the edges, but in a sexy kind of way. Just a touch of stubble, and rolled out of bed hair made him sexy all over. Dressed in jeans, and a black t-shirt, he made Sam feel overdressed. She went all out for the first date, with a traditional look, little black dress and matching three-inch heels.

Quietly getting her hopes up, they were quickly dashed when he passed her table without the slightest glance. He headed straight for the bar. *Well I should have known better. He looked only a couple years older than me anyway, that couldn't have possibly been Christopher. Wishful thinking got the better of me, yet again.*

While she was distracted with the mystery man, Christopher walked in and had made his way to her table, startled by his sudden appearance, Sam jumped

"Sam? Hi, it's so nice to meet you, I'm Christopher." He thrust his hand in her direction, and she quickly tried to regain her composure.

"It's nice to meet you too." Saving her from having to think of anything else on the spot, the waitress returned with her drink.

"Can I get you something, sir?" Sam stifled a laugh. He was definitely a "sir". Sam wasn't young by any definition of the word, she was long past her twenties. This year she would be 35 in May, but Christopher had to be close to 50, on a good day. Polite as her mother always taught her, she wouldn't ask, but her assumption was plenty close enough for her.

"Yes of course, I'll have two fingers of Scotch, on the rocks." He even ordered in a way that suggested his age. *What has my mother gotten me into? This is going to be a disaster.*

Attempting to push her negativity out of her head, she needed to make the most of this. "So, Christopher, my mom didn't tell me much about you. Why don't you tell me a little about yourself?"

"Oh, what kind of beer are you drinking?" Christopher flipped the conversation back to her. At first, she didn't find that odd, but her opinion would soon change.

"Oh, I just got a Miller Light. I'm not a fancy drinker." *Especially on first dates*, she added, but not out loud. He just smiled enthusiastically, and proceeded to keep control of the conversation.

"So, what is your favorite show on MTV?" That made Grace get a little concerned. How old was this guy, and how young did he think she was?

"I'm not sure, I guess I watch a video here or there, but not any particular show per say."

"Oh yeah, I love those music videos they are very...dope."

Sam fought a cringe, as she was slowly coming to terms with what was happening here. It felt like she was stuck in the Twilight Zone. What was her mother thinking? This guy is obviously trying too hard to prove that he is younger than he really is, but failing miserably. Without waiting for her to add to the conversation, not that she knew what to say anyway, he carried on.

"So, did you see Friends, last night? It was my favorite episode, where Ross gets his teeth over whitened and a horrible spray tan."

"No, I'm afraid I missed that. I had to work late," she added hopefully he would ask her about work, and forego this ridiculous line of outdated questioning.

"Oh, that's a shame it was a good one. Well, I was reading about Justin Timberlake and Britney Spears the other day. I sure wish they would get back together. Do you think that will ever happen?" Right then, the waitress brought his drink and Sam slipped her a piece of paper. This wasn't planned, but since she had no one else to turn to at this particular moment Sam hoped she got the hint.

"Justin and Britney? Uh, I guess I haven't given them much thought, recently. I guess they made a cute enough couple, but that might have been right before her crazy period, and probably was for the best that they split before things got too nuts." *This is officially the strangest date ever. Why did I agree to let my mom fix me up?*

Christopher lifted his drink to his mouth and sipped slowly. "Mmm, that drink is Chuck Norris approved." Sam didn't know what that meant, but decided it wasn't worth any clarification. Luckily, she was saved by her phone as it chose that moment to burst into Taylor Swift's, Shake It Off, at full volume. Glancing at the screen, she didn't recognize the number, but that wasn't going to stop her at this point.

"I'm so sorry, I should take this," Sam said to Christopher as she swiped her phone to answer.

"Hello?"

"Sorry it took me so long, I had wait til I could take a quick break. Sounds like a real winner you've got on your hands." Sam recognized the voice of the waitress.

"Oh no, it's fine. I understand," she replied vaguely not wanting to give too much away to her self-centered time-warped date.

"Want me to have someone walk you out? I'd hate for you to be stuck with him any longer than necessary."

"No, I'll be there right away. I'm glad you got ahold of me so soon. I would have hated to have missed it. Thanks for calling." With that Sam hung up the phone, and turned to her date who was lost in his own world, completely unaware of her conversation.

"Sorry about that, I don't usually leave my phone on during dates. I must have forgotten when I got here. That was my best friends husband, and she is in labor."

"OH! Well you should head right over to the hospital. Do you need a ride? I could take you there myself."

Sam bit the inside of her cheek to hide the lie she was about to tell. "No, I drove so I'll make a run to the ladies room, and head out. I really enjoyed meeting you Christopher."

"Yes, this has been a great date. I'll call you soon, if that's ok? Maybe we can set up another date for dinner soon."

Avoiding that answer, Sam stood up abruptly and shook his hand awkwardly. Without another word, she made her way to the lady's room to hide. She waited ten minutes to give Christopher time to realize she wasn't coming back out to say anything to him. She opened the door slowly, praying not to be confronted by anyone outside the door. Pleasantly, the hallway was empty so she made her way to the bar to get another drink after that disaster. Then she would take a cab home and try and sleep off this mess.

As she approached the bar, she passed the waitress who saved her. Sam made her way up to her, "Thank you so much! I owe you one, that's for sure. What a mess tonight has been, I'm just glad it's over."

"You betcha! I'm just glad you slipped me your number when you did. I couldn't imagine sitting as long as you did before that with him. Was he like that the whole time?"

"It just kept getting worse. He was making out of date pop culture references, and expected me to have an actual response to them all. Not to mention, he was old enough to almost be a father to me, or an uncle at least. I should have known better than to let my mother fix me up."

Wow, there are no words to express the level of insanity that you just spilled. I've got your back anytime."

They parted ways, and Sam continued on her way to the bar. She grabbed a stool, and wasn't surprised that the bar wasn't dead, but it had a few people here and there spread out. It took the bartender a couple minutes to make his way down to her, but when she looked up to place her order she was stunned into silence. The man that stood in front of her was none other than the mystery man from earlier, when she was waiting for her date.

"What can I get you?" a husky voice drew her out of her stupor.

"Vodka and Cranberry Juice, please," she said on a sigh. This night had done her in, and she was exhausted, but this new development was making her evening one for the memory books.

Dear Loyal Readers,

Thank you for taking the time to read Dangerous Calculations. I know you are probably anxious to find out what happens next and with those teasers you are likely cursing me right about now. I understand, but so I'm writing as quickly as I can. One of the new books will be released before you know it. Not to mention, I can't silence the voices in my head for too long. They are already screaming to have their stories told and released so all of you wonderful readers can get lost in their worlds.

That said, in the meantime, I would you please go and leave me a review on Amazon and/or Goodreads? What you don't realize is this helps not only other readers, but me as well. I get to know what you loved and what you hated of each story and this helps me grow as a writer. I'm never going to have everything completely figured out. There will always be something I can improve upon. You can assist me by telling me all these things in a review.

I'm not asking you to write a book or anything crazy or untrue. I want an honest opinion of your reading experience. This can be as simple as "I loved it" or a complex review detailing the synopsis as you see it. No review is unworthy as long as it comes from your heart and is the truth you won't upset me.

Reviewing is what helps other readers decide if something is for them or worth it for them to try. Everyone has a different viewpoint and yours might influence someone along the way.

Thank you again and I hope you will follow me on social media and on my Amazon author page. Links are included in the front of the book for you to find easily. You will be first to hear about new releases and possible beta/ARC opportunities. I love to share my books with everyone and can't wait to hear your opinions!

Acknowledgements

It's so hard to know where to start. Each person who helps every step of the way is important, but I think this time I should start with my hubs. He is a trooper and has to endure late nights alone in bed. TV night dates turned, "Did you see that?" me: "Uh, no sorry." I don't mean to ignore or neglect him, but sometimes writing trumps everything else.

A huge thank you goes out to Erica, Tess and Deborah without you ladies the editing process would have been subpar actually whatever is beneath that is more accurate. I'm guessing pond scum is a good place to start. I have been given the gift of writing and a love hate relationship with semi colons and run on sentences. You ladies improve the way others see me and make me look way better than I actually am. You can't go wrong with a good editing team.

Once again, thank you to my sister-in-law, Jessica for the amazing pictures she takes of me. It's amazing how pretty I look with the help of photoshop!

To all my beta and ARC readers, what would I do without you? To write something and be the only one who has read it is scary. You all have done a wonderful job of reading past my errors (before final edit) and seeing the story beneath. Without you who knows what kind of product would be released. You are also my first reviewers and your opinion matter!

Last but not least thank you to my readers from the bottom of my heart. Your time spent in my world and sharing that with other is beyond compare. I do what I do FOR YOU! Knowing you are out there waiting, not so patiently, for my upcoming releases motivates me beyond belief. I know without you joining me in my imaginary world it wouldn't be worth it, so THANK YOU!

About the Author

Erin Thornton for the past 13 years has been a mom first. Now with six kids, she felt like she'd lost her own identity. She no longer had a first name and was always someone's mom or her husband's wife. It became very discouraging.

Erin has been telling stories since she was a kid. Her mom always told her to write her stories down, but she just rolled her eyes and moved on. As an adult, instead of reading a book for a bedtime story or on a long drive she would tell a made-up story to her kids. Keeping them sometimes captivated for hours. Some of them were amazing works of fiction and fantasy. Others were awful, and her kids still remember their insanity to this day. She wasn't afraid to take the stories to their most abstract point just to get a laugh from her kids.

Instead of letting her identity crisis overtake her, last summer Erin decided to write a novel. A story that was for her, not for her kids.

With her days spent on 100 acres with chickens and kids that act like the chickens most days, Erin writes whenever she can get a spare moment. Between musical practices, sports, and just plain mom life to distract her she tries to get in her words for the day with Disney Princess movies in the background or while her youngest naps.

All jokes aside, Erin Thornton is a true writer at heart. This won't be the last book she writes. The stories in her head are always screaming to get out. The only way to free her mind is to put them on paper.

Other books by Erin Thornton
Dangerous Series (Romantic Suspense)
Dangerous After Dark
Dangerous Calculations

· · · ·

Standalones
Disaster In Love (Romantic Comedy)